I0762039

A
WALK
BETWEEN
RAINDROPS

also by amalie jahn

The Clay Lion Series

The Clay Lion

Tin Men

A Straw Man

Under the Rainbow – A Prequel Companion

Brooke's Time Travel Notebook

Phoebe Unfired

The Next to Last Mistake

Before Checkmate – A Prequel Companion

The Sevens Prophecy Series

Among the Shrouded

Gather the Sentient

Beyond the Sanctified

Let Them Burn Cake!

(A Storied Cookbook)

A WALK BETWEEN RAINDROPS

amalie jahn

BERMLORD PUBLICATIONS

This is a work of fiction. All characters, organizations, and events portrayed in this novel are either products of the author's imagination or are used fictitiously. Any resemblance to actual persons, living or dead, events, or locales is entirely coincidental.

www.bermlord.weebly.com

BERMLORD, Charlotte, North Carolina

ISBN-13: 978-0-9910713-9-5 (BERMLORD)

First Edition, June 2023

Typeset in Garamond
Cover design and artwork by Natalia Lavrinenko
Author photograph courtesy of Bitmoji

for laura

"But the love of sisters needs no words.
It does not depend on memories, or mementos, or proof.
It runs as deep as a heartbeat, it is as ever-present as a pulse."
-Lisa Wingate

I've never wanted to throw up more than I do in this very moment.

Beneath me, the clack-clack-clack of the wheels against the coaster's steel runners is enough to send my already churning stomach into a full-blown regurgitative maelstrom. The seat beside me is empty, and I consider a possible trajectory should I become sick before the train returns to the platform. The front car is about to crest the peak of the first drop, and my sister Wylla lurches forward as we ascend. She's six cars ahead—second from the front—leaning against the arm of a cute stranger. It's just like her to meet someone at this stupid event.

That girl is always in the right place at the right time.

Her head disappears over the peak, and I brace myself for the fall. It's the sixty-seventh time I've descended the almost hundred-foot drop this morning, and as ready as I am to abandon the whole endeavor and never ride another roller coaster again, I can't stand the thought of giving up before my sister.

She's already better than me at everything, and I'll be damned if I'm gonna let her add another accomplishment to her list.

At the bottom of the Blaster's first hill, I concentrate on her head, a single point of focus as another wave of nausea washes over me. The train climbs again before careening sharply to the right, and the g-force makes me wish I could've left my stomach back in the spectators' booth with my best friend, Nia. She's the one who encouraged me to participate in the first place—seeing my time on the coaster as an opportunity to drum up financial support for our upcoming band competition.

"My dad said all the news stations will be covering the contest," she told me over tacos in the cafeteria last month, the week after I was announced as one of the lucky participants. "If you wear your marching band t-shirt and I hold up a poster on the sidelines, we're bound to get some publicity."

It seemed like a good idea at the time, but now I'm feeling less and less confident in my decision with each loop around the track.

The Blaster is the oldest coaster at one of the first amusement parks in the nation, Drury Park. To celebrate their 100th anniversary, they orchestrated this publicity stunt to encourage locals to purchase season passes. The owner's been gifting tickets to our family ever since Mom sold his summer house a few years back, which is how my sister and I were automatically entered into the lottery. A couple months ago, during the live press conference when the names were announced, I almost died when I was selected as one of the forty lucky pass holders in the running to win an all-expense-paid trip around the US to ride some of the fastest, tallest coasters the country has to offer.

This morning, at Nia's suggestion, I've been mugging at the news cameras in my neon green South Perry High School Marching Band t-shirt each time the train pulls into the station to let the quitters off, but at this point the whole ordeal's become about way more than winning the grand-prize or even drumming up support for our band competition.

Now, I just want to outlast Wylla.

The coaster zips beneath a canopy of trees, and I spot my former seatmate's black and yellow Steelers ballcap on the ground. I tried convincing him it was never gonna survive the contest before we loaded, but he refused to listen and sure enough, it flew right off his head during our seventeenth loop. The moment he lost it, his receding hairline (and reason for wearing the hat) were exposed, and he ended up bailing shortly after—doubled over and blinking back tears as he vacated the seat beside me at the end of our thirty-first trip.

Two dips are followed by a hard bank to the left, and as the coaster pulls into the station, the woman in the seat behind me calls for the attendant to release her restraint. She's been gagging over my shoulder for the past ten minutes, and I'm glad to see her tumble onto the platform. At least now I won't get barf down my back.

Nia and I are wearing matching bright green marching band shirts, emblazoned with the school's mascot—Go Tigers!—so it's easy to find her beside my mom in the viewing section. They offer small waves which I return with a sigh. The first few laps brought cheers and applause from the spectators, but much like watching a toddler on the carousel, my appearance draws less enthusiasm from them with each return.

One person noticeably missing from the platform is Wylla's boyfriend, Jackson. If he was here, he'd be pissed about her proximity to the guy sitting beside her, whose arm is now casually draped across the back of their seat. And since I'm the only one who knows the real reason she's riding today, I wouldn't blame her for being annoyed at him for not coming out to cheer her on. Watching her shift uncomfortably under the restraint, there's no way she would have agreed to this ridiculous stunt if Jackson hadn't begged her to win it for him.

"You got this, baby," I heard him crooning in the student parking lot at school the day after the announcements were made. "Do it for me."

While everyone else within earshot probably assumed he was being colloquial, I knew he was making a literal request. I'd seen a text from him that morning begging her to win the trip and gift it to him. He knows how much she hates roller coasters—ever since she wet her pants on the SooperDooperLooper in Hershey Park when she was seven—but that didn't stop him from guilting her into competing for him.

Love must be a powerful drug.

Tremendously powerful if her body's feeling anything like mine right now.

As the attendants give the all clear for the relaunch, I do a quick passenger headcount. Of the original forty participants, only seventeen remain.

The last seven win the trip.

Because seven, of course, is a lucky number.

The train pitches forward, and as I pass the news crew on my way out of the station, I give feeble shout out to the marching band. "Help us bankroll our competition," I call, pointing to my shirt. At this point, however, they're no longer filming. Probably saving their batteries until the winners are announced.

The familiar route of the coaster follows: up, up, up, down, down, bank left, bank right, loop, loop, up, up, down, up, down, bank, bank, down, bank.

With my thumbs pressed into my temples, attempting to relieve the pressure inside my skull, I glance ahead at Wylla, trying to decide whether the brain damage I'm sustaining is worth the satisfaction I'll get from having this one accomplishment to hold over her head. It helps imagining how I'll casually bring it up at dinner or in the hallway at school.

"Remember that one time you couldn't hold out long enough on the stupid Blaster to win a trip around the country? I mean, no offense Wylla, but it's practically a children's coaster."

There are two problems with my daydream scenario, though. One, even visualizing the dejected look on my sister's face isn't enough to distract from the throbbing headache and severe motion sickness I'm currently experiencing. And two, with her self-proclaimed hatred of coasters, I never honestly thought she'd make it this long.

Going into this thing, my only goal was to stay on long enough to get some publicity for the band, and I planned to bail out long before the end. But here I am, a couple hours into this ridiculous ordeal, unable to get off because of Wylla.

And she's showing no signs of giving up.

She must really love Jackson.

Or maybe she's just trying to outlast me.

By lap one hundred, my breakfast is barely staying down. I don't know why I thought eating a bagel and banana before climbing aboard was a good idea, but they're still churning undigested in my stomach all these hours later, as if my internal organs have all gone on strike. As we pull into the station, two of my fellow passengers call to be let off, and I want desperately to join them. The appeal of solid ground beneath my feet is overwhelming—every inch of my body screaming for relief from the jarring motion of the train. I stare at the back of Wylla's head, boring into it, willing her to get off the coaster. If she would just give up, I could survive a few more laps to solidify my victory before making my triumphant withdrawal from competition.

But she stays in her seat.

And so do I.

"You're doing great," Mom calls. The desperation in her eyes overshadows the sad smile pulling at her lips. I haven't told her otherwise, so she probably assumes I want to go on the trip. She'd never ask me not to, but the prospect of being left alone if Wylla and I both win must have her wondering how she'll manage if the two of us head off across the country without her.

She doesn't meet my gaze, and as the coaster takes off on the next loop, the guilt of abandonment tightens my already knotted stomach. She needs me around. She needs my sister around. Because despite the fact Wylla and I haven't spoken to one another in almost six months, we still both take responsibility for Mom. I want to let her know Wylla's gifting her trip to Jackson, and that I have no intention of leaving, but there's no way to communicate this information to her now.

By the four-hour-mark, numbness has taken over, and for a long time all I do is concentrate on the back of Wylla's head. Her wavy, chestnut hair sparkles in the sunshine, whipping around in the breeze. I don't envy the snarl of knots she'll need to comb through tonight with her coconut-scented detangler. I have no idea why she left it down—God forbid she wear a ponytail, even when it's practical.

I also don't know why—after all this time on the coaster—she hasn't turned around to face me, not even to acknowledge the solidarity of our situation. I'm still trying to suppress my annoyance when the train comes to a screeching halt and my lap restraint releases unexpectedly.

"Congratulations to our winners," Mr. Blankenship, the owner of the park, announces over the loudspeaker.

I shake my head, forcing myself out of a self-imposed daze, and look around. To my right, Mom and Nia are applauding.

She motions to my t-shirt. "Turn toward the cameras. They're rolling."

I scan the platform for the news crew and wave my arms to grab their attention, thrusting my chest forward and straightening my shirt across my shoulders. I stand cautiously, uncertain of my footing, and step off the train. Around me, the other winners follow suit, and Wylla steps from her car onto the platform, smiling broadly. At that moment, she turns to me for the first time all day, our eyes lock, and she mouths the words, "I win."

CHAPTER 2

The only time Wylla ever darkens my doorstep is when she wants something, which is why her persistent loitering in the hallway outside my bedroom makes me suspicious. I don't necessarily want to be the one to break the silence between us, ending our standoff after all these months, but this might be the opportunity to clear the air I've been waiting for.

I'm still on the fence, deciding whether to speak, when I notice her puffy, red eyelids and the balled-up wad of tissue in her left hand.

Wylla never cries.

There's never anything in her life to cry about.

Which makes me hopeful she might finally be ready to make amends.

She passes by the door a fourth time, and I pull a striped Henley out of my laundry basket nonchalantly, snapping it in the air to the release the wrinkles before folding it into thirds, Marie Kondo-style. I don't want to appear too eager so I keep my eyes down, like I can barely be bothered. "You need something?" I ask. My words come out harsher than I intend, and I worry for a moment she'll walk away like always.

But this time, she doesn't.

Instead, she takes my question as an invitation to step inside, whether it was or not, and I smother a groan as she throws herself across my bed's green plaid comforter the way she used to when we were kids, crumpling my clean laundry beneath her. Her lithe limbs sprawl from pillow to footboard, and memories of all the Saturday mornings we spent holed up in my room together, watching cartoons, hiding from the wrath of Dad's inevitable weekend hangover come flooding back. Now, as she rumples my favorite tank top, I suppress the urge to yell at her and force myself to focus instead on how grateful I am she's finally reaching out.

Is it possible she's missed me as much as I've missed her?

When she doesn't respond, I kick my hamper under my bed and smooth the wrinkles beside her before taking a seat. "What's going on?"

She wipes the back of her hand across her eyes and blinks back tears. "I want to go on the roller coaster trip."

Her admission feels like a punch to the gut. Of all the confessions for her to make, a desire to spend two weeks of her summer vacation riding roller coasters with a bunch of strangers takes me by surprise, and I struggle to keep the disappointment in my heart from spreading to my eyes where she can see it. I'm an idiot for thinking she was here for me, and as I work to make sense of her true motivations, realize there's obviously a lot I don't understand about my sister these days.

What clearly hasn't changed in the months since we last spoke is her unwavering belief that she stands at the center of the universe. I was naïve to think her sadness could have anything to do with me, and this understanding ignites a spark of anger inside of me, reducing the sprig of hope I'd been nurturing to ash. She rolls to her back with a heavy sigh, knocking a pair of freshly laundered jean shorts off the bed, and when she makes no attempt to pick them up, I snatch them off the floor myself, lashing out.

"So, go," I say.

She sniffles and releases a heavy shudder. "I can't."

"You can. Just keep the trip for yourself and don't give it to stupid Jackson like you were planning. It's not hard." My voice slices the space between us, and at this point, I honestly don't care if I piss her off.

Her nostrils flair, an indication she either doesn't agree with my assessment of the situation or is confused about my knowledge of their agreement.

"How'd you know about that?"

I avert my eyes with a shrug. She may have cut me out of her life back in the fall, but with her track record of poor decision making, I couldn't let her navigate freshman year without a big sister, even if it meant keeping tabs on her from a distance. And it's not like I've been spying on her or anything, but when you live in the same house and go to the same school, you hear stuff. Still, I can't tell her about the text I saw, or she'll accuse me of snooping, and we'll get into another one of our infamous blowouts.

"You guys weren't quiet, talking about it in the parking lot that day," I say, offering a plausible explanation. "And unless you have something in writing, legally, you're not required to give the trip to him. You won, fair and square."

Her eyes set like stones. "I'm not giving the trip to Jackson."

The determined tone of her voice surprises me. If there's one thing my sister's known for, it's doing whatever it takes to please her man, which is why something about her new resolve doesn't add up. Her dedication to Jackson and her hatred of roller coasters should make gifting the trip a no-brainer. I refold my shorts and place them on top of my Hello Kitty pajamas, stalling as I try making sense of the situation.

There's got to be a reason she suddenly wants to go on the trip. Maybe she assumes I'm going and wants to hang out after all.

My pulse quickens just thinking about the possibility of a reconciliation.

"If you're keeping the prize for yourself, what's the problem? Just go on the trip."

The wadded-up tissue falls into her lap, and she tucks her chin to her chest, like she's embarrassed to look at me. "Mom won't let me go unless you go, too."

I replay her words in my head a second and a third time, letting them sink all the way in. It was stupid of me to assume she had any intention of making amends. I should've listened to my instincts.

She's only here because she needs something *from* me, not because she needs me in her life.

I open my mouth to tell her I'm not going. To destroy her with the knowledge that I never intended on claiming my prize in the first place. That riding the tallest, fastest coasters in the country before I die is not on my bucket list.

And that goes double for riding them with an ungrateful kid sister.

Then I catch a glimpse of pain tucked behind her resolve, and it disarms me. The way she's looking at me now—with swollen eyes and snot dripping from her left nostril—tugs at something primal deep inside me. She's hurting. She's in need. And for some reason she thinks going on a dumb trip to a bunch of amusement parks will make her feel better.

I scan her face for the truth. I can't ask her, of course, but maybe there's a clue in the deep-set lines carved between her eyes or the set of her jaw.

As I study her, the familiar longing for connection rematerializes, and although I'm inclined to suppress it—no good can come from hoping—I allow it to fully form. Maybe she *is* finally ready to make amends and sees this trip as an opportunity for us to fix what's broken between us.

Or perhaps she's simply looking for new and exciting ways to ignore me all over the country.

I narrow my eyes at her. "Why do you even want to go? You hate roller coasters. And haven't you and Jackson made big plans together all summer?"

Her lip trembles at the mention of her boyfriend's name, and just like that, the truth of the situation comes into focus. This sudden desire to go ride coasters doesn't have anything to do with forgiving me. It's about him.

Did they have a fight? A falling out?

Could I have missed a break-up?

Jackson is one boy in a long line of suitors she's entertained over the years. Her first boyfriend, Declan, gave her a bracelet. For Valentine's Day.

In kindergarten.

It's hard to imagine what it would be like to have a boyfriend, much less one who gives me holiday jewelry. But, of course, Wylla's always been lucky in love. Hell, she's always been lucky in everything, which is how I know whatever's going on with Jackson now won't derail her for long. She'll be on to the next adventure before summer vacation even starts.

Still, if she's willing to leave him behind for two weeks, she must be pretty angry at him.

Maybe even angrier than she is at me.

I want to reach out. To console her in some small, physical way, but I know better. "Did something happen between you and Jackson?"

She sniffles and blots her mascara with the Kleenex. "That idiot doesn't deserve my trip." She swallows hard. "And he doesn't deserve me."

I purse my lips, suppressing surprise at her revelation. Jackson hasn't been by to visit in a while, but I figured he was busy with lacrosse practice and his part-time job at the Y. Now it seems there might be trouble in paradise, and although the last thing I want is a backstage pass to her relationship drama, I can't squander the opportunity to reconnect. "You wanna talk about what's going on?"

She shakes her head, picking at a nonexistent thread on her floral skirt. "What I want is to get outta here. Out of this Podunk little town of ours. And this trip is my ticket out, at least for a little while." She bites at her bottom lip and gazes up at me through her lashes, which aren't the least bit clumpy, despite all the crying. "But Mom says I can't go without 'supervision.'"

So as not to be caught off guard by life's unexpected twists and turns, I take great care in preparing for every worst-case scenario. That way, I'm pleasantly surprised if things work out better than expected.

But Wylla wanting to go on the roller coaster road trip is one plot twist I didn't see coming.

How was I to know she and Jackson were suddenly gonna go on hiatus?

I pick up the stuffed cow beside my pillow and hug it against my chest. "I honestly wasn't planning to go. You know that, right?"

"Then why'd you even bother showing up to the contest? And why'd you stay on the coaster so long?"

My breath catches inside my throat. There's no way I can tell her the truth, that my pride wouldn't allow it. "You know I was helping raise money for the band competition."

"Yeah. But you guys didn't get enough so now you're not going." She shrugs matter-of-factly, as if there's nothing else going on in my life to prevent me from leaving with her.

She's partially right. Even my fifteen minutes of fame as one of the contest winners, wearing my South Perry High School Marching Band t-shirt on live television, wasn't enough to drum up the donations we needed to subsidize our big trip to Washington DC for the Bands of America competition. We did, however, raise enough to fund a crummy end-of-year banquet at Golden Corral.

Chocolate fountain. Whoopee.

"I've got work." My job at the fro-yo place refilling tubs of Oreo pieces and chocolate sprinkles is less than glamorous, but college isn't going to pay for itself. And besides, I'm not sure how thrilled my boss would be about me leaving for two weeks.

Her nose crinkles. "You hate that place."

"I need the money."

"So, tell him you'll start after we get back. That's what I'm doing." The desperate whine in her voice takes me by surprise. I've never heard her make a case for anything she's wanted in her life. I don't think she's ever had to.

"You love teaching swim lessons at the Y." As the words come out of my mouth, though, I remember the reason she chose to apply there this summer instead of the community pool where she usually works.

Jackson Pollock.

No wonder she's looking for a way to escape.

I expect her to well up, but she merely shrugs before squaring her shoulders and righting herself against my headboard. "The kids'll be fine without me for a few weeks. Let someone else struggle to get them in the water for a change. I'll be back in time to teach the actual strokes." She's gazing at me now, her bottom lip thrust into a manipulative pout.

My head swims with the strangeness of the situation—of all the reasons I have for saying no. Wylla and I haven't willingly hung out together since middle school, but it's not hard to imagine what spending two weeks on the road with her would be like.

Probably a lot like the last time we slept over with our cousin Kora in her family's camper three years ago.

Back when I was in elementary school, my aunt and uncle bought a Winnebago RV, and Wylla, Kora, and I started having monthly 'camp outs' in their driveway the night they brought it home. The third Friday of every month, we'd pop popcorn in the little microwave tucked inside an overhead compartment and rearrange the banquette into a proper bed for us all to sleep on. Then we'd stay up way too late laughing and watching movies on the flip-down TV until the sun peeked through the miniblinds the next morning.

It was fun while it lasted, but by eighth grade, Kora and Wylla started finding excuses to bail on me. And when they would show up, they'd purposely pick movies they knew I hated, hogged the cheddar salt all to themselves, and whispered about how annoying I was, just loud enough for me to hear.

The memory of their rejection strengthens my resolve to stay home. I'm not gullible enough to believe Wylla wants to spend time with me—she's only looking for a way to avoid Jackson—and this trip is a convenient alibi. Not to mention, I saw the way she cuddled against the guy beside her on the coaster. She knows he's gonna be there, and my gut tells me she's looking at him as potential rebound material.

Lord knows I would.

"Please, Elise." She twists the tissue in her hand and skootches a bit closer to me on the bed. "I'll never ask you for another favor again. I promise." A huge sigh escapes her lips and tears pool at the corner of her eyes. "Please come with me."

"No."

"Elise, please. I need to get away for a little bit."

"I'm not going."

Her face contorts into a desperate grimace, and I turn away to stare instead at my chipped, blue toenail polish. Silence fills the room, and when she shifts away, I allow myself to hope she's given up.

"But you owe me." Her voice is barely above a whisper.

My head snaps up, and I level a glare at her. "Owe you?"

"Yes. Owe me. Remember the whole Christmas ornament fiasco?"

I run my hands through my hair which is now slick with perspiration. I should've known when she took the blame for breaking Mom's favorite ornament last Christmas it would come back to haunt me eventually. At the time, the gesture seemed genuine, like she legitimately didn't want me to get in trouble. She knew my holiday band trip was coming up, and that I'd be grounded for destroying my great-grandmother's ceramic angel, so she confessed before I had the chance.

Things between us didn't used to be this complicated. We weren't always so competitive, and we didn't used to keep score. Not for the first time, I wish we could go back to when things were simple, and it was enough to just be friends.

I might be imagining it, but as I look at her now, the intensity of her gaze suggests she might feel the same. Either that or she's still holding something back. Some deeper, darker reason for wanting to get away.

Did Jackson hurt her?

Could she be pregnant?

I glance at her midsection which remains perfectly taught; though to be honest, I'm no expert when it comes to gestational milestones or the fluctuating state of her abdomen.

In any case, it's obvious that if I don't do this for her, I might regret it for the rest of my life. We have a lot of history together, both good and bad, and this may be the last chance to fix everything that's gone wrong between us.

Or at least find out what's really going on with her.

"You really want to spend two weeks of your summer vacation traveling in a stinky bus, sleeping in one-star hotels, and riding roller coasters with a bunch of strangers?"

She shrugs. "You're not a stranger."

I shake my head. Why the hell am I agreeing to this? "It's gonna break Mom's heart, both of us leaving together."

Her face brightens. "She's a grown woman. And it's only a couple weeks. She'll probably be glad to have the house to herself for a little while."

I highly doubt it. She might not miss me, but she'll definitely miss Wylla. Between their *Great British Baking Show* binge watching and weekly cucumber facials, the two of them are practically inseparable. "Listen, if I go along, don't expect me to chauffer you around for the rest of the summer when we get back. I've got my own stuff going on." It's a total lie, but I'm determined to maintain some dignity in all of this.

"I promise. No more favors." She springs off my bed and backs away toward the door, tossing her hair across her shoulders. "Thank you. Thank you so much. You won't regret it."

She breezes into the hallway, everything right with her world, as it should be. Not for the first time, however, I'm already second-guessing my decision.

CHAPTER 3

"So, that's it, then. You're leaving me for two whole weeks." Nia scowls beside me as we assemble our clarinets in the band room Monday morning. She's been the first chair to my second chair since sixth grade, and when we play together, it's almost as if the rest of the woodwinds section doesn't even exist.

In the usual pre-class commotion, the others buzz around us, but I'm wholly focused—determined to help Nia understand my motivation for leaving without disclosing the truth. If I tell her I'm only going as a favor to Wylla, she'll try to talk me out of it.

And it'll probably work.

"I'll be back before you'll even know I'm gone. And think about all the extra cash you'll make taking over my shifts."

She rolls her eyes, dumping the contents of her clarinet case onto the floor, most likely in search of a fresh reed. "That's supposed to help me feel better? Instead of working together, I'll be stuck doubled up with Crusty Carl."

Crusty Carl is the owner of the fro-yo shop where we both worked for the past three summers. Everybody knows he's short-tempered, especially with customers who waste yogurt or ask for too many samples, so Nia and I serve as the face of the company for the summer crowd. I've seen his month-to-month sales reports, and I'm certain the increase in profits from June to August have as much to do with him not being there, hovering over everyone's topping selections, as it does the hot weather.

All this is to say, she has a point.

I pull my own reed from my mouthpiece and hand it to her. She's lucky I always carry extras. "Look, I really think it would be good for me to get away for a little bit. A change of scenery and all that."

She thanks me for the reed and secures it to her mouthpiece before meeting my gaze. A strange look of understanding crosses her face. "You're probably right. It might be nice for you to have a few weeks to yourself. Maybe meet some new people. See some new sights." She looks away with an unsettled cough. "Maybe you'll finally be able to get out of your own head for a little while."

Nia's one of the only people who knows the truth about what went on between me and Wylla this past fall. She also knows about my recent therapy sessions for PTSD—the only lingering reminder of the car accident I had back in March. My car was broadsided at an intersection and completely totaled, but I was lucky enough to walk away with only minor injuries. In the weeks after the accident, though, every time I got behind the wheel my heart would race so severely, I'd almost pass out. Mom took me to the doctor where we discovered over ninety percent of people who walk away from accidents the way I did don't end up with long-term mental health issues.

Lucky them.

"You think so?" I'm grateful Nia's coming around. It'll be

way easier to leave knowing I have her support.

"Yeah, I mean, the other people who won seem nice. Especially that cute guy from the car up front. Did you see his eyelashes? You know I'm a sucker for a guy with thick eyelashes." She blows an off-key note on her clarinet. "What was his name? D-something, wasn't it?"

I can't believe she's bringing him up. Not with the way he and Wylla were practically sitting in each other's laps by the end. If he's going to be interested in anyone, it won't be me.

"His name's Dustin. And yes, I noticed the eyelashes." I don't add that I also noticed the broadness of his shoulders and the adorable way he kept tucking his hair behind his ears as the winners posed for pictures after the contest.

I dig through my bag for sheet music and prepare my stand for class. Beside me, Nia releases a heavy sigh, her shoulders sagging.

"Just promise you won't have too much fun without me, okay?"

I laugh aloud. "Who am I gonna have such a great time with? The old guy, Travis, with the mutton chops?"

"You never know. He might lure you in with his Harley."

I shake my head.

"There's the other girl, what's-her-name."

"Chloe?"

"Yeah. She seemed okay." Nia gazes up at me through her lashes. "And really pretty."

I try to picture Chloe, the third winning girl, conjuring a vague image. She'd been sitting behind me on the coaster, and since turning around made me sick, I didn't get a good look at her until the press junket, after the contest ended. By that time, though, the only person holding my attention was Wylla.

"She's way older than us. Like in college, I think, so I doubt she'll want to have anything to do with me." My voice carries a dejected tone, and I remind myself this trip isn't about making friends. It's about doing right by Wylla, helping her through whatever mess she's embroiled in, and potentially fixing things between us.

Nia tilts her head to the side and grins. "The other two guys looked younger. Maybe one of them will sweep you off your feet."

I refrain from throwing my sheet music at her. "First of all, who even uses that expression? What are you, a hundred? And secondly, Seamus and Mikal aren't really my type."

"They seemed friendly during the news interviews."

Friendly, yes, but a bit too extroverted for my taste.

The guys I'm drawn to are typically quiet and even a little broody. Like Logan, my childhood BFF and quintessential boy-next-door.

After all the drama last fall, though, there's no chance the two of us will ever be a thing.

I sigh. "So, what you're saying is, you want me to make friends but only have a little fun with them, is that it?"

"Something like that." A small smile pulls at the corner of her lips, releasing the dimple in her left cheek "Ten parks in fourteen days. It's gonna be wild."

"The wildest."

She counts on her fingers. "Pennsylvania, Ohio, Tennessee, North Carolina, Virginia, Maryland, and New Jersey. That's a lot of states."

"It's a lot of time on the road with a bunch of strangers."

"Lots of time to clear your head."

"Or get lost inside it."

She nods sympathetically. "I'll make you a new Spotify playlist. All our favorites to help you pass the time. And promise you'll text me every day and send me pictures of all the parks."

"I will."

"And the cute guys. And girls."

"I will. As long as you check in on my mom. I'm worried about leaving her alone."

She agrees, remembering how bad things were for Mom after Dad left. All the nights she agreed to stay over, helping me clean the house and make dinner in an attempt to coax Mom out of her room.

Nia swears her Beef Wellington is what finally did it, but I'm more inclined to credit the counseling and anti-depressants for her improvement.

Then again, maybe it was all three.

The late bell rings, effectively ending our conversation, and as I adjust the reed of my own clarinet, release a heavy sigh. Because with Nia's help and her own medication, Mom might not miss me at all.

CHAPTER 4

The afternoon of my departure, Mom sits at the kitchen table clutching a nearly empty mug of coffee. I set my faded orange duffle on the floor beside her and help myself to a banana from the counter. "You sure you're not upset about me leaving? You're gonna be okay?"

She works her face into a neutral expression and takes a sip from her World's Okay-est Mom cup—a gag gift from me and Wylla a million years ago. It was funny then, but today it just seems sad. "It's fine. A change of scenery will be a good thing for you. But only if you promise to keep taking your pills."

The banana is green and bitter. I can't force myself to swallow so I dump it in the trash, hoping it's not an omen of things to come. "I'll take them. I promise."

But the bottle of Zoloft is only tucked in the bottom of my toiletry bag because it's too risky leaving it here at home for Mom to find. I stopped taking them when they started upsetting my stomach about a month ago, but I still haven't found the courage to tell her the truth. And I get it—the pills were a godsend for her, which explains why she's pinning all her hopes on them for me. But at this point, it's been weeks since my last panic attack, so I'm pretty sure I don't even need them anymore.

Mom glances at her watch and with a fractured tone, announces it's time to go. It's obvious she's wrecked about us leaving, but God forbid she deny Wylla, even at the expense of her own mental health. I want to say something. Want to tell her she can still change her mind about letting us go. But as she pushes away from the table, the chair's feet screeching against the linoleum floor, the moment to speak passes by. She grabs her keys from the hook by the door, and I unzip my duffle, scanning the contents to make sure I haven't forgotten anything one last time. My phone charger's missing, and I pass Wylla coming down the stairs with her bag as I race to retrieve the cord. She doesn't say anything as we brush by each other on the landing, but there's no denying the nervous set of her eyes, like she's suddenly having second thoughts about going.

Something more than a simple fight with Jackson is forcing her through the door.

Moments later, cord in hand, the kitchen door clicks shut behind me, and after racing across the weed-stricken yard to the car, I find Mom and Wylla in the middle of an animated discussion. The rolled-up windows muffle their voices, but something about Wylla's uneasy glance in my direction suggests they're talking about me. Mom notices my approach and falls silent, all but confirming my suspicions.

Between Wylla and her gear, the entire backseat is taken, so I climb into the passenger's seat beside Mom.

She clears her throat, backing out of the driveway. "You know the rules. Keep your phone on you at all times. Lock the hotel room while you're inside. Stay with the group. Don't go off alone." She pauses, glancing into her rearview mirror for more time than it takes to merge. A private conversation passes between her and Wylla, and a deep ache settles in my chest. "And have fun, okay?"

We both agree to have a good time and to check in with her frequently. This won't be a problem for Wylla since the two of them text each other constantly. It'll be more of a stretch for me and Mom, though, since the only time we text one another is to coordinate when and where I should pick up Wylla from her friends' houses or dance class or work.

But at least I know she's got my number.

Save for a large, green van parked near the entrance, Drury Park is strangely empty as we pull into the lot. Wylla bounds out of the car, blowing a kiss to Mom and slamming the door without so much as a glance in my direction. I, however, stay locked inside, the stale air from the AC scratching at my lungs.

"You'll have fun." Mom's hand is on my arm. The warmth of it settles my stomach.

"What if I don't? What if I have one of my attacks? What if no one likes me?"

What if this doesn't fix my relationship with Wylla?

"Stick together and everything will be fine." She squeezes three times like she used to when I was little. One for each word.

"I love you, too," I say, opening the door.

She throws me a sad wave as I step onto the blacktop and make my way to where the other winners are loading their bags into the back of the van.

An elderly guy in a ball cap and torn pair of cargo shorts peers out from behind the rear door as I approach. "Well, now, since you're the last to arrive, you must be Elise." He tosses someone's floral shoulder bag into the back of the van and takes the worn duffle from my hand. "My name's Ernie, and

I'll be chauffeuring you folks around in this here chariot for the next couple of weeks."

I introduce myself, forcing a smile. "So, this is our *bus*?" I ask, peeking inside.

"No, not a bus, per se." He rearranges someone's luggage to make room for my duffle and slides it in. "But the budget was tight so Mr. Blankenship thought the most economically sound decision would be for us to take one of the park shuttles."

"In case you're wondering, there aren't any TVs," Dustin interjects from the side of the van without looking up from his phone. His shaggy blond hair's a little longer than it was the day of the contest when he was so eager to cuddle beside Wylla. Now, though, it's almost as if he's making a point to ignore her in favor of Chloe, the oldest—and sexiest—female of the group. "If anyone needs me, I'll be streaming Netflix on this tiny screen, I guess."

Chloe rolls her eyes and heaves a sigh. "Who cares about TV when there's no bathroom? How are we supposed to drive thousands of miles with no place to pee?"

Travis, the older dude with an Alaskan bushman sort of vibe, pulls a penknife from his jeans pocket and drags it beneath his thumbnail. "We'll pee at rest stops with the truckers, the way real long-haulers do."

For some reason, his comment makes me smile, and a trickle of relief spreads through me. Wylla isn't going to voluntarily spend all of her time with me, so the only way this trip isn't going to completely suck is if I find a way to connect with everyone else.

I glance around at my traveling companions, trying to keep them all straight.

A couple are easy. Like Chloe. She's the only other girl—beside me and Wylla—and she's kind of hard to ignore, not only because she looks like an anime doll, but because she's loud. Like, super loud. "What is this? Pleather?" she calls out now, inspecting the van's cracked vinyl seats like she's genuinely expecting an answer.

The old guy, Travis, is super easy, too. Although, with so much wiry, grey facial hair, his face is barely visible.

The three younger guys are harder, though, and for some reason, even after meeting them at the press junket back in March, it's tough keeping them straight. They're all sort of milling around now, noses in their phones, not really talking, so it surprises me when Mikal, the black guy with the sharpest edges I've ever seen, clears his throat.

"You know who else got around in a van like this?" he asks out of nowhere.

"The Manson family," Dustin deadpans.

Mikal chuckles. "Yeah. I mean, I guess they did drive something similar, but I was thinking of Scooby Doo and the gang. You know, the Mystery Machine."

Beside me, Wylla smirks. She knows I loved Scooby Doo as a kid and even had something of a crush on the show's animated heartthrob, Fred. I hold my breath, waiting for her to call me out, but before she has a chance to open her mouth, Ernie the driver gives the all clear to load on.

Chloe climbs in first, calling over her shoulder. "Well, if we're the Scooby gang, I call Daphne."

Dustin pushes past Mikal through the side door. "I guess that makes me Fred," he says, settling beside Chloe in the back seat.

"So, I'm Shaggy?" Mikal rolls his eyes and flops down in the second row. "Zoinks."

When I don't make a move for the van, Travis takes his cue and slides in next to Mikal. "That means I'm Scooby." He sets a leather fanny pack on the floor at his feet before glancing up at me as I hoist myself into the van. "And I guess you'll be our Velma, the brains of this operation." For a second, I'm surprised he chooses to single me out over Wylla since she's rarely overlooked, but when he adds, "You've got the glasses for it and everything," it all makes a bit more sense.

Wylla and I take the first of the three bench seats, right behind the driver. She's been quiet since we arrived, and I'm pretty sure it's because Dustin hasn't given her the time of day and is clearly smitten with Chloe. Not that a guy being interested in someone else has ever stopped my sister from going after who she wanted in the past, but having another beautiful, witty coed in the group will make winning his affections more challenging.

The last to enter the van is Seamus, who's barely taller than I am and about the same age. He reminds me of a Weasley—the eighth wizarding sibling perhaps—sporting a mop of red hair and one of those forgettable faces, with wideset eyes and sparse teenage boy stubble that's too awkward to be considered sexy. He glances at me briefly as he steps into the van, like he's considering whether he'll be welcome beside me and Wylla, before dropping his pack on the floor beside Travis instead.

"Mind if Scrappy sits back here with Scooby and Shaggy?" he asks.

Travis gives him a hardy clap on the back. "The more the merrier."

Ernie shuts the door behind Seamus and after ambling around the front of the van, takes his seat behind the wheel. He buckles his seatbelt and adjusts the side mirror before turning the key in the ignition. "First stop, Kennywood Park. Should be there in a few hours, about dinnertime. Now, I know you all are anxious to settle in for the drive, but there's a bit of housekeeping we need to go over to make sure things remain copacetic over the next fourteen days."

Of course, we've already signed a number of disclaimers indemnifying Drury Park and everyone involved in the contest should something go wrong on the trip, so I'm not sure what he's referring to.

"One of the first things we need to settle is the sleeping arrangements."

Behind me, Mikal blows out a breath.

"Like I mentioned before, the budget is tight, so we're only allotted three rooms per night. The way we've broken it down is: Dustin, Mikal, and Seamus in the first room, me and Travis in the second, which leaves you girls to share the third."

Beside me, the tightness in Wylla's muscles releases—she's happy Dustin and Chloe aren't officially paired in the same room together—but I don't share her relief. There are three of us girls, which means she and I will be expected to share a bed. It's gonna be awkward sleeping beside someone who hasn't willingly spoken to me in almost a year.

If she doesn't ask to bunk up with Chloe instead.

I wouldn't put it past her.

"The second thing we need to discuss," Ernie continues, "is a special surprise, care of Mr. Blankenship himself." He pauses, glancing in the rearview mirror as if he expects some sort of enthusiastic reaction from us. When he's met with the indifference of our collective gaze, he gives a sad shake of his head and continues. "When we arrive at each of the ten parks, an employee will hide two Drury Park tokens somewhere on the premises. You'll be given a clue at the start of the day about the tokens' location. The two of you who collect the most tokens over the course of the trip will receive Fast Lane vouchers for the rest of the season at Drury Park when we get back."

A beat passes while I consider this opportunity along with everyone else.

"Can we work together with another person?" Dustin asks.

Ernie shrugs. "Sure. You can team up with as many people as you want, but only the two people with the most tokens at the end will get the vouchers."

Almost immediately, Chloe starts conspiring with Dustin in the backseat. For the briefest moment, I consider partnering with Wylla—a common goal might be the jumpstart our reconciliation needs. But it's a stupid idea. She hates amusement parks and probably cares less about those vouchers.

Behind me, Travis lowers his voice to just above a whisper. "Either of you boys wanna work together with me? I'm a real good puzzle solver. I bet we can find them all."

Mikal remains silent, and a moment passes before Seamus responds. "Let's see how it goes. I don't know if I wanna waste my time searching for tokens when I could be riding the rides, you know what I mean?"

Something about the way he says it, with such diplomacy, draws my attention. It says a lot about this wannabe Weasley's character that he's inclined to let Travis down easy instead of rejecting him flat out. I turn to face him, and when our eyes meet, he gives me the smallest indication of a smile, like he might be interested in partnering with me instead of Travis.

Then he glances at Wylla, and I'm forced to admit he may not be holding out for me after all.

A painful knot forms beneath my ribcage as Ernie drones on

about meals as well as expectations of being on time and staying with the group. He passes around a written daily agenda, and instead of fixating on Seamus, I focus instead on something meaningful to talk about with Wylla once Ernie's lecture eventually comes to an end. I could ask her to help me find the tokens, but that would probably be a short conversation. Or I could tell her about the list of 'low thrill' options I compiled for each of the parks, hoping to entice her onto some of the less vomit-inducing rides. I've been waiting for the right moment to share them with her, but as Ernie finishes his spiel, she pops in her earbuds and turns her attention out the window. The volume's so loud, I can almost make out the lyrics of the newest song by her favorite K-Pop boy band. As the van chugs down the highway, I find myself wishing the tune was loud enough to drown out the nagging voice in the back of my head telling me this entire trip is a huge mistake.

CHAPTER 5

After dinner at a McDonald's outside the Kennywood Park entrance, Ernie checks into the motel while the rest of us wait at the van. I'm still stressing about how the whole sleeping arrangement's going to work out when he arrives back in the parking lot with three sets of keys.

"For you." He hands the first set to Dustin before holding out the second keychain to me. "And for you girls."

I thank him, grab my bag, and follow Wylla up the stairs to the second-floor. She steps aside for me to unlock the door, letting out an audible gasp as she takes in the room.

"This is disgusting. I can't stay here."

I push past her and toss my bag on the bed closest to the door. The mattress sags under its weight, puckering the brown and yellow floral bedspread. I run my hand across the nightstand. "It's not dirty. Just dated."

"It's gross."

I roll my eyes. "Think of it as kitschy, but in a good way. Like maybe this is supposed to be a Steeler's themed room."

She steps across the threshold, glancing at the rusted-out A/C unit under the window. "Does this thing even work?"

"It's pretty cool in here now," I say with a shrug.

She kicks at it with her foot, stubbing her toe in the process as the door shuts behind her. I collapse onto the bed, digging through my bag for my toothbrush and phone charger. Across the room, Wylla dumps her bag on the cracked laminate dresser and begins organizing her belongings, lining up each of her toiletries just so: body lotions and sunscreens and perfumes and exfoliants. Only my sister would pack enough beauty products for an entire YouTube makeup tutorial on a trip touring amusement parks with a bunch of strangers.

I bite the inside of my cheek as she unwinds the cords to her curling iron and her flat iron, lining them up with the other items on the dresser. She sets two stuffed makeup caddies beside them before finally stepping back to assess her stash.

She sighs.

"Did you forget something?" Even though I don't mean to sound sarcastic, the question takes a mocking tone.

She bristles momentarily before regaining her composure. "No. I'm just… I dunno. I guess I'm a little worried about riding the coasters tomorrow."

She's probably thinking about Dad and Hershey Park and how she freaked out on the SooperDooperLooper all those years ago.

Or maybe she's worried about the pregnancy disclaimer attached to every ride.

"You did a great job on the Blaster. I mean, you stayed on long enough to win this trip, so you've obviously conquered your fear."

She shakes her head. "I'm not so much afraid as I am nervous about getting sick."

"Sick?"

"Yeah, like, I don't want to get nauseous and throw up the way I do in the car sometimes."

She got sick riding in the back of the rented Suburban during our last trip to the beach. Mom had to stop twice for her to throw up along the side of the road—not her finest moment. She didn't seem to have any issues sitting in the front of the van with me today, though, but she's probably right to be concerned about some of the more aggressive coasters. "Maybe you should get some anti-puke medicine."

"Like Dramamine?"

I nod. "It might help. I mean, I made lists of some of the low-thrill rides at every park, and if you want to do those instead, I don't mind riding with you. But if your heart's set on coasters, you should get some Dramamine."

She sighs again, overwhelmed by the prospect.

"I saw a Walgreens not far from here as we were driving in. It wouldn't be too long of a walk." I nod at the door, hesitating when she doesn't immediately agree. "I'll go with you."

"Yeah?"

"Yeah." I fish my wallet from the small zippered section of my bag and pocket the room key on my way to the door. "But we should try to find Chloe on the way out."

Wylla raises an eyebrow. "Why?"

"Because she might need to get in here while we're gone. We should leave her the key."

She shakes her head like going to find Chloe is the dumbest thing she's ever heard. "Listen. It's not our fault she headed off with Dustin and still hasn't made an appearance. As far as I'm concerned, she can stay wherever she is until we get back." She follows me out the door into the muggy night air. "If she wanted to get into the room right away, she should've come with us from the get."

"Fine," I say. "But at least let me leave her a note."

While I scribble off a message to Chloe on the back of my McDonald's receipt, Wylla checks Google maps to confirm we're heading in the right direction. Once our trajectory is established, we set off across the parking lot to an uneven sidewalk rife with gaps and errant weeds. I've never been particularly superstitious, but as we fall into what feels like a weirdly amicable silence, I find myself avoiding the cracks to keep from jinxing our delicate truce.

She kicks a bottlecap into the gutter as we pass in front of a Wendy's. "Travis seems—interesting."

"I can't figure out what his deal is." He spent most of the trip eating from an enormous bag of licorice while doing crossword puzzles with a pen. "We learned in chemistry that black licorice has this compound that causes heart problems. What if he craps out on us on a ride or something?"

Wylla shrugs. "He looks like one of those guys who can smoke and drink and eat nothing but fast food and still live to be a hundred. He'll probably die in a poolhall fight when he's ninety. Pool cue to the cranium or some mess."

"And you should see the other guy."

This gets a chuckle out of her, and a strange sort of relief spreads through me. I never imagined when she first stopped speaking to me back in September that I would eventually miss her the way I do now. It snuck up on me, I guess, the longing. At first it was like the tide coming in—so gradual I didn't even know what it was when I felt it lapping at my toes. As the months went by, though, it started knocking into me, throwing me off balance, especially when I needed her. Like the day Dad showed up drunk at our front porch on Christmas Eve, yelling for Mom, and I didn't know what to do. Wylla would've known how to handle him. She would've known what to say. What to do. But, of course, I locked the front door and hid in the kitchen, crying like a baby.

I consider telling her about it now, but bringing up something from months ago seems stupid, especially since she'd be pissed to know I ignored him. Still, the more she talks, the less time she has to think about all the reasons why she's so angry with me in the first place.

If only I had something meaningful to say.

We round the corner, and the Walgreens finally comes into view. "Seems like Dustin has a thing for Chloe, huh?" she says.

I swallow hard, knowing she could take any number of responses the wrong way. Setting her off now will disrupt the balance of our tenuous relationship, so the only sure bet is to redirect the conversation to someone else. "That guy Mikal's cute."

She scoffs. "Mikal's gay."

I glance at her, the streetlight from above creating a halo effect around her face. Her skin is pale with dark circles shadowing her eyes. How long has she looked this way? How long haven't I noticed?

What the hell is going on with her?

"No, he's not," I respond, unable to keep the indignance from my voice. "There's no way."

She shakes her head. "He showed up today in pink pineapple shorts and a Sailor Moon t-shirt. Plus, his bag is one giant rainbow flag. He's gay, Elise. He won't have any interest in me, if that's what you're thinking."

What I thought was his shorts were adorable. Because who doesn't like pineapples? And I figured the rest was some hipster stuff.

When I don't reply, she stops midstride. "Oh my God, do *you* like him?"

The way she says it—the mocking tone—keeps me from immediately responding. When she acts this way, I've learned to ignore her, which is why I keep walking. I mean sure, what I want to do is turn on my heel, get right up in her face, and explain how ridiculous it is to think I could possibly like a guy I've literally known for five hours.

But the truth is, it's not Mikal who grabbed my attention, even if he does seem funny and smart and adorable. It's Seamus who made my heart swoon, listening to him tell the others about delivering baby goats on his grandfather's farm. But I won't confess this to Wylla. If she knows I like someone, even as friends, she'll end up sabotaging it, whether she intends to or not.

Because why would any guy want to hang out with me when they could be with Wylla instead?

A moment later, her sneakers pound the pavement behind me as she catches up, her breath raspy. "It's just like you to fall for the guy you can't have. It's honestly a solid plan, though, because if you spend all your time pining away for someone who's too gay like Mikal or too popular like Logan, you don't have to worry about being rejected by someone you might actually stand a chance with."

I'm supposed to be using our time together on this trip to make things right between us, but when she says stuff like this, I just can't. Here I am, going out of my way to make accommodations for her, but instead of appreciating my effort, she pisses on me the way she always does.

Why do I even bother?

I slip a ten-dollar bill from my wallet and toss it at her before heading back toward the motel. "Get the Dramamine yourself. I'm out."

At the end of the block, I check over my shoulder for her, but of course, she's gone and isn't coming after me. She's always been a firm believer in 'telling it like it is' regardless of whether or not the truth needs to be told. And maybe I *didn't* understand back when we were still kids playing H-O-R-S-E in the driveway that my best friend Logan would eventually grow up to be way out of my league. But by middle school, I'd gained enough self-awareness to realize the boy next door was never gonna fall for a girl like me.

His feelings for Wylla were another story altogether, though—until I managed to ruin everything for all of us.

The walk back to the motel feels endless—stuck inside my own head, trying to convince myself Wylla's wrong about me. I don't care if Logan was never more than a friend because our childhood together was enough. Like the time he stood up for me when I started wearing glasses in first grade, telling the kid who called me Four Eyes to back off. Or the year my dad left, when we weren't poor enough for free lunch but were too poor to pay, so he shared his turkey sandwich and chips with me every day.

It didn't matter if he liked Wylla in ways he never liked me.

And after all these months, when it came to choosing between his future or hers, I still stand by my decision.

There's no light peeking out from between the drawn curtains as I approach the motel room, and it dawns on me that poor Chloe's been locked out this whole time. Instead of going to find her, though, I leave the deadbolt unlatched and hole up inside by myself. She's probably hanging out with

Dustin in another room anyway, and at this point, I lack the strength for small talk.

With the bathroom to myself, I prepare for bed, lingering in the shower—hoping if I give the water long enough, it'll wash away the sting of Wylla's words. But of course, it doesn't, and they're still rolling around inside my head when I eventually crawl between the covers and turn out the light.

But sleep eludes me, and instead of closing my eyes, I lay there quiet in the stillness compiling a list of all the bad things that could happen to Wylla between the pharmacy and the hotel. It would be just my luck if something were to happen to her on my watch.

CHAPTER 6

Hours later, I'm startled awake by someone hollering outside the window as the door swings open. Chloe stumbles into the room, cursing under her breath, and as she makes her way to the bathroom, I glance at the clock on the nightstand.

It's just after two in the morning.

I roll over, burying my head beneath the pillow in an attempt to muffle the gargling sounds from the other room, when I remember Wylla. I bolt upright, but as I'm fumbling around the nightstand for my glasses someone stirs in the other bed. She's there, of course, hair splayed across her pillow in gentle waves, breathing softly through parted lips. My gut reaction is to be offended that she chose to sleep in the second bed instead of crawling in with me, but considering how quiet she must've been not to wake me, I reconsider.

Maybe her decision wasn't meant as a snub. Maybe she genuinely didn't want to disturb me.

Several minutes later, the toilet flushes, and the bed creaks beneath Chloe as she climbs in beside my sister, who doesn't rouse in the slightest. I don't know how long I lay awake, listening to them breathing on the other side of the room, but when the alarm on my phone goes off at nine o'clock, it feels like I've been run over by the Mystery Machine.

Chloe and Wylla barely stir, so I snag the bathroom first. On the edge of the sink, there's a Walgreen's bag with a bottle of Dramamine. The sight of it makes my stomach drop. I'm glad she has something to stave off the nausea, of course, but a little part of me was hoping she wouldn't be able to manage on her own. Clearly, though, that wasn't the case.

She didn't need me after all.

By the time I'm finished getting ready for the day, they're both up and dressed, mindlessly scrolling through their Instagram feeds. I purposely avoid making eye contact with them. "I'm all done in there, so I'm gonna head outside to wait for the others."

"M'kay." Chloe throws her legs over the side of the bed and stretches, lithe and lethargic like a cat. "See you out there."

I hesitate for a beat, waiting for Wylla to acknowledge my existence, but she doesn't. Instead, she just lays there, scrolling and scrolling, as if I was the rude one last night.

I let the door slam shut behind me and without regard to my sleeping neighbors, stomp down the metal staircase to the parking lot. Mikal, Seamus, and Travis are already sprawled across three lounge chairs beside the pool, sunning themselves. The pool itself looks less than inviting—something toxic and green is growing on the surface—but Ernie still hasn't made an appearance, and the pool deck seems a good a place as any to wait for him.

Way better than my room.

Travis spots me across the parking lot and stops combing his beard long enough to wave me over. "Morning, Elise. We saved you a seat."

No other guests are occupying any of the deck loungers, so there are literally a dozen other chairs to choose from, but I grab the one he's reserved for me just the same.

Carrot-topped Seamus finishes applying a coat of sunscreen to his freckled nose and cheeks before wiping the excess onto his athletic shorts. There's a stack of papers on the chair between his knees, and I'm curious about what he's printed out.

"How'd you sleep?" he asks.

"Alright, I guess." I don't tell him about being woken up in the middle of the night by Chloe. I don't ask if he was with her or if she was off with Dustin as I suspect.

Travis stashes his black plastic comb in his fanny pack and leans back in his seat. "Mikal, Seamus, and I were sitting here, planning our day. Which rides we wanna hit and which foods to try. And, of course, working on a strategy for finding those tokens. Mikal and I are gonna work together on that." His eyes cut to Seamus then back to me—an invitation. "So, maybe the two of you wanna work together?" He shrugs. "Either way, we can all four tag along together on the rides if you'd like."

I hesitate, considering their offer. After our argument last night, I'm glad I never got around to asking Wylla if she wants to help me find the tokens, because at this point, I'd rather search by myself. Spending all day with these three seems a lot more fun than hanging out with my bratty sister, anyway.

A twinge of guilt picks at the corner of my selfish logic, but screw it. I'm doing her a favor by simply being here. I never promised to stay with her every minute of every day.

"What rides are at the top of your list?" I ask Seamus.

He hands the papers in his lap to Mikal who hands them to me—printouts of the Kennywood map from the website with about a dozen locations circled. "The coasters, of course:

Sky Rocket, Exterminator, Jack Rabbit, Phantom's Revenge…" He trails off. "Then, I dunno, you guys might think this is weird, but I have sort of a soft spot for the classic carnival rides." He's marked a bunch of them with yellow highlighter.

"The Whip, Musik Express, the Pirate… we have all of these at Drury," I say.

Seamus shakes his head, pointing to the map with conviction. "Not all of them. We don't have the Kangaroo. It says on the website it's the last of its kind."

I glance at him, expecting to see a smirk like he's kidding about the whole conversation, but his face is inscrutable, and I consider the possibility he's being sincere. He catches my gaze and before I can look away, something flickers inside his eyes. A hint of longing or the desire to be understood? Either way, his passionate delivery is enough to sell me on the classic appeal of carnival rides—a return to innocence and simpler times when it was enough to spin around and around and around.

"I'll ride the Kangaroo with you," I tell him. "And I'll work with you to find the tokens if you want."

Seamus agrees to our partnership, his pasty complexion crimsoning, and Mikal raises a perfectly shaped eyebrow at Travis in an 'I told you so' sort of way. Now would be the time to ask about the possibility of Wylla tagging along, but I honestly don't want to let her anywhere near this blossoming circle of friendship. Not Travis. Not Mikal.

And especially not Seamus.

"The other page is the first token clue." Mikal rolls the hem of his shorts. "We were about to look at it when you showed up."

I pull it from beneath Seamus's map and read it aloud. "Everyone enters two by two."

Mikal lowers his sunglasses, peering over them at me. "Girl, that's it?"

I turn the paper over to make sure there's nothing else written on the back. "Yup. Everyone enters two by two."

"Maybe it's a ride where there are only two people to a seat," Travis says.

Mikal sighs. "So, like, most of them."

I glance up at Seamus, and he's grinning at me the way Nia does when she knows we're about to nail a performance. He's already figured out the clue, and I suppress my own smile, knowing better than to give this bit of information to the others. It's a competition after all, so I change the subject as a way out of the token conversation.

"Cool shirt," I say to Seamus, eying the Pikachu on his chest.

He glances at it before raising an eyebrow at me, like maybe my compliment isn't really a compliment. "Yeah. Pokémon. It's cool, right?"

Travis pipes up. "My boys used to collect those cards when they were kids 'Bout took me broke buying the damn things."

"I gave my cards to my little nephews," Mikal says. "But I still watch the TV show."

I pull out my phone to put Pokémon on my Netflix watchlist as Dustin, Chloe, and Wylla cross the parking lot together. I don't mean to stare as they stroll casually from the motel to the van, but the way the three of them look together, like they own the place, knots my stomach. Wylla's laughing along with Chloe at something Dustin's said, and it's clear she won't be asking to tag along with me.

"They certainly seem to have hit it off," Travis says in the same tone my dad uses when he's trying to sound relevant around Wylla and her friends. Still, I can't tell if he thinks their budding friendship is a good thing or a bad thing.

That makes two of us.

Before anyone can respond, however, Ernie pops out of the motel office, van keys jingling in his hand. "Let's hit a drive-thru for breakfast, then head straight to the park. It opens at ten thirty, and I don't want you all to miss a minute of the excitement."

Although Ernie's forced enthusiasm brings an eyeroll and audible groan from Mikal, it makes me smile. He seems like the type of person who's able to put a positive spin on just about anything, which is one of the qualities I love most about Nia and will miss while we're apart.

I drag my bags over to the van behind the guys and after everyone's gear is loaded, we pile inside. My sister gets in the back with Chloe and Dustin, so I'm left in the front, alone. I shouldn't be surprised she's abandoned me already since it's kind of her MO, but I still find myself staring a hole through the window at the Pittsburg suburbs, fighting to hold back tears.

Until Seamus slides in beside me.

"It's the Noah's Ark ride," he whispers with a wink. "We should head there first thing."

I nod in agreement and force a smile, replacing the disappointment of Wylla's rejection with the possibility of a new friendship with this quirky ginger.

After a trip through the drive-thru for breakfast sandwiches, the van is silent but for the sound of quiet munching until Travis finishes, clearing his throat with the gusto reserved for someone announcing the queen. "So,

Dustin, right? Why don't you tell us a little about yourself, young man?"

Dustin, who until now hasn't spoken to anyone but Chloe and my sister, considers Travis smugly as he swallows a bite of his sandwich. "What'd you want to know?" he asks condescendingly.

Travis brushes a few biscuit crumbs from his beard onto the floor before turning around, draping his arm over the seatback. "No need to take that kinda tone," he says. "I'm just interested in getting to know you young folks a bit, that's all. We are gonna be spending an awful lot of time together over the next few weeks. Figured we should know a little bit about one another."

Dustin, Chloe, and my sister exchange a look—the same look she throws at me whenever she's annoyed by something I've done.

"I'm Dustin Cobbs," he says with a shrug. "College junior. Starting second basemen for my school's baseball team. I still haven't decided on a major, but maybe after this trip it'll be mechanical engineering. You know, so I can design coasters and stuff."

Beside him, Wylla swoons like designing roller coasters is the sexiest job on earth. I'm all set to be irritated, except she does kind of have a point. I wouldn't turn down an opportunity to hook up with a dude who designs roller coasters, so I suppose in this particular case, her obvious flirting is justified.

Travis seems appeased by Dustin's response and moves on to Chloe. "What about you, little lady?"

It's not that I'm uninterested in what she has to say, but as soon she starts droning on about her part-time job at GAP and legions of sorority sisters, I tune her out, focusing on my own concerns instead. Because if Travis's interrogation continues around the van one person at a time, he's gonna get to me eventually. And when he does, what the hell am I gonna say?

Do I mention my all-county clarinet title?

How I totaled my car in an accident that made the front page of the local paper?

The Zoloft I'm supposed to be taking twice a day for my PTSD?

Or maybe I should lead with how my sister's barely spoken to me since I singlehandedly destroyed our relationship with our childhood best friend, Logan, last fall?

Luckily, before Chloe finishes describing how her recent spring break experience led her to consider a career in modeling, Ernie announces we've arrived at Kennywood. He parks in the drop-off, handing us our entry passes and food vouchers as we exit the van.

"Don't lose these because I don't have extra." He holds onto Dustin's ticket a few extra seconds, for emphasis. Although it's somewhat reassuring to know he's as leery of this guy as I am, it also gives me pause. Agreeing with the old dude about Dustin's character is wholly indicative of the prudish behavior Wylla's always accusing me of. "And remember, we're meeting back here in the parking lot at seven o'clock tonight. If you're not here, you're on your own getting to Ohio."

"Wait," Mikal says when Ernie climbs back into the van. "Aren't you coming into the park with us?"

He gives a shrug. "Like I said, the budget was tight. You all go on without me and have a great time."

My heart breaks a little for our driver who won't get to experience any of the 'thrills and chills' he's been talking so much about. It doesn't seem fair, but then again, my life has never been fair, so maybe that's just the way it is for some of us. Things always seem to work out for people like Wylla, though, which is why I'm surprised to catch a wisp of jealousy flicker across her face when Chloe threads her arm through Dustin's. My sister adjusts her course, tossing her backpack across one shoulder as she sidesteps an oncoming car, and for a second, I assume she's ditching them to come with me instead. Tension releases in my neck and shoulders—maybe today will be the day we can start anew—but the familiar stomachache returns the moment she takes Dustin's other arm, her winning smile plastered across her face.

Once again, she's leaving me behind.

CHAPTER 7

Kennywood, it turns out, is a lot like Drury Park, in that it's old and a lot of the rides are half-a-step above carnival grade. This includes Noah's Ark, which is an eighty-year-old walkthrough funhouse full of quirky gags about all the animals gathering before the Great Flood. After entering through a gigantic pink tube, designed to simulate the mouth of a whale, it only takes Seamus and I about twenty minutes to find the red token bag, tucked away behind the tail of a bird at the end of the ride.

He pockets the first token and hands the second to me as we emerge from the darkness of the ark back into the sunlight. "After that pathetic ride, I'm in the mood for something with a little more speed." He pulls his map from his backpack and hands it to me. "Maybe we should hit our first coaster."

It's still early, so we ride the Steel Curtain before its line grows into a three-hour wait. Happily, the coaster with world's tallest inversion does not disappoint, which is exactly what I tell Travis and Mikal when we run into them on the other side of the ride photo line.

"How was it?" Travis asks as the four of us set off on a stroll along the midway together.

"Amazing," I tell them. "Scary good."

Seamus raises his hands to the sky like he's a Baptist praying to Jesus. "It was awesome. Face down, two-hundred-feet up, with only a harness strapping you in—nothing like confronting death head on to make you feel alive." He lowers his ballcap across his forehead to shade the sun before tuning to Mikal. "And also, if you guys are still looking for the tokens, you can stop."

Mikal claps Travis on the back. "Told you they got them." He turns to me. "They were in the ark, weren't they?"

"Two by two," I say with a grin.

"Two by two," Travis repeats.

The sugary aroma from a nearby funnel cake stand distracts me as Seamus pulls the token from his pocket. The guys gush over him like he's discovered the holy grail, and they're so focused on the coins, I half expect them not to notice the approaching herd of teenage girls—not a ponytail in sight, with perfectly winged eyeliner and shorts more suited for clubbing than coasters.

But Travis sees them.

And he sees me seeing them.

He takes as step in my direction and lowers his voice, cutting his eyes to Mikal with a shake of his head. "I feel sort of bad, you know? Poor kid's stuck schlepping around with my old ass all day, instead of, well…" He hesitates, looking after the girls as they saunter past, the scent of cotton candy lingering in their wake. "Hanging out with me is probably cramping his style with the ladies, that's all I'm saying."

On the far edge of the sidewalk, Mikal's head is thrown back, laughing at Seamus's impersonation of the ark's giraffe.

"He doesn't seem disappointed to me," I say.

My voice must carry above the roar of the closest coaster because as Seamus tucks the coin back into his pocket, he gives me a quizzical look. "Who doesn't seem disappointed?"

I glance at Travis for an indication of how to respond, but he's already draped his arm around Mikal in a fatherly embrace. "I was just saying, I thought you might be kind of disappointed about being partnered with me instead of a pretty girl like Elise."

He waggles his eyebrows, and my jaw falls open. How am I supposed to react to that?

Luckily, Mikal doesn't miss a beat—clearing his throat as he extracts himself from Travis's armpit. "Hanging out with you isn't keeping me from having some romantic summer fling with Elise or any other girl, if that's what you're thinking."

"Well, now, why the hell not? She's a good-looking lady."

Glancing at Mikal, with his hip thrust to one side and head cocked to the other, it occurs to me that Wylla might be right about his sexual preference. And now I'm super uncomfortable because they're speaking about me like I'm not standing beside them which is pretty much an analogy for my life.

"It doesn't matter how amazing Elise is, or any other girl for that matter, because I'm gay. I like guys." He gives me a good-natured pat on the shoulder. "No offense to you, Elise."

"None taken," I tell him sincerely.

He kisses the air between us and continues. "I didn't come on this trip to make a love connection. I've got an amazing boyfriend waiting for me at home. I just wanna ride some great coasters and make some new friends. That's it. So please don't think hanging out with you is a letdown."

At this point, all eyes have turned to Travis who's now staring at his sneakers like they've become sentient and hold all the answers to the universe. It's obvious I wasn't the only one who didn't figure out the truth about Mikal on my own—damn you, Wylla—because Mikal's declaration clearly caught Travis off guard. When you're gay, it must be hard figuring out who's an ally and who's not, and it honestly feels to me like Travis could go either way.

He wipes a bead a sweat off his brow with the bandana he keeps tucked in his back pocket, like he's considering an exit strategy—maybe a feigned illness paired with an Uber ride back to the hotel. "Why don't you all go on without me for a bit. I'm feeling a little weak and better go grab myself a Coke before my blood sugar gets too low." When none of us move, he continues. "Go on, now. I'll catch up with you in a bit."

Mikal protests, but Travis waves him off before heading in the direction of the nearest drink stand. After a brief discussion about whether we should go after him, the three of us continue around the paddleboat lake in silence until a familiar voice grabs my attention.

"Hey, guys! D'you ride the Steel Curtain?" Chloe jogs toward us, her flip flops slapping the concrete, Dustin and Wylla following close behind. "Being upside-down that high up almost made me pee my pants."

Mikal gives all three of them a once over. "You sure you didn't?" They're soaked, head to toe, and have evidently ridden the Pittsburg Plunge or Raging Rapids in the last hour or so.

Missing the joke, Chloe raises a confused eyebrow but doesn't respond. Instead, she thumbs over her shoulder toward the other side of the park. "We were just heading over to Ghostwood Estate to bust some ghouls. You guys want to come along?"

The other half of our traveling party disappeared just beyond the main gate when we first arrived, so I haven't seen Wylla in hours. I scan my sister's eyes for some indication of remorse for bailing on me, but her perma-grin is plastered smugly on her face, right where it always is. If she's missing her boyfriend, Jackson, she doesn't show it. If she's the tiniest bit upset about the way things went down between us last night, she's hiding it well.

And, of course, she doesn't think to ask about Travis's whereabouts.

"Yeah, sure." Seamus inspects his trusty map and turns in the direction of Ghostwood Estates. "It's this way, past the pizza place."

Ghostwood Estates, as it turns out, is a mash up between a ride-thru haunted house and a video game, like if Disney World combined the Haunted Mansion with Buzz Lightyear's Space Ranger Spin. The guys spend our time in the cue searching YouTube on their phones for ways to max out their scores on the ride while Chloe scrolls through her Snapchats, leaving Wylla and I to pretend we aren't purposely ignoring one another. Luckily, the line moves quickly, and I barely have time to worry about how I'm going to finagle my way into the four-person car with the guys.

As we approach the loading area, however, Chloe elbows her way to the front of our group with Dustin and hops into the front seat beside him before I can object. The attendant ushers Seamus and Mikal into the back, and as the car takes off, Seamus gives a sad wave and mouths the word, "Sorry."

The next empty car approaches, and Wylla follows me into the front row. Behind us, two preteen boys clamor on, smelling of sunscreen and gym socks, and for a second, I'm grateful to have a little sister instead of a little brother. I lift my gun from the closest slot, and wrap my fingers around the plastic, worn smooth by the thousands of hands that have come before. The green paint on the barrel is chipped on both sides, and I give the trigger a squeeze to make sure it works, eliciting an electronic sounding 'pew.'

Wylla follows suit, the muscles in her arm tightening against mine as she tests her own gun. Without a word between us, the change in her demeanor is palpable. I should've known how she'd react to being placed in a competitive situation. She can't pass up an opportunity to outshine me, even if it's on a stupid amusement park ride with two eleven-year-old witnesses.

Inching toward the ride's entrance, a door swings open and an ultra-cold blast of air-conditioning raises goosebumps to my flesh. I shiver and draw my legs together, wincing in pain as I peel the back of my thighs from the plastic seat. Beside me, Wylla's pursed lips and narrowed eyes speak to her anticipation. Part of me considers holstering my gun. Why should I give her the satisfaction of beating me? But the other part—a bigger part—wants to wipe the floor with her.

Guns drawn, we enter the first room, where it's clear we're supposed to aim for the illuminated discs. I line up my first shot, and when it connects, a spider dances above my head. Wylla doesn't notice, of course, because she's too busy opening fire at every disc on her side of the car. Around us, skeletons and ghosts of every shape and size come to life, animated by our direct hits.

There are dead pirates in the next room, and although I want desperately to sneak a peek at my sister's score, I can't risk missing my own targets. Even more distracting are the boys behind us, who—thanks to the sulfurous smell of a fog machine—are now making fart sounds with every shot they take, laughing hysterically at themselves. I want to be annoyed at them for breaking my concentration, but instead a lump forms in my throat; envious of their ability to simply appreciate the ride, not caring who gets the higher score.

We continue deeper into the house, through a library and a sitting room, where the ghosts seem to be egging us on. I could stop now. Simply put down my gun and enjoy the rest of the ride without regard for my final score. If I do, though, she'll assume I gave up because I couldn't beat her.

She'll take the win regardless.

I continue shooting, disc after disc, room after room, until I'm no longer truly aware of what's going on around me. I'm running on instinct, and my mind wanders to one of the many times the universe conspired to pit us against one another in competition.

When I was eight, I asked for a new bike from Santa—the only thing I truly wanted—so of course I was thrilled when a shiny Schwinn with a big red bow was waiting for me beside the tree Christmas morning.

Until I saw a matching bike with an identical bow waiting for my six-year-old sister on the other side of the tree.

Acid churned in the pit of my stomach as my elation quickly turned to rage. Wylla hadn't asked for a bike. Worse still, she couldn't even ride without training wheels. That didn't stop her, though, from following me out to the driveway after breakfast to test out our new presents. She watched while I clipped on my helmet, nearly pinching her fingers adjusting her own.

"Will you wait for me?" she asked as I took off toward the street.

"Keep up if you can," I called back.

I was determined to leave her behind, punishment for the way she sullied the joy of my gift. I'd begged for months for the new bike, a replacement for the rusted, thrift store hand-me-down I'd been riding around the neighborhood with my best friend Logan since I was Wylla's age. But the rasp of her labored breathing and rattle of her training wheels grew louder as she began catching up, and I channeled the mounting anger into my legs, spinning them faster and faster, not wanting her to overtake me. She would never know the embarrassment of riding a worn-out bike with missing handle tassels and a ripped banana seat. Worse still, now the other kids, including Logan, would know her as the girl with the cool, new bike.

A moniker which was supposed to have been mine.

I sped around the block, faster than I should've been going. Luckily, it was Christmas morning, and the roads were abandoned. Maybe that's why she was able to catch me before I made it all the way around the block. Or maybe her legs were just stronger than mine. Either way, with Mom watching from the front porch, I was determined to beat Wylla home.

But she passed me on the straightaway, startling me so severely, I crashed into our mailbox.

Of course, Mom and Wylla both rushed over to make sure I was okay. There were a few scrapes and bruises, but no major injuries. My bike, on the other hand, didn't fair nearly as well. The front wheel was bent and the rim busted, like my dreams of being a neighborhood celebrity. Snot ran down my face as I sat on the front lawn, sobbing into my jacket, not only for the destruction of my gift but for my wounded ego as well. What I needed in that moment was for my mom to acknowledge my loss in a way that centered my feelings. What she said instead was, "Who knew Wylla was gonna come up on you so fast, huh? She's a real little racer, that one."

Beside me now in the final room of the ride, my sister's intense focus has spread to the boys in the back seat, who have stopped goofing off and are now trash talking one another about their scores.

"Six thousand? Were you even trying, you loser?"

"Dude, my gun was barely working. It's not even fair."

For the first time, I chance a glance at Wylla's score, hoping her gun might not be working either, and we can pretend this whole ride never happened.

But it's working. And she's crushed me.

"Nice job," she says as I follow her out of the car. I have no idea whether she means it sincerely or if she's only saying something so I know she knows she beat me.

I force myself to smile and meet her gaze. There's something there. An invitation, perhaps. An opportunity to let things be without having to acknowledge one of us is better than the other.

For the first time in my life, I take it.

"You, too." I say.

"Listen, folks, if we're gonna make it to the other nine parks in the next thirteen days, we gotta make tracks. That means getting to the van on time in the evenings so I'm not stuck behind the wheel until after midnight every night."

Ernie's looking at all of us like it wasn't just Dustin, Chloe, and Wylla who were late. But it was, and they're all wet again, riding the whitewater rapids last like a bunch of idiots. Now I'm stuck waiting in the parking lot while they change their clothes in the back of the van.

Mikal and I are still discussing dinner options with Ernie and Seamus when Dustin throws open the sliding door. "We're finished. And I'm starving, so let's go."

Seamus rolls his eyes, drawing a smile from me. Is being annoyed by the same person a solid foundation for a friendship? Because it seems to be working so far.

"So, where are we heading?" Ernie asks. "Did you guys decide on a place to pick up some dinner?"

Chloe pipes up from the back seat. "Chick-fil-A?"

"That's a hard pass from me," Mikal says.

"You have something against waffle fries?"

Mikal turns around in his seat to address her face-to-face. "No. Waffle fries are fine. What I take issue with is the company's stand on same sex marriage and their continued policy of giving financial support to anti-LGBTQ groups."

Behind me, Travis purses his lips, and even though we caught up with him later in the day, I'm still not sure how he feels about Mikal's sexual orientation.

Dustin, however, is quick to offer his opinion.

"It's just food, dude. Not everything needs to be political."

"It's not political. It's…" Mikal hesitates in a weary sort of way which speaks to an overwhelming exhaustion.

I open my mouth to defend him as Seamus clears his throat. "It's basic human dignity," he says, finishing for Mikal.

A strange sort of relief settles over me. At least Seamus isn't a jackass.

I chance a glance at my sister, expecting her to weigh in. She loves Chick-fil-A sauce in a way that borders on obsession. It's her go-to condiment and given the opportunity, she'll put it on just about anything. She's smart enough not to speak up against Mikal and Seamus, though, and her restraint elicits a twinge of pride.

"I'm actually in the mood for a nice burrito," Travis says. "Anyone else want to hit a Taco Bell or something?"

"There's a Chipotle right off the interstate." I pull up the location on my phone. "It's couple of exits from here, Ernie."

He glances at me in the rearview mirror. "Everybody good with Chipotle?"

Wylla nods enthusiastically, and even Chloe gives a begrudging thumbs up.

A murmur of thanks passes between Mikal and Travis.

I guess now I know where he stands.

Ernie orders the food to go and the rest of us compare favorite rides and opinions about the newest coaster as we eat. Travis works hard to keep the conversation going, and although it shouldn't seem funny that the guy who looks most like he could kill you with his bare hands is the peacemaker of the group, he keeps surprising me at every turn.

"I don't know, guys, the Exterminator was pretty awesome," he says. "It was an experience, not just a ride, you know? With the animatronics and strobe lights and audio. Definitely the best ride in the park."

"Plus, the darkness made the hairpin turns intense," Dustin adds.

Wylla nods in agreement, and as she takes a bite of her burrito, the entire back end busts open, dumping rice and beans all over her lap. Of course, she'd spill on herself now when Mom's not here to see it.

Of the two of us, I've always been the messy eater while Wylla's someone to be emulated when it comes to table manners. My whole life has been a symphony of 'why can't you use your napkin properly like Wylla,' and 'how hard is it to keep your food in your mouth while you're chewing the way Wylla does?' It's not that I don't try to be careful, but somehow, I always manage to spill something on myself at every meal.

I'm tempted to say something snarky to her now, but as she scrambles to salvage what's left of her dinner, I simply hand her my napkins instead.

She smiles, and the relief on her face is worth having kept my mouth shut.

***

The sun sets below the horizon, and Ernie, Wylla, and I are the only ones still awake as mileage signs to Cleveland begin peppering the landscape. We haven't spoken directly to one another since our strange little truce at the end of the Ghostwood Estate ride, and the last thing I want is to create turmoil between us now. But she needs to know why the comments she made to me last night were hurtful, and despite everything that's happened, she can't continue taking passive aggressive shots at every turn.

I know better than to lead with my grievances, though. Wherever Wylla's concerned, it's best to back into the conversation.

With that in mind, I skootch down in my seat and lean toward her until our shoulders touch, hoping the hum of the engine will be enough to drown out my voice. "How'd it go with Chloe and Dustin today?" I whisper.

She keeps her face turned to the window. Shadows from the overhead lights dance across her profile. "It was fine." She shrugs. "They're pretty nice, but honestly, it felt like they thought I should be grateful they let me tag along with them all day."

The truth of her confession sinks in, and I'm surprised she has the self-awareness to see her position in their group objectively. Still, this doesn't prevent a strange defensive reaction from stirring inside of me. "Were they mean?"

She turns from the window, resting her head against the seat beside mine. Being inside her personal space feels strange, and I can't remember the last time I was close enough to count the freckles on her nose or see the tiny flecks of gold in her hazel eyes. "No. Nothing like that. Just…" She breaks off, her voice catching. "I'm sick of always being treated like everyone's little sister."

I stifle a laugh. They're treating her like a kid because they're six years older than she is. They're technically adults, and she's still a child. But the real reason she's upset has nothing to do with the age difference and everything to do with Dustin's attention. She wants him to take an interest in her over Chloe.

But he hasn't.

Fifteen is way too young for a college junior—which he obviously realizes even if she can't—leaving me with two options moving forward: be brutally honest or say something empathetic to soften the blow. Our tumultuous history would justify taking a swipe at her, but I'm no monster.

"Maybe they sense you're in a weird emotional place right now, and they're just trying to give you some space." I raise my brows at her, but she brushes off my analysis with a shake of her head. This is the perfect opportunity to expose her real motivation for leaving home, though, so I continue prying despite her annoyed expression. "Have you said anything to them about Jackson?"

The road noise carries the silence between us as she pulls away. "No. Why would I?"

"I dunno. I mean, I thought you might have shared your reasons for coming on the trip. If you told them about what's going on with him, it might explain why they're acting kind of parental."

I have no idea what transpired between them, but as anger flares in her eyes, it's obvious she won't tell me now.

"What's that supposed to mean? You think they're treating me like a kid because my boyfriend issues make me sound childish? Jesus, Elise, at least I've had boyfriends."

I wasn't braced for the blow, so her shot hits me square in the heart. Why does she always assume I'm coming for her? That every comment I make is a snub, designed to bring her down?

If I text Nia about this conversation later, she'll be disappointed if I can't report that I didn't at least try standing up for myself. Not that she'd expect me to throw a tantrum or anything, but she's constantly encouraging me to let people know how I feel instead of staying silent.

"Speak up for yourself," she told me recently when I was passed over for a spot on the debate team for what seemed like the hundredth time. "And for Christ's sake, stop being so level-headed."

But I suck at showing my emotions. And it's not that I don't get angry because let's face it, rage is getting to be my default setting these days. It's just that in my family, putting my feelings on display only gets me in trouble, and things usually work out better if I keep things to myself.

Now, though, Nia's words reverberate in my head, pushing me into action.

"Look, I didn't mean anything by it. I was just trying to come up with a plausible explanation for their behavior." I don't add that Dustin and Chloe are clearly into one another and probably wish she'd leave them alone.

Her fists ball in her lap. "Why are you always so mean to me? What did I ever do?"

Mikal's foot presses into the back of my seat as he adjusts his sleeping position against the window. I lower my voice to keep from disturbing him. "Excuse me, what? *I'm* mean to *you*? Name one time I've been anything but nice."

She scoffs before shooting an icy glare in my direction. "I could name about a million, but how about we start with last night when you left me stranded in the middle of a strange city all by myself. That was tremendously un-nice."

"Are you kidding me right now? I left *you* stranded? No. Just no." Every instinct in my body tells me bury the hurt and the anger and keep my mouth shut, but look where that's gotten me. I shift away from her, needing space. "First of all, you weren't stranded. You were always within walking distance of the motel. And secondly, I only left because *you* were mean to *me*, and I didn't want to blow up at you. But maybe I should've."

"Mean to *you*? *I* was telling the truth." Her voice carries around the van, threatening to wake the others. A glance at the rearview mirror reveals Ernie staring back at me, his lips pressed into a tight line.

So much for keeping our conversation private.

A beat passes, and when I finally find the words to respond, my voice is barely above a whisper. "Sometimes, instead of brutal honesty, it would be nice if you could keep your hot take opinions to yourself."

"Look, if you don't want to face the truth about yourself, that's on you." She throws her hands up in defensive apology. "But when it came to you and Logan, everyone was laughing at you behind your back because you didn't stand a chance with him. You know that, right? It was embarrassing for you. I did you a favor."

My jaw hurts from the pressure of my molars grinding against one another. "It was embarrassing for *me* or it was embarrassing for *you*?"

"For God's sake, Elise, it was embarrassing for both of us. And everyone knows why you ratted him out. He publicly rejected you, and if you couldn't have him, nobody could. Including me." She swallows. "Especially me."

She assumes I turned on him because I was angry at her for being the one he chose instead, but that's not it at all. I've attempted explaining the truth to her at least a dozen times, but she never lets me finish, so trying again now won't do any good. Still, memories of that muggy September evening in his basement linger—the way my hair plastered itself to the back of my neck, thick with sweat caused by the anxiety of what I needed to do.

Did I like Logan? Of course.

Did I love him? Probably, yes.

But at the end of the day, I loved my sister more, and she had gotten in too deep. Sacrificing him for her was the only way to keep her from destroying the rest of her life.

In the months since, I've asked myself a million times if I could have done something different—something that might have protected Wylla while still preserving our relationship—but there was no other way. Maybe, *maybe*, if the three of us wouldn't have been so entrenched in each other's lives since we were babies, we'd still be speaking now. But I underestimated how much she loved him.

Or maybe I simply underestimated how little she loved me.

There's nothing left to say, and I wish like hell I wasn't stuck beside her in this stupid, smelly van for the next hour. But there's nowhere to go and no one else to talk to, so all that's left is to turn away. I shift toward the door, setting my daypack on the seat between us the way we would when we were children so neither of us crossed over the invisible line into the other's space. I pull out my phone to text Mom and Nia when her screen illuminates in her lap.

A text from Mom.

Hey hon. Just checking in. Hope you're having a good time. Please stay safe and call me when you get a chance.

Glancing at my own screen, the air in my lungs feels like sand inside my chest. I count off the seconds: one, two, three, four. She texted Wylla first, which is fine. No big deal. But how long does it take to copy/paste the same message to me? Ten seconds? Maybe she got distracted on Facebook. Or needed to use the bathroom. Still, it should be coming anytime now. If I'm patient and wait, she'll reach out. She cares about me, too.

Right?

Right?

A minute passes. Then a second and a third. Beside me, Wylla fires off a response.

Everything's good. We're almost to Cedar Point. I'll call you in the morning.

Mom replies immediately.

Okay. Have a good night. Love you.

Love you too.

My own phone lies expectantly in my lap. I glance at the signal strength—full bars—and the battery which is at twenty-six percent. If she wants to find out how *I* am, there's nothing stopping her from getting through.

Except maybe not caring.

CHAPTER 9

I sleep with my phone charging beneath my pillow all night, and by sleep I mean lay awake listening for my phone to vibrate, alerting me to a text from Mom which, of course, never comes.

It's almost a relief when the alarm goes off at five-thirty. At least starting the day means I'll have something to distract me from my position as the runner-up daughter in my family.

Wylla stirs beside me as I climb out of bed, but she doesn't wake. The thinnest hint of sunlight slices its way between the curtains and brightens the room just enough for me to see my way safely through the minefield of luggage to the bathroom. I ease the door shut behind me before cutting on the light and am dismayed by the haggard teenager staring back at me in the mirror. Dark circles shadow the hollows beneath my eyes and despite spending the previous day in the sun, my skin is blanched like a dried-out seashell. I rake my fingers through my hair and pile it on top of my head with an elastic before realizing, after riding coasters the day before, I should take time to comb out the knots properly and do something more proactive to protect it from today's adventure. After a quick shower, I plait two Dutch braids along either side of my head, and although my fingers are cramped by the time I finish, I'm pretty pleased with the result.

I brush my teeth, and as I'm spitting into the sink, catch a glimpse of the Zoloft bottle in the bottom of my toiletry bag. Mom's voice echoes in my head. Something about being consistent. Something about giving the medication time to take full effect. I ignore her, though. I've been panic-attack-free for so long, I'm certain I no longer need the stupid pills.

Both Wylla and Chloe are dressed by the time I finish using the bathroom, and I try my best to make small talk with Chloe as she brushes mascara across her lashes.

"They should've disclosed this part of the trip with us up front," she says. "Not that I wouldn't have come or anything, but forcing us to get up at five-thirty for some stupid 'Sunrise Thrills VIP Tour' is ridiculous."

I shrug. "It might be cool. I mean, when else are we gonna have a chance to go behind the scenes at one of the greatest amusement parks in the country?"

She swipes a layer of gloss across her lips and puckers hard. "Yeah, I guess. But why can't they do the tour at like noon or something?"

Her question is rhetorical, so I don't remind her there are lots of good reasons they can't take guests into the restricted sections of the park while it's open.

Once Chloe and Wylla finish primping, we meet the guys in the parking lot, and of course, Seamus has the park's website pulled up on his phone to educate everyone about what's in store.

"We get to climb to the top of the Valravn and see the mechanicals of the Millennium, the Maverick, and the Steel Vengeance. It's gonna be epic."

Ernie unlocks the van and opens the back for us to toss in our bags. While the others climb inside, Wylla chews at her thumbnail—clearly nervous about all the coasters she's expected to ride today. I'm about to say something to her about taking the Dramamine but stop short, remembering her accusations from the night before.

Screw it. If she gets sick, she gets sick.

Lips pursed, I slip into the van, taking the window seat. As we pull out of the parking lot, the sky brightens into layers of blues and oranges and pinks beyond the tree line. Daylight glistens across Lake Erie, and I fish my prescription sunglasses from my bag. Beside them, my phone buzzes with a notification.

Good morning Elise. Don't forget to take your pills. And have a fun day.

I swipe across the screen, dismissing the text. I should respond to her so she knows I'm okay, but when I notice she's texted Wylla as well, I ignore her. Let her favorite daughter keep her abreast of our situation.

At the park entrance, we're greeted by a middle-aged woman in pleated khaki shorts and a red Cedar Point polo. "Welcome," she says with a wave of her clipboard. "My name's Sandy, and I'm the operations supervisor for the rides department. I'll be facilitating your tour here today. Now, who's ready to head with me to the top of the Valravn?"

The guys respond with enough gusto for all of us, and after a short safety briefing about the dangers of falling and mechanical parts with the potential to sever limbs, I'm fitted with a safety belt and tether and led two-hundred-twenty-three feet to the top of the tallest, fastest, longest Dive Coaster in the world.

It's windy at the top, which shouldn't be a surprise, but somehow still manages to take my breath away. Sandy attaches my tether to a rail, and I'm encouraged, along with the others, to follow single-file around the perimeter of the platform. Dustin and Chloe are the first onto the walkway, and if the sparkle in her eyes is any indication, she's no longer upset about the early hour.

She calls back to us, hands cupped at her mouth. "You guys! Hurry up! You can see everything from up here."

Mikal, Travis, and Seamus follow them onto the platform, leaving Wylla and I alone with only our safety belts and tethers between us. The wind tosses her hair across her face, but I don't need to see her eyes to tell she's scared.

She's cemented to the metal platform like her shoes are made of magnets, but my tether is hooked behind hers so if she doesn't move, I can't either.

She's probably thinking, like I am, about our trip to Hershey Park with Dad in elementary school, when he bribed her with ice cream to ride the SooperDooperLooper. She was petrified of falling and told him she didn't want to go, but he made her anyway, forcibly dragging her onto the train. Fraught with anxiety, she wet her pants on the ride, and when Dad noticed the stain, he yelled at her, making a scene in front of all the other families.

I washed out her clothes in the bathroom sink while she stood sobbing in her underpants, everyone around us gawking. When I couldn't get them completely dry with paper towels, I spilled water my own shorts in solidarity.

It didn't completely stifle her embarrassment, but at least she knew people were staring at me, too.

Now, part of me wants to unhook my tether and take off across the platform without a single word—let her stand there and wait by herself until it's time to head back. But another part remembers that small, frightened little girl at Hershey Park and simply can't walk away.

"Come on." I hold out my hand and give a nod toward the lake. "The views must be amazing from the other side. I know it's high, but we're tethered and you can hold onto the rail. Or me if you want."

She turns, tears pooling in the corners of her eyes—from the wind or maybe something else. There's only ten minutes left until we head back down, so every second she stalls is a moment of wasted opportunity.

The sun has risen fully over the horizon now, and many of the park's other coasters are springing to life in preparation for riders later this morning. I pull out my phone, resigned to grabbing a few shots of the view from my less-than-stellar vantage point when Wylla takes a hesitant step forward. Her knuckles blanch as she grips the rail on her left, and with a sigh of relief, I follow her across the platform.

Her pace quickens as we venture closer to the coaster's largest drop off, and I let her go on without me. The other's call to us, but the breeze carries their voices out and away. Near the end of the line, Mikal and Travis count the surrounding coasters aloud, seventeen in all, and Dustin drapes his arm casually around Chloe's shoulder.

Alone for the first time all morning, I allow myself to take it all in: the pungent smell of decaying aquatic life wafting up from the lake below, the roar of the coasters racing along their tracks to my left and right, and the warmth of the sun on my face in perfect juxtaposition to the crispness of the morning air against my bare skin. Gooseflesh prickles my arms, and I release the rail to hug myself, venturing a bit closer to the lake. Large waves lap the sandy shore as a pleasure boat passes by off the coast. I squint into the sun, hoping to catch a glimpse of the people on board, but they're too far away.

Like everyone in my life.

Wylla's caught up with the guys now, and the four of them watch a flock of pelicans skimming the surface of the water for fish. How carefree they look, gliding effortlessly along, searching for breakfast.

Below me, two employees in matching lanyards and polos laugh together. I wonder how they'd react if a body appeared between them from above, a casualty of this morning's Sunrise Thrills VIP Tour.

If I jumped, would anyone even miss me?

Nia.

And maybe Mom.

But thanks to the mess with Logan, that would be about it.

Hand on the tether release, I'm still thinking about how loneliness can make us ponder unimaginable things when Sandy and the others appear by my side.

"Let's head back," she calls over the wind. "Last one up is the first one down."

I take a hesitant step onto the first tread. The stairs seem a lot steeper now than they did coming up, and putting one foot in front of the other demands my full attention. I'm holding tight to the rail when something tickles the back of my arm, disturbing my focus. It's probably my braids brushing against me, but when I feel another tap after pulling them forward, I find Wylla gazing at me, eyes soft and appreciative. It's no surprise she was able to overcome her fear without incident—somehow, my sister always finds a way to survive—but her grateful smile feels monumental, like a small wave at the changing of the tide, and for the first time in a long time, I allow myself to feel hopeful I might not always be alone.

CHAPTER 10

The rest of our tour takes us behind the scenes of the park to the places the public never gets to see, like the storage facility housing the dummies they use to weight down the coaster seats so they can hit their maximum velocity during test runs. We're also shown the special harnesses the park provides to patrons who are missing arms or legs so they can ride the coasters safely.

"And this is the computer timing system which controls the hydraulic brakes," Sandy says. I'm standing with the rest of the group beneath the undercarriage of the Millennium Force, and she motions for us to cover our ears as the train screeches past. "Another interesting fact about this coaster is that a member of our maintenance staff climbs a three-hundred-and-ten-foot ladder to press a button at the top of this hill at least once every twenty-four hours."

"Or it explodes?" Dustin says with a laugh.

"Or it stops." Sandy shields her eyes with one hand as she points to the top of the coaster with the other. "If someone doesn't push that button every day to let the ride operator at the manufacturer know it's been inspected, they'll shut it down, simple as that."

Travis gives a nod of understanding. "Like in *Lost.*"

"Something like that," Sandy replies.

Travis and Sandy start talking about airplanes and jungles and time warps, and I gaze at the others who seem as confused as I am.

"What's lost?" Chloe asks.

Travis shakes his head. I half expect him to come out with 'kids these days,' but he doesn't. "It was a television show that went off the air over a decade ago," he explains without an ounce of superiority in his voice. "About these people who survive a plane crash on a deserted island. Anyway, at one point they find this guy who's been stranded on the island for a while and his job is to sit at this antiquated computer and type in a numerical sequence every hundred and eight minutes."

"Does the island blow up if he forgets?" Mikal asks with a nod to Dustin.

"No." He pauses. "The whole world."

Everyone's silent for a moment. "Jesus," Dustin says. "That show stream anywhere? Netflix? Hulu? It sounds pretty good."

I'm still gathering intel from Travis about this mysterious old TV show as we sit down to breakfast at the conclusion of our tour.

He swallows a bite of his egg and cheese sandwich. "You know another great show from about the same time was *The Office.*"

"My older brother used to watch that," Chloe says.

Unlike *Lost*, Wylla and I know lots about *The Office*. We watched all nine seasons of the documentary-style comedy following the lives of a paper company staff with Dad when we were little. Wylla's smiling now. Is she remembering that time Michael Scott's goofy catch phrase got us in trouble?

"Seven times eight. That's a hard one," Mom said, flipping over another of my multiplication flash cards as we did homework together one afternoon.

Wylla looked up from her worksheet about the lifecycle of a butterfly, crayon in hand, and when our eyes met, we cried out, "That's what she said!" in unison, before dissolving into a fit of giggles.

"Enough with that, Elise," Mom scolded.

I swallowed hard, turning from my sister, eyes narrowed. "But Wylla said it, too."

"Yeah, Mommy. I said it, too." Wylla stuck out her chest defiantly, not wanting to be left out, even if it meant getting in trouble.

Mom ignored her, though. "She's only mimicking you, Elise. If you stop, she'll stop."

In that moment, the responsibility associated with being Wylla's big sister became clear. If I was a good girl, Wylla would be, too. If I got in trouble, she'd follow me into certain ruin.

Looking back, the dumbest part of the whole ordeal was we didn't even know what that stupid phrase meant. But it didn't matter. We thought it was the funniest joke ever. It was our special thing.

I smile at her now, and after a few seconds, she stops picking at her greasy hash browns and looks up.

Her eyes brighten. "That's what she said," she mouths.

"So, who'd Ernie give the token clue to this morning?" Mikal asks, changing the subject with a glance around the picnic table.

Dustin grins at Chloe who winks in return. "Three point eight," he says.

Seamus kicks my foot under the table, but I don't dare look at him. He must know what it means, and I don't trust myself to keep a straight face.

"That's it?" Mikal takes a sip of his coffee. "Just the number: three and eight tenths."

Dustin shrugs. "That's all it said."

Beside me, Travis wads up his sandwich wrapper and collects the rest of his trash onto his tray. A look of understanding passes between him and Mikal. They've obviously figured it out, too. He squeezes himself off the picnic bench with a grunt, and fastens his leather fanny pack around his waist.

"Leaving already?" Dustin gives the smallest nod across the table at Chloe and my sister. "They said we could eat as much as we want. Don't you want to grab another sandwich or two for the road?"

Mikal shoves the last bite of glazed donut into his mouth and nearly topples over getting up from the table. Around me, a quiet sort of panic settles in as everyone collects their belongings in hushed anticipation.

Another kick from Seamus startles me into action. "Let's go," he mouths.

I slip my arms through my backpack straps and race across the eating pavilion behind him, tray in hand. We dump our trash into the receptacle on the way out, and by the time we hit the pavement, Seamus has broken into a full-on sprint.

"They're all ahead of us," he calls back to me, his voice thick with alarm. "We gotta beat them."

Travis and Mikal are only a few yards ahead, but I've nearly lost sight of Wylla, her hair billowing behind her as she races across the park to our destination.

A destination I'm still very much in the dark about.

But there's no time to ask where we're heading now.

During breakfast, the park officially opened, and now keeping up with Seamus is extremely difficult. Still, even with the growing crowd, I do eventually pass Travis gasping for air under a shade tree. Mikal's nowhere to be seen, though, having evidently gone on without his partner.

I pass Camp Snoopy, dodging and weaving between strollers and toddlers and am relieved when the Gemini midway opens up, revealing the rest of my competition.

I hope wherever we're going isn't far because my stomach's cramping something fierce.

"Come on," Seamus calls again with a wave of his hand. "Dustin's already getting in line."

By the time I make it to the Top Thrill Dragster entrance, Dustin, Chloe, Wylla, and Mikal are all a full loop ahead. Short of cutting the line, there's no way we'll get to the tokens before them, unless by some stroke of luck they pass them by.

We need a plan, but I allow myself a few seconds to catch my breath and while my heartrate returns to precardiac levels. "You sure this is the place?" I ask.

He nods. "Three point eight can only mean one thing—the number of seconds the Dragster takes to go from zero to 120 miles per hour."

"Excuse me, what? And we're going on it now?"

He sets a hand to his stomach. "Yeah. I know. This has the potential to end poorly for all of us, but what choice do we have?"

I stand on my tip-toes to see how far it is to the front of the line. "Maybe our breakfast will digest by the time we get to the ride."

"Or we could always bale once we get there."

Our eyes lock, considering this option, but when his mouth curves into an impish smile, it's clear we're both thinking the same thing.

Neither of us is gonna bale.

"So, where should we look?" I ask.

He scans the cue and part of the loading platform. "Unlike the ark yesterday, there aren't a lot of great hiding places on this ride. We've got the railing here in line and a bunch of trashcans along the way, but other than that, I don't know where else they might have stashed them."

We shuffle forward as the next group of passengers boards. I glace ahead, wondering how scared Wylla is—this coaster's a thousand times more intense than the SooperDooperLooper —but she's laughing with Dustin about something on his phone, seemingly unfazed by the task ahead. With a shake of my head, I shift my focus to Mikal, who's feeling along the underside of a nearby rail. Of course, Travis isn't in line at all, and I'm starting to worry about him. He looked ghost-like under the tree as I passed, and something tells me I should go after him to make sure he's okay. I scan the line for an escape route and am about to tell Seamus where I'm headed when I notice several bleachers filled with onlookers near the ride's exit.

Travis sits in the front row, haggard but all right. I wave my hands above my head to get his attention, but he's not looking in my direction. In fact, he's not looking at the ride at all.

He's feeling around under the seats.

"Seamus, what if the tokens aren't on the ride." I cut my eyes to the bleachers. "What if they're over there, in the viewing stands?"

He nods, noticing them for the first time. "It makes sense." He scans the crowd waiting with us in both directions. "If they're up there, we should duck out of line and go try to find them. If we leave now, though, it'll mean waiting through this entire line again if we want to ride later."

"Not to mention, Travis is already over there searching."

"He is?"

I point him out—halfway up the far side, crawling around on his hands and knees.

We stay the course in line, watching Travis excuse himself past onlookers and waiting for others to move along so he can check for the tokens beneath their seats. We're almost to the platform when he pulls the same red plastic bag we discovered the day before from under the bleacher, an enormous smile spreading across his face.

Seamus shrugs. "Well, if it can't be us, at least it'll be Travis and Mikal today. Better them than the others."

"Yeah."

"You know what this means, though, right?" I turn from Travis to meet Seamus's gaze. His eyes twinkle with determination as he rests a hand on my shoulder. "Tomorrow's tokens are ours, no matter what it takes."

CHAPTER 11

Wylla, Dustin, and Chloe are the last to arrive at the van for the second day in a row. Ernie glances at his watch in obvious frustration as they approach a full twenty minutes late.

"It's almost two hundred miles to Kings Island, and we gotta check into the motel before eleven, which means now we won't have time to stop for a proper dinner along the way. The rest of you have our tardy friends to thank for that."

The three of them grumble apologies—something about being told an inaccurate wait time for the line they were in—as they squish past me into the backseat of the van.

"I mean, we were almost to the front, so we couldn't just leave, could we?" Chloe whines.

"Um, yeah. That's exactly what we did," Mikal says with a shake of his head. "It's called common courtesy. Look it up."

Chloe whispers something to Dustin, and they laugh to themselves. Wylla, however, doesn't join in, setting off my big sister defenses. Are they including her in their conversations or still treating her like a tagalong? Either way, God only knows how poorly they'll have to treat her before she eventually decides to spend some time with me.

"We need gas, so I'll stop at a Circle K down the road, and you all can run inside to grab some snacks for dinner. That's all we have time for I'm afraid."

Five minutes later, Ernie pulls the van into the gas station parking lot. No one complains outright about our situation as we trudge single file into the market, but Chloe's slack jaw expression tells me everything I need to know about her affinity for convenience store fare.

Travis, on the other hand, is the proverbial kid in a candy store, basket in hand as he peruses the aisles beside me. "Oh, Slim Jims sound good." He tosses a couple into his pile. He's already grabbed two bags of hot Cheetos and, of course, several bags of black licorice. "What're you getting?" he asks.

I hold up a premade egg salad sandwich from the refrigerated section.

"The rest of the van's gonna love you," he says with a grin. "But at least it's not tuna fish."

I chuckle, having considered the stench when making my dinner selection. "At first, I was just looking for something nutritious, but if egg salad serves as some sort of lingering reminder there are consequences for not making it back to the van on time, I'm fine with that, too."

"I like your style, kid."

Travis picks up a pack of cheddar cheese Combos, and while he's deciding whether to get them, my phone chirps inside my pocket. I pull it out to discover a text from Nia.

How was day 2? Did you find the token again? I'm gonna be so jealous if you get that fast lane pass.

I shoot her a quick reply.

Had a great day. Lots of amazing rides but no token. Those two guys Travis and Mikal I told you about got them. Hopefully Seamus and I will find them first tomorrow.

Travis chucks the Combos into his basket and glances at my phone. "Is that your folks checking in?"

Something about the way he says folks all casual like everyone in the world has them tightens a knot inside my chest. Having parents and having 'folks' feels like two very different things to me.

"My best friend, Nia," I tell him. "Wondering if Seamus and I found the tokens."

This draws a smile from Travis. "Didn't do too bad for an old timer today, huh? All you young'uns ran off, left me in your dust, but sometimes it's better to be smart than fast."

"You're not wrong." I grab a bag of Lays off the shelf to accompany my sandwich. "Did you tell your family about your big score today?"

He's silent for a beat, and when I glance up from the chips, now he's the one who looks like he's been sucker punched.

"Sorry, I…"

"No, no, don't apologize. Ain't nothing to apologize for. I got three grown kids and an ex-wife who keeps life interesting, but there's nobody keeping tabs on me the way people are checking in with the rest of you. Hell, they probably don't even know I'm gone." He shrugs off his initial reaction. "I'm pretty excited about that token though, and I'd be lying if I said I wasn't gonna fight you for the rest of them."

I try to imagine him in his Led Zeppelin t-shirt, leather fanny pack, and cut-offs skipping to the front of every line in Drury Park. "You must really like riding coasters."

He nods. "Gives me something to do all summer during the off-season."

"Off-season?" My voice is skeptical. "You some kind of athlete or something?"

"Math teacher, actually. Seventh grade."

While we've been chatting, Seamus and Mikal have wandered into the aisle and seem as taken aback by Travis's confession as I am.

"No way you're a teacher." Seamus unwraps a Snickers and takes a bite. "I've never had anyone like you behind the desk in any of my classes."

"Yeah," Mikal agrees. "I might've enjoyed middle school if I'd had someone like you for a teacher."

Travis turns toward the front of the store, attempting to hide the red crimsoning the tips of his ears. "That's enough of that," he calls over his shoulder. "Now let's get outta here before Ernie leaves us behind."

I make my way to the register where I check out before loading back into the van. Wylla takes the window seat behind Ernie, and I have no choice but to slide in beside her. As she unwraps the foil from her hot dog, I suppress the urge to make some snarky comment about slumming it in the front with me.

"I can't eat back there," she says with a glance over her shoulder. "All the bouncing gives me a stomach ache."

I shrug, taking a bite of my sandwich. "Suit yourself." As I watch her squeezing mustard onto her dog, I can't help but wonder if the nausea she's experiencing is plain old car sickness or some other kind of pregnancy related illness.

An awkward quiet stretches between us as we scarf down our respective meals, and not for the first time I wish we were still the type of sisters who were best friends and shared everything.

But those days are long gone.

Somehow, over the course of the past few years, life found a way of pitting us against one another over and over and over. Our friendship never stood a chance.

Which is why I'm surprised when she's the one who breaks the silence now.

"Your hair looks pretty like that," she says.

It takes a second to realize she's talking about the braids I wove this morning to protect my hair from the knotting effects of the coasters. I pull one of them around to inspect the damage and am pleased to discover they seem to have survived the day.

"Thanks," I reply, waiting cautiously for her to continue. Because with Wylla, there's always something more to be said.

Your hair looks pretty like that, *but* are you sure you want to draw so much attention to your ears?

Or—Your hair looks pretty like that, *but* it makes your face look kind of fat.

Instead of adding a footnote to her compliment like I'm expecting, though, she squirts another dollop of mustard from the Heinz packet onto her dog and takes an enormous bite.

My brain races for a way to keep the conversation going. All I come up with is, "Yours looks pretty, too."

As soon as it comes out of my mouth, I want to take it back. It's a ridiculous thing to say considering her hair's in a messy ponytail, tucked under one of dad's old Philadelphia Phillie's baseball caps.

She raises a suspicious eyebrow. "Thanks?"

"I mean, you always look so cute in hats. I can never pull them off."

She lets out a contented sigh and considers me. It's the golden hour, and the entire van is bathed in a warm glow, illuminating my sister's sun-kissed cheeks. Looking at her now,

I remember all the times I wanted to trade places with her. All the times I watched our mother brushing through the soft waves of her hair.

"I know you're disappointed no one asked to the dance tonight, Elise," she'd said, pinning Wylla's hair up for Homecoming last fall. "You're so smart and funny. It's just, if your put yourself out there a little more or tried wearing a bit of makeup, maybe the guys would take more of an interest in you the way they do with Wylla." She reached over, rubbing her thumb against my cheek, her eyes soft and remorseful. "Think about it, huh? Then maybe you wouldn't be stuck here at home with your boring old mom all the time."

She honestly thought my ponytail and lack of eyeliner were the reasons Jackson asked Wylla and no one asked me. If she only knew how it all went down after Logan. If she only knew how my sacrifice turned me into a social pariah.

Or that the stupid Homecoming dance was the least of my worries.

"The reason hats don't look right on you is because of your bangs," Wylla says now. "You gotta brush them back if you want to wear a ball cap. They'd look cute if you wear them down with a slouch beany, though. It's too hot for those in June, but I can show you how to wear them the right way when it cools off."

For the first time since agreeing to this stupid trip with her, there's more than just a spark of something. Like maybe our relationship isn't completely doomed, and we just need time to figure things out.

I thank her, and she nods before turning to gaze out the window. I'm left staring at the silhouetted back of her head.

What exactly does she want from me? And what exactly is going on with her?

CHAPTER 12

I'm still rubbing sleep from my eyes when a quiet tapping at the motel room door draws my attention the next morning. Beside me, Wylla snores softly against her pillow, and on the other side of the room, Chloe doesn't stir at all. It might be housekeeping, but if the cobweb in the corner above my head is any indication, it's not. I sit up and lean toward the window just far enough to get a peek at who's waiting behind the curtain.

It's Seamus, dressed for the day in a Flash t-shirt and tan cargo shorts, nervously biting his bottom lip as he waits for a response. Seeing him standing there, looking so vulnerable, stirs something unexpected inside of me. A twinge of excitement? Anticipation?

Joy?

Regardless, my instinct is to throw the door wide open and invite him inside, but I'm dressed in nothing but an oversized t-shirt, and there are the others to consider. So instead of opening the door, I pull back the curtain so he can see my face and tap loud enough to draw his attention.

When his gaze meets mine, the relief in his eyes causes my

stomach to flip flop in a most surprising way. Is it possible this guy actually likes hanging out with me?

I hold up a finger to indicate I'm gonna need a minute, and he gives me a thumbs up in return. The curtain drops between us, leaving me with a dilemma. Do I make him wait on the sidewalk while I take time to fully prepare for the day, or do I simply throw on a bra and shorts and head out there?

Past me wouldn't have given it a second thought. She would've put on whatever was necessary to pass for 'decent' and gone out. But these days, I don't even need to glance at Wylla to hear her voice inside my head.

"Guys like when you made an effort for them, Elise. They're not going to pay any attention to you if you always look like you just rolled out of bed."

But Seamus isn't really a guy I care about impressing. And even if he was, it feels like he might already be a little bit interested since he's knocking on my motel room door at the crack of dawn.

I split the difference, slipping on a bra and shorts before splashing some water on my face and giving my mouth a quick once over with my toothbrush.

Out on the sidewalk, Seamus sits with his back against the room's sputtering air conditioner. A smile spreads across his face. "Good morning."

"Hey." I slide down the brick wall beside him. "To what do I owe this early wake-up call?"

He glances at his watch, then back at me. "I guess it is a little early, huh? Sorry about that. It's just—Ernie gave today's token clue to Travis when we got in last night, and I snuck a peek. I stayed up half the night thinking about it, and I couldn't wait any longer to talk with you. I'm hoping we can work it out together because I'm not about letting him and Mikal get it again."

I can't help smiling at his single-minded enthusiasm, even if working out the clue is more important to him than I am. "So, what is it?"

He shakes his head. "Sixteen spin out."

"Sixteen spin out?"

"Yeah. That's it. And unlike the first two, I have no idea what this one means." He hands me his computer printout map of Kings Island. Half-a-dozen rides are already circled.

"You think these are possibilities?"

He shrugs. "They're the ones I'm certain you spin around on. The carousel, of course. And the Scrambler's a given, too. The Zephyr's one of those swing rides that goes around in a circle. I have no idea what the sixteen's referring to, though."

I trace my finger from the others to their descriptions on the page. "Oh, God, it looks like this Delirium one spins around while it spins around. Maybe we should put it at the top of the list."

"Maybe." He points to the Monster. "This one does, too."

After a full inspection of the ride descriptions, we determine there are no fewer than seven possible contenders for the token clue. "We might spend a lot of time searching the wrong rides while we could be riding coasters," I say.

He takes back the map with a nod. "Yeah. I thought the same thing. The good news is, this park doesn't have a ton of great coasters. The Banshee holds the world record for having seven inversions, and you sit facing other riders on Invertigo which seems pretty cool. Oh, and the Diamondback has stadium seating so you can see the front from anywhere on the train. Other than those, it's a bunch of wooden stuff."

Around us, motel guests are waking up, and the family of four who emerge from the room next door give us the stink eye as they roll their luggage past on the way to their car like we're some sort of hoodlums. Last time I checked, it wasn't illegal to have a conversation in a public space, but with the way the parents hurry their children along, they must think we're passing around a joint instead of an amusement park map. I glance at Seamus. An unspoken bond of solidarity spreads between us, and we sit together in silence until they leave.

An uncharacteristic giggle escapes my lips as they pull away. It feels nice to share something private with Seamus. "So, what's the plan, then?"

"I guess it depends on how committed we are to finding the tokens."

He's been sitting with one leg tucked beneath him this whole time, but as he pulls it out to find a more comfortable position, his hand grazes my fingers. A tingle runs up my arm, and I gaze at the spot where we touched, wondering if he felt it, too.

"I, uh… I guess I'm as committed as you are." I don't want to let him down, but I'm not sure what summer will hold for me once we get back home. What my life will hold for me. Even if I end up winning the fast lane vouchers, it's not like I'll have anyone to use them with. Nia's never been able to afford a single day pass to Drury Park, much less a season pass. Since the fall, she's the only friend I've got, and lord knows Wylla isn't planning any sister trips to the park.

"If you don't mind tagging along, I'd like to look for them today, at least for a little while. And honestly, sometimes the other rides are as much fun as the coasters, don't you think?" He raises his eyebrows expectantly.

I nod in agreement, remembering his affection for carnival rides. "What if we give it 'til lunchtime, and if we haven't found the tokens by then, we'll go do the coasters."

"Sounds like a plan." He hoists himself off the concrete and holds out his hands to me. I hesitate and am on the verge of overthinking the entire thing when he pulls me to my feet by my wrists.

We're face to face and inches apart, just the minty scent of his toothpaste between us. "Ernie, Travis, and I are headed out to Dunkin Donuts for breakfast. What kind do you want?"

I don't even need to think. "I'll take a cruller."

He raises an eyebrow. "A cruller?"

"Yeah. You know, the twisty kind."

He shakes his head, skeptical. "Are they any different than a regular donut?"

"No? Yes?" I shrug. "I dunno. I like them better, though."

"Then maybe I'll get one, too." He starts across the parking lot toward the guys' room. "See ya when we get back."

I thank him, throw a wave over my shoulder, and head inside to get ready for the day.

CHAPTER 13

Powdered sugar spills all over my lap as I eat my cruller on the way to the park. Behind me, Travis and Mikal whisper conspiratorially about where to look for the tokens, and Seamus presses on the back of my seat with his knee when they mention heading to the Scrambler first. We hoped they'd forgo the hunt and opt for the coasters instead, but they're obviously not giving up that easily.

"The Scrambler, huh?" Dustin pipes up from the back of the van. "You think that's the one?"

"Maybe." Mikal glances dramatically over his shoulder at him, eyes narrowed. "You have another idea?"

Dustin shrugs. "The Scrambler's not a *bad* idea…"

"But?" says Travis.

"But nothing. If it's on your list of possibilities, who am I to convince you otherwise."

Chloe giggles beside him through a bite of Boston crème, and I replay it in my head, listening for some lyrical nuance which would be indicative of Dustin's intentions. I chance a glance at Wylla to see if her expression gives any indication of what she knows. Does Dustin legitimately think the tokens aren't hidden on the Scrambler or is he trying to throw us off the right path because he knows they are? Her lips are set into a thin line, and she's sending someone a text like she's not even paying attention to the conversation going on around her. I don't want to check the name at the top of her screen, but my eyes flick to the word *Mom* before I can stop myself.

Of course, they're texting one another this morning.

Because, why wouldn't they be?

Mom barely had two minutes for me when I called her last night. Something about being tired. Something about not having a lot of time to talk because she had to put together a purchase offer for one of her clients before morning.

And, of course, something about making sure I was taking my Zoloft.

Now, though, she's got plenty of time to chat away with Wylla. I take out my phone and pull up my contacts. Part of me wants to text Mom, too, to see if she'll respond, but the fear of being disappointed sits like a rock in my stomach, and I slip my phone back into my pocket without typing a single word.

While I've been ruminating on my family dynamics, the conversation about where the tokens are hidden has continued on without me.

"You've got it all figured out, huh? You know what the sixteen means?" Mikal challenges Dustin about his theories.

"Even if we did, we wouldn't tell you about it," Chloe says.

"Exactly," Wylla adds, not looking up from her screen.

Her declaration is followed by another kick to the back of my seat from Seamus. I know what he's thinking: Chloe, Dustin, and my sister don't have any more figured out than we do. It's going to come down to which one of us gets lucky and stumbles onto the right ride first.

Listening to the others bantering back and forth, something occurs to me. When we arrive at the park, I pull Seamus to the side to share my revelation. "Of the rides that spin around, which ones might have numbered seats?"

He scans his map as we make our way across the parking lot toward the front entrance. "The Delirium might. And also, the Windseeker." He chews the inside of his cheek as he thinks. There's something so innocent and childlike about it, almost endearing. "What about the carousel, though? You think the horses are numbered?"

I try to remember if they're numbered at Drury Park. "Probably not. Names, maybe, but not numbers."

He nods. "I bet you're right. Based on your numbered seat theory, we could scratch the carousel off our list."

"Or at least move it to the end."

He makes an adjustment to our planned route on the map with his pen. "That leaves the swings, the Scrambler, and Shake, Rattle, and Roll, all of which may or may not be numbered."

"Are there any you're certain of?"

He shakes his head. "No. They could all be numbered. Or not. There's no way to know for sure until we see them, so we should stick to the route we decided on and skip the ones that aren't numbered."

We pass through ticketing and head left toward Delirium. I don't know whether to feel disappointed or relieved when the rest of our group heads straight down International Street toward the Eiffel Tower, but Seamus, who is obviously one hundred percent committed to our plan, doesn't give them a second look. Upon arrival, we discover Delirium's seats are, in fact, numbered. The trick, however, is going to be making sure one of us gets to sit in seat number sixteen.

We move forward in the cue, checking the railings and trashcans for the tokens along the way to be sure. When it's our time to board, there are only five people in front of us.

"Can you see which one's seat sixteen?" I squint into the sunlight, shading my eyes with my hand.

"Nope," Seamus says. "Can you?"

I shake my head. "When they open the gate, you run to the left, and I'll run to the right. Whichever of us gets seat sixteen, we need check every inch while we have time on the ground. It'll be impossible once we get spinning."

After what seems like the longest three minutes of my life, the ride comes to an end and a group of nauseous looking people disembark. Seamus and I stand together in hushed anticipation, the electricity palpable between us. To my left, the attendant moves toward the gate, and Seamus reaches across the space between us, squeezing my palm against his.

He grins. "Let's find those tokens." It's the cheesiest thing to say, almost cringeworthy, but the way he says it, like we're on a mission to save the world, makes me feel like, at least when it comes to finding tokens, I might actually be capable of accomplishing something.

"Let's do it."

As the gate opens, he lets go of my hand and takes off at a run. I head in the other direction and about halfway around, on the far side of the ride, spot seat sixteen. I bolt for it, lowering my restraint quickly so I have plenty time to feel for the tokens.

There aren't many places for the them to be hidden—under the armrests and along the edges of the seat. I don't feel anything, and panic sets in as the attendant makes his way around to secure my restraint. I slide my hand along the padding beneath my thighs and the beside my shoulders, but there's nothing. Not a single token to be found.

The attendants give their 'all clear,' and I'm forced to give up the search, grasping the handles and bracing myself for what's to come.

The ride is intense—a huge swinging pendulum with a rotating wheel on the end. The seats face outward, and the wheel spins around, with the pendulum carrying it into the air: up and down and up and down. As we reach maximum height and velocity, I say a silent prayer my cruller has had time to properly digest. I'll have more to worry about than finding stupid tokens if my breakfast reappears.

The instant my feet touch the ground, I resume my search, knowing it won't be long until I'm forced off the ride. I'm still sliding my hand along every crevice I can reach when Seamus appears.

"Nothing, huh?"

I shake my head, still searching the backside of the restraint which is now above my head where I can see it properly.

"It's okay." He turns to walk away. "If it's not here, it's not here. We've got other rides to search." His voice is optimistic, but it feels as though I failed us both already. Realistically, I can't find something that simply doesn't exist, but it still takes all the way to the next ride for me to shake the disappointment.

CHAPTER 14

The Monster, the Scrambler, and the Zephyr follow, one after another along the Coney Mall section of the park. Although each of them has at least sixteen cars, none of them are numbered.

Seamus leans against the rail outside the giant swings as the passengers zip past. "What do you think we should do?" he asks.

Sun bakes my bare shoulders, and I pat at them with my fingertips, making sure the Delirium's restraint didn't rub off my sunscreen. Sweat gathers under my ponytail along my nape, and the breeze of the passing swings seems particularly inviting. But every moment we spend riding non-token rides is a moment we give the others to find them.

"I think we go on to Shake, Rattle, and Roll. It's right around the corner."

"The seats might not be numbered."

I doubt they are, but I'm determined to remain optimistic. There's something sweet about Seamus's crooked smile. "Only one way to find out."

After striking out on the first four rides of the day, he can't contain his excitement as we approach Shake, Rattle, and Roll.

"The cars are numbered. And this one spins while it spins." The normal tenor of Seamus's voice climbs to an almost soprano level.

My eyes ricochet inside their sockets, trying to read the numbers as the cars speed past. After two rotations, the ride slows, and I spot number sixteen. "There it is."

He follows my gaze as the current group of passengers reaches the ground, and with an excited punch to the air, takes off for the ride's entrance.

It occurs to me, as I race to catch up, that his initial ambivalence about finding the tokens was an absolute lie. And I have no idea why he's so desperate to win the fast lane voucher, but for some weird reason, I want to help him.

My theory is confirmed during our excruciatingly long wait, as he analyzes every inch of the cars while the riders in front of us load and unload.

"See the area where your feet go up front? It looks like there might be a place for them to be tucked up inside. And, oh, see underneath the seat there? That's definitely a possible hiding spot."

He's still droning on about all the places we need to check when Dustin, Chloe, and my sister join the back of the line. I don't know if they've seen us yet and can't decide if I should point them out to Seamus.

Finally, I break down. They're gonna notice us eventually, and it's probably best if we don't let them see us searching. Better to let them wonder whether we've already found them. "Don't look now, but we have company."

His head whips around so fast his vertebrae cracks. "Where? Who?"

"I said *don't* look."

But it's too late. Chloe waves at us sweetly, fingers fluttering in our direction.

He sighs. "Well, the good news is they must still be looking, too, otherwise they'd be off on the coasters already."

"True," I say. "And they started from the other direction, so it's possible they've already checked where we're headed."

He pulls out the map to do a quick scan. "Maybe they went all the way out to the Windseeker first. It's the last one we haven't checked."

We don't have time to discuss this possibility because a moment later, it's our turn to board. At this point, he's practically turned himself inside out with anticipation. "You know what? The Windseeker doesn't matter. It's gonna be here. This is definitely the one."

He's memorized the layout of the ride and knows exactly where number sixteen has stopped. He nearly knocks over two elementary schoolers, racing to the car before anyone else can snag it. I pick up the pace, swerving around a couple holding hands as they stroll along, ignorant of our mission. Of course, he's already face-down in the car by the time I arrive.

"Anything?" I ask, feeling along the bench seat as discreetly as possible.

A muffled voice replies. "No. Nothing yet."

I move out of the way as he checks beneath the seat, prying at a soldered panel.

"Maybe it's behind this."

I suppress a giggle, feeling along the underside of the car's nose as the ride attendant approaches. "It's welded solid."

"Did you guys lose something?" he asks.

Seamus glances up at me and purses his lips. "A contact?"

"Oh, bummer." He scrunches up his nose. "The ride's pretty gross. Like, people throw up on it and stuff. You might wanna give up on the contact, if you know what I mean."

A look of resignation passes between us as the attendant pulls the safety bar across our laps. "Hope you brought your glasses," he says, walking away.

The car picks up speed, restricting my search from behind the bar. I spend the entirety of the ride checking every crack and crevice but ultimately come up emptyhanded.

Seamus's shoulders slump as the seat bar lifts and disembarking instructions play over the loudspeaker. "They're not here."

"We can still check the Windseeker." The forced buoyancy of my voice draws his gaze, and when he looks at me with those pouty lips, any reservations I had about wasting time on the tokens melts away. I have no idea why he's so invested in this silly mission, but there's something strangely appealing about his dogged determination. He isn't budging from the seat, though, so as the next set of riders files in around us, I grab his hand, pulling him to his feet. "Come on. Those tokens have gotta be here somewhere."

Unfortunately, after an exhaustive search of seat number sixteen, we don't find them on the Windseeker either.

What we do find is Travis and Mikal.

Travis is quick to bring up the missing tokens as we search for a lunch spot together. "No luck on your end, either?"

Seamus shakes his head. "No. Nothing. And we've been on every ride we can think of."

"Us, too," Mikal says with a sad sigh. "I'm gonna be pissed if Dustin finds them. I don't know about the rest of you, but that guy rubs me the wrong way."

I did know. So did everyone else. "I don't think they've found them yet, either," I say. "They were in line behind us on Shake, Rattle, and Roll."

Travis stops in front of the *Tom + Chee* stand, and along with the others, I fall into line behind him. "Riding carnival rides instead of coasters is a good indication they're still looking," he says.

Seamus's eyes flick in my direction like he's trying to communicate via ESP. He makes a tiny zipping motion with his hand in front of his mouth—a clear indication he doesn't want me giving away our strategy. I respond with a wide-eyed shrug. I'm not convinced sharing intel with them would be such a bad idea.

We order a few grilled cheeses with a couple side salads to share, and find a bench under a shade tree to eat.

Mikal takes an enormous bite of grilled cheese and swallows before giving a nonchalant wave of his napkin. "What've you guys ridden so far?"

I don't need to look at Seamus to know he's glaring holes through my head, so I let him do the talking. The last thing I want is to mess this up for him.

"Oh, you know. A little of this and a little of that."

Travis chuckles before responding, his tone playful. "It's gonna be like that, huh? We give you two a little competition, and now we're not helping each other out anymore."

"No. Not at all." Seamus takes a sip of his Coke. "It's just… We've run out of ideas and are probably giving up."

"Bullshit," Mikal says.

"Seriously," Seamus tells him. "We've checked every ride on our list."

Travis names all the spinning rides, and Seamus eventually relents, confessing what we found—or rather—didn't find.

"Between the four of us, we've checked all the spinning rides," Mikal says. "The only possible explanation is the others found them before we did."

Seamus nods along, but I don't share their confidence. I know my sister. If they'd already found those tokens, I would've gotten a text from her. She never misses an opportunity to rub it in when she's shown me up. I don't say any of this, though, because as the guys have been talking, I've thought of another ride to check.

"I don't know about you guys," Travis says, swallowing the last bite of his sandwich, "but I could use a pit stop before we head to the Diamondback."

We all agree a trip to the restroom sounds like a good idea, but after throwing away my trash, I waylay Seamus, grabbing him by the arm. "We gotta go," I tell him.

"Yeah, I, uh, thought that's what we were doing."

I let out an exasperated sigh as the men's room door shuts behind Mikal and Travis. "No. Not to the bathroom. We need to go to another ride. And we can't go with them."

His brow pinches in confusion. "Another ride? Which one?"

"We passed it earlier, and I didn't give it a second thought, but I was stupid." I wave over my shoulder for him to follow and take off at a run for the other side of the park. A moment later, he catches up, and together we cut and weave our way through the crowd to Dodgem where I step into line.

Seamus frowns. "The bumper cars? But they don't spin."

I lean against the rail to catch my breath, watching the cars ricochet around the rink. "No. They spin *out*." In front of us two cars crash into one another, each sending the other spiraling out of control.

"And the cars are numbered." Excitement returns to his voice. "There goes number sixteen now."

By the time the attendant ushers us through the gate, it's all Seamus can do to control himself. "You take sixteen," I tell him with a wave of my hand.

A moment later, I'm strapped into car number eleven, hands poised on the wheel as Seamus searches his car for the tokens. Instructions to remain seated and follow the directional signs carry over the loud speakers, and in the seconds before the ride begins, a triumphant Seamus waves the red token bag above his head.

"I've got them!" He has just enough time to tuck them away before a puckish-looking middle schooler in a Cincinnati Bengals hat rear ends his car, thrusting him forward into the wall.

I'm trying not to laugh when a nearby car hits me head on before I even have a chance to react.

In the moments that follow, I'm vaguely aware of what's happening on the ride around me, and it isn't long before the music, the screeching tires, and the laughter fade. The chaos of the amusement park gives way to the memory of my recent accident—most specifically, the quiet stillness of suspended animation following the impact.

The pungent smell of burnt rubber and gasoline.

The pain in my shoulder.

The blood on the dashboard.

Lizzo continued blaring out of the radio about taking a DNA test as if nothing had happened. But something had happened.

Something terrible.

I tried catching my breath that day, but the seatbelt cut tight across my chest making it nearly impossible to fill my lungs. My seat was bathed in sunshine, and the broken glass from the driver's side window twinkled like diamonds in a puddle of crimson blood.

This isn't the first time I've been thrust back to the scene of the accident—the intersection of Third and Hawthorne in the center of my tiny rural town. What's strange about my memories, though, is they don't include any of the day's details before or after the collision.

And the incident itself is only a little less fuzzy.

Mom says the unseasonably warm day—not a cloud in the sky—inspired her to invite our neighbors over for an impromptu cookout. During a pantry inspection, I discovered our last onion had gone bad, so I volunteered to run to the grocery store across town for a fresh one.

I have a vague recollection of the intersection where the accident occurred. After looking both ways at the stop, I was in the middle of my left-hand turn when the sound of squealing tires drew my attention. I turned to look out the passenger's side at the exact moment my body was thrown against the driver's side door. The window broke, and my shoulder throbbed as tiny shards of glass embedded themselves into my flesh.

My ears rung so loudly, I could barely make out the person beside me, crying out my name.

"Elise."

"Elise, can you hear me?"

"Elise."

Now, instead of a medic, Seamus calls for my attention.

"You're gonna get whiplash if you don't start driving and get out of the way." He's laughing, eyes wild with excitement as he plows toward me at top speed.

I don't know why I thought riding the bumper cars would be a good idea, but now the trauma of the accident has overwhelmed me, and there's nothing left to do but brace for impact. I white knuckle the steering wheel, close my eyes, and tuck my chin to my chest as my heart races inside.

I prepare for the blow, muscles rigid against the seat back, but nothing happens.

I open my eyes to discover Seamus pinned between two other drivers, the result of a collusion between a little girl with pigtails and some dude with a manbun. My whole body's still shaking, but I force myself into motion—wriggling myself free of the shoulder harness and taking off on foot across the rink. The attendant calls out for me to remain seated, straining his voice over the electric motors and squeals of delight, but I don't stop and I don't look back.

With both hands on the railing, I steady my breathing and plan a plausible explanation for my behavior. I can't tell Seamus the truth about being triggered. He'll think I've lost my mind.

I've nearly picked my cuticle raw by the end of the ride when he appears by my side. "You okay?" His brow wrinkles in concern. "One minute you were right in front of me, then you were gone. Did something happen?"

I kick at a rock with my shoe, eyes trained on the ground. "Yeah, I… my car must've been busted or something because I couldn't get the stupid thing to go. I didn't feel like getting smashed into for five minutes, so I bailed."

He narrows his eyes. "You sure it's nothing more than that? You look pale. Clammy even."

"I'm fine," I say, pressing memories of the accident from my mind. "I'm just hot and thirsty."

"Then let's get a drink." He glances over at a nearby refreshment stand. "Slushies, maybe. My treat."

I follow a step behind him across the midway, wishing I could simply enjoy our time together. But I can't help wondering if he'd be as willing to hang out with me if he knew all the messed up stuff inside my head.

CHAPTER 15

With three parks down and seven to go, the following day is allocated for travel and rest. It's a five-hour drive from Kings Island in Ohio to Dollywood in Pigeon Forge, Tennessee, so after a fairly good night's sleep, Ernie sets a course due south on Rt 75.

Wylla's hunkered next to me in the front seat. She blames her relocation from the back on the long drive and proclivity for car sickness, but I'm certain the real reason she's slumming it up front with me has more to do with avoiding Dustin and Chloe's egregious PDA. If I sit too straight, an image of them cuddling together stares back at me in the rearview mirror, so I slouch way down in the seat until I'm nearly falling off.

Behind me, the guys busy themselves in various activities: Mikal watches anime on his phone, Seamus researches every ride in Dollywood—because tokens—and Travis works on a Sudoku puzzle while plowing through another bag of licorice.

Wylla gazes out the window at the Kentucky countryside, one grassy swatch after another. It's hard imagining what must be going through her mind. She hasn't spoken a word about

Jackson or her friends or missing home, but, then again, she hasn't done much talking to me at all one way or the other.

Still, it hasn't kept me from trying to reconnect. Not having much in common makes it difficult, but I might have found a way.

"Hey." I move the backpack from between us and scoot across the seat. "Ernie said we're gonna have some time in Pigeon Forge to explore this afternoon, and I was wondering if you wanted to go somewhere with me?"

She turns away from the window like she's coming out of a trance. "Where?"

In a perfect world, the prospect of sharing an experience with me would be enough.

"I'll give you a hint."

She rolls her eyes and returns to the window. "I'm done with stupid clues. What is with you people and your puzzle obsession?"

A pinch of resentment twists in the pit of my stomach, but I ignore it along with her comment. "There was room on the door for Jack."

This grabs her attention, her head whipping around. "Jack as in *Titanic*?"

I nod.

"Is Leonardo DiCaprio in Tennessee?"

I pull up the web browser on my phone, open it to the Titanic Museum's website, and hand it to her.

She scrolls through, eyes widening with each new page. "Wait. Is this place in Pigeon Forge?" The tone of her voice releases the ball of tension inside of me. There's no way she'll turn me down.

"Yup. I already talked to Ernie, and if you're interested in going with me, he said he'll drive us over after we check in at the motel."

She returns her attention to my phone, pulling up a list of all the exhibits inside the museum. I knew when I saw the brochure tucked away in a kiosk at the last rest stop, she wouldn't say no. Because if the world's only half-scale replica of the Titanic, complete with almost five million dollars' worth of artifacts isn't enough to lure her in, nothing is.

"Remember watching the movie together at Dad's when we were in middle school, and how I totally fangirled over Jack and made Mom take me to the library so I could check out a million books about the ship?" She giggles, and when I giggle back, for a moment we aren't estranged anymore. We're just two sisters sharing a memory. "Oh, and remember how pissed Mom got about the part with the boobs and the sex in the car when she found out we saw it? Like we'd never seen a pair of tits before."

I wait for her to remember the rest of the story. The part about Mom's reaction that still knots my stomach when I think about it.

"I don't like how your father leaves you girls unsupervised all the time," Mom said that afternoon, a kitchen towel wrung between her hands like she wished it was his neck. "And you should've known better too, Elise. Your sister is a child. She's got no business watching R-rated films."

Wylla puffed out her chest and squared her shoulders the way she did whenever she wanted to appear older. "Elise told him you were gonna get mad, but he said it wasn't R. Only PG-13."

"Well, you're not old enough for either." Mom might have been speaking to Wylla, but her eyes were locked on me.

Disappointment oozed from her. I'd let her down. Contributed to the corruption of my little sister.

I thought for sure Wylla'd remember my failure, but listening to her reminisce about all things Titanic now, she seems to have forgotten all the bad parts. It gives me hope that if I can fool her into spending some time alone with me on this trip, I might still be able to fix what's broken between us.

"You want me to get us tickets?"

She glances up from the phone. "I thought you already did."

Ernie drops us off with instructions to call him for pick up when we're done. We climb out of the van, eyes locked on the world's largest Titanic museum attraction—a replica of the front half of the illustrious ship seemingly dropped on the side of the highway.

"This is intense," Wylla says as I slide the van door shut behind her. "I can't wait to see what's inside."

We hurry across the parking lot, but by the time I make it to the entrance, Wylla's fallen behind. I spot her halfway down the sidewalk, trying to snap a selfie in front of the ship. As I step out of line to wait for her, a huge tour bus pulls up to the curb. It'll take us forever to get through the museum if they get in front of us, so I call for her to hurry up and approach an employee at the door, dressed in a suit and tie.

"Welcome to the Titanic's maiden voyage." He scans the digital vouchers off my phone screen. "Two?"

"Yeah." I toss a glance over my shoulder at Wylla who's now racing to beat the tourists off their bus. "My sister's right behind me."

He hands me two squares of paper. "Okay. Well, here are your boarding passes, which include the names and stories of actual Titanic passengers. At the end of the exhibit, make sure you visit the memorial room to discover whether or not your passenger survived."

I thank him, and as I enter the building Wylla slips in behind me. "Good thinking getting in front of that tour," she says, taking the boarding pass from my hand. "What's this?"

I explain about being assigned a passenger, and she skims the paragraphs describing her girl's experience on the ship.

"I got a kid. Catherine Nellie Johnston. A third-class passenger from Sussex, England." She glances over at me. "Who'd you get."

"R. Norris Williams. First-class passenger. Twenty-one years old. Says he was traveling with his dad."

Her eyes go wide as the rotunda and grand staircase open before us. "Wonder if either one of them made it?"

I shrug. "I guess we're about to find out."

Around the museum, some employees are dressed as the ship's crew in naval blues, complete with badges and insignias adorning their chests. Chambermaids wear simple black dresses with crisp white aprons skimming their ankles, while others represent actual passengers from the ship in vintage three-piece suits and bustled dresses.

"All of the four-hundred-plus artifacts on display were either salvaged as floating debris or donated by survivors." An employee dressed as the unsinkable Molly Brown, complete with her feathered hat, points out a pocket watch, frozen in time at two thirty-six. "Most of the smaller artifacts, like this one, were discovered inside floating trunks salvaged by the USS Carpathia."

Watching my sister swoon over the shelves full of leather-bound books and ornate inlaid furniture makes me feel nostalgic for a time when we were both still innocent of the ways of the world. When neighborhood kids were the only friends we needed and no one dreamed of asking us to break the law for them. If they had, we never would've been stupid enough to agree.

In addition to actual relics, the ship also houses hundreds of movie props, like Kate Winslet's red-sequined 'you jump, I jump' dress and Leonardo DiCaprio's tan overalls. Wylla's face lights up as we pass a third-class hallway, water rushing through it. "It's just like the hall Kate and Leo ran through in the movie."

Although the ship itself is only built to half-scale, the individual rooms and halls inside are full-size, crafted with the same care and precision as the original ship, with heavy moldings and elaborate detailing. Wylla runs her hands against the rich woodwork as we make our way to the Promenade Deck, which of course, was only accessible to first-class passengers on the maiden voyage. A giant white boulder fills the space now.

"This is supposed to be the glacier, I guess." She presses her palm against the synthetic slab of ice. "And look, you can put your hand in the sea water." She touches it but immediately recoils. "It's freezing."

I test the water myself imagining what being submerged would feel like. The desperation of it. The pain. It's surprisingly easy, and I let the numbness spread through my fingers, up my hand, and into my wrist. How long would I need to stay submersed before paralysis set it? Thirty minutes? An hour?

How long before death?

There's no time to consider further because Wylla has left my side and is moving on to the next part of the museum. I pull my hand from the water and wiggle my fingers to return the blood supply before drying it with my shirt.

Together, we wind our way through the remaining cabins, staterooms, and galleries, eventually finding ourselves in Memorial Hall.

"Woah. Look at all the names." Wylla approaches the wall listing the individuals who lost their lives when the Titanic sank. "Do you think our people are on here?"

"I'm a first-class passenger, but a man, so I could go either way. You're third-class, but a child, so there's a good chance you got on a lifeboat."

We scan the wall of passengers and crew who lost their lives, and it occurs to me how fleeting life is. How you can be sailing along on an unsinkable boat, and the next thing you know, you're drowning at sea. My fingers trace the letters in their names. How many of them left words unspoken? How many of them never got a chance to share all the truths they were holding in their hearts?

"Wylla?"

She turns to me, blinking like I've interrupted something. "Yeah?"

"I'm sorry about everything with Logan. I know you two were close."

Her eyebrows furrow, and she takes a step back. "Jesus, Elise, I thought we were having a nice time. Why do you always have to ruin everything by bringing up stuff like that?"

"I just…" I shake my head. Every time we get to this part—the part where I explain why I did what I did—I shut down because I'm afraid she'll walk away. But today, there's nowhere for her to go. She's stuck here in this museum with me, in public, and she won't cause a scene. Her teenage sensibilities won't allow it. "I only agreed to work with the police to protect you."

"Please." She scoffs, her eyes like daggers. "What you're saying is *I'm* the reason our best friend is in jail? Thanks. That makes me feel so much better."

I'm determined to speak my peace, so when she starts across the hall toward the museum exit, I take off after her, grabbing her by the arm. "Stop, just hear me out. There are things you don't know. He had priors and was going to jail whether I helped the police or not. But if I hadn't, you'd probably be in there with him."

This gets her attention, and when she stops, I release my hold on her arm. "What are you talking about?"

For months, I've practiced this speech in my head. The one where I tell her everything.

Even the horrible parts.

I head for a nearby bench, and she follows, taking the seat beside me.

"Look, you obviously think I'm the bad guy in all of this, and maybe in some ways I am. But Nia overheard her dad talking about this whole sting operation his unit had planned. How they were gonna raid Logan's house and arrest him. I knew you were involved because I saw you giving stuff out for him at school. And, yeah, maybe I was a little disappointed he didn't ask me, too, but that's not the reason I did what I did."

I rest my head in my hands, pretending the rejection of not being cool enough for Logan's inner circle doesn't still sting. But it does. All the time we spent together as kids meant nothing to him once we got older. Not the sand castles we built in my backyard sandbox or the Kool-Aid popsicles we made with twice the recommended sugar. Not even all the fireflies we caught on summer evenings, when the freshly mown grass would turn our bare feet completely green. Our past didn't matter because he had a bad boy reputation to uphold and hanging with me would've tarnished his shine.

Wylla sighs, wearily, as if rehashing the whole ordeal might break her. "Then what was the reason, Elise? What possible explanation could you have for turning our best friend in to the cops."

"They had your name, Wylla. They had everyone's names. All the people at school who were distributing for him. You were all going down—they were talking jail time, not just fines—and I couldn't let that happen. So, I made a deal."

"A deal?"

After being bottled inside for so long, the story pours from me as the memories of that day in Nia's kitchen come rushing back. Sitting across from her dad at their farmhouse table, my eyes kept shifting to his biceps which threatened to burst through the seams of his police uniform.

"Nia said you wanted to talk to me about Logan Meyers." His voice was deep and authoritative. It was no wonder he got so many criminals to confess.

"Actually, my sister."

He nodded, giving a sidelong glance at Nia across the kitchen. She took a ton of heat for telling me about the sting operation in the first place but didn't mind getting grounded if there was a chance of saving Wylla.

"She's one of the names we've tagged for arrest. Distribution is a serious offense."

"I understand." The slow leak of the faucet drip, drip, dripping into the sink behind me felt almost torturous. I swallowed hard, swiping at the bead of sweat pooling against my hairline. If I continued on, there would be no going back. I'd be choosing my sister over my best friend and our lives would never be the same. "Nia told me because of the priors, you're looking for a way to catch Logan in the act instead of arresting him for intent."

"That's correct." His gaze was unflinching. There was no way to tell whether he'd even take my offer into consideration.

I pursed my lips and forced myself to speak. "If I was able to get the evidence you need, would you consider taking my sister's name off the list?"

His eyes flicked to Nia, and the look passing between them confirmed she'd already told him everything, and they'd discussed my plan. "You think you can do the job? Wear a wire? Have him sell to you?"

I nodded.

"It's not as easy as it looks, betraying someone's confidence."

His words settled upon my shoulders, heavy as a weighed yoke, threatening to crush me. Sacrificing my best friend for my sister wasn't going to be easy at all. I'd be sealing Logan's fate. Sending him to prison.

And even if he got a short sentence, I'd still lose him forever because once all was said and done, he'd know I was the one responsible for ruining his life.

But Wylla… Wylla's life would go on. She'd be safe.

So, it was worth it.

Looking at her on the bench beside me now, I take a deep breath and let it out slowly, unable to gauge her expression. "I'm sorry Logan took the fall, but I don't regret protecting you. I couldn't allow you to become collateral damage because having a criminal record would've ruined your future, you know that, right?"

Tears of appreciation pool in the corners of her eyes, and a wave of relief washes over me.

This is it. She finally gets it. She's finally going to forgive me.

Then her gaze shifts in my direction, cold and hard.

"All this time you've woven this tight little narrative inside your own head," she says. "Called yourself as a saint. Fooled yourself into believing your motives were completely pure. But even if the main reason you sold Logan out *was* to protect me, you know it wasn't the *only* one. You resented our closeness. You hated the way he looked at me and talked to me and touched me. You hated that we were together." She sets her jaw, ignoring the tears running down her cheeks.

My face grows hot like I've been slapped, and I open my mouth to object to her lies. But I stop.

Because she's speaking the truth.

Part of me did resent her relationship with Logan. And if I'm being honest, Mom was part of the equation, too. If my sister got in trouble, I knew she'd find a way to blame me for Wylla's involvement.

If I'd 'been a better sister' or 'kept better tabs on her,' maybe she wouldn't have gotten wrapped up in Logan's mess.

Both were selfish motivations woven alongside the pure one.

I lay a gentle hand on her shoulder. "You're absolutely right. It *wasn't* just about saving you. On the other hand, if you hadn't been mixed up in all of it, I never would've gotten involved in the first place." I release a long slow breath, composing myself. "You might never agree with what I did or even why I did it, but I'm hoping you might be able to find a way to eventually forgive me. My heart was in the right place, you gotta know that."

She swipes at her eyes with the back of her hand, sniffles once, then stands, effectively ending our conversation. "Come on. We should go check to see if our people are on the Survivors' Wall of Stories."

Sadly, although R. Norris Williams survived the sinking of the HMS Titanic, the body of seven-year-old Catherine Nellie Johnston was never recovered. We don't acknowledge the resulting melancholy that settles over us as the tour ends, but by the time Ernie pulls the van to the curb for pick up, I'm convinced my relationship with Wylla may be nearly as tragic as Catherine's short life.

CHAPTER 16

The next morning, Wylla's already holed up in the bathroom before my alarm even goes off. I take her early rising as a good sign, and as I lay staring at the popcorned ceiling, waiting for her to finish showering, I'm strangely hopeful after our time together at the museum, she might be ready to abandon Chloe and Dustin to tag along with me instead.

But when she eventually emerges from the steamy bathroom, hair wrapped in a towel, she offers me nothing more than a curt hello, making it difficult to remain optimistic. I smile sweetly, sliding past her near the foot of Chloe's bed, and pray the condensation fogging up my glasses is enough to mask my disappointment. Minutes later, however, their boisterous laughter cuts through the door while I'm brushing my teeth, confirming my attempts at connecting with her have had absolutely no effect.

Even the Titanic Museum wasn't enough.

I'm still stewing about a way to get through to her as I pack my duffle, wondering if I ought to ask Nia for some suggestions, when a text alert chimes on my phone. It's embarrassing the way my stomach clenches in the seconds before checking the screen, while I still don't know who it's from. I'm unapologetically hopeful it might be Mom checking in, but it's not, of course, and I force myself to swallow the rejection as I read the text from Ernie instructing me to meet him by the van in ten minutes so he can give me today's token clue. I tell him I'll be there and shoot off a quick text to Seamus.

Apparently it's my turn as keeper of the clue. Getting it from Ernie in ten minutes. I'll let you know as soon as I have it.

His reply is immediate. *I'll meet you by the ice machine on the first floor. And I'll bring the Dollywood map.*

Ernie's grinning ear to ear as I cross the parking lot. "Here comes our token leader. You gonna snag another one today?"

My ears heat. "I'll try, but honestly, I wouldn't have two if it weren't for Seamus. He's the real brains of the operation."

Ernie holds out a slip of paper but resists when I reach to take it. "Oh, no. That's not what he says at all. To hear him tell it, you singlehandedly solved the bumper car clue at Kings Island, and that was a tricky one."

"He said that?" An unexpected warmth spreads through me as I take the paper. Being appreciated feels nice.

Really nice.

Ernie checks his watch before glancing over his shoulder. "He did. And hey, make sure you don't take too long sharing this with everyone, huh? Don't want certain folks getting their panties in a wad about not having adequate access and all that." He gives me a wink. "For what it's worth, though, I'm rooting for you."

I thank him and after rounding the corner, spot Seamus slouched against the wall beside the ice machine. I jog over and hand him the slip.

"Burgers and fries?" he asks.

"I know. What the hell? It's gotta be hidden in a restaurant or something, right?"

He pulls his trusty paper map of Dollywood from the back pocket of his cargo shorts. "Three days ago, I would've agreed, but after the Kings Island fiasco, I'm thinking maybe not." He traces a circle around the map with his finger.

"Is there a food-related ride?" I take a step closer to get a better view of the map and trip over a crack in the sidewalk. The map crushes beneath me as I tumble into his arms, but Seamus manages to keep us both from collapsing to the ground. My cheek presses against his chest, and his muscles tighten under his t-shirt. He wraps his arms around my waist as he rights me, but instead of being immediately embarrassed by my clumsiness, I take a moment to bask in how nice it feels to be held.

Eventually, though, the reality of my awkwardness sets in, and I let out a nervous laugh. "I'm so sorry." My tank top's ridden up in the back, and I focus my attention away from him as I adjust it, bracing myself for the ridicule that's certain to follow. I'm used to it, though, since this is the part where Logan would've teased me for being a klutz.

"Don't be sorry," he says. "If anyone should be sorry it's the stupid sidewalk. That thing's a real hazard."

I stare at him dumbfounded as he smooths his crumpled map on the side of the ice machine. He didn't make fun of me. Not even a little bit. I don't know why I thought he might—nothing he's said or done in the time we've spent together would indicate he's the type of person who relishes the opportunity to put another person down—but still, his kindness takes me by surprise.

In the chaos, the clue has fallen to the ground, so I pick it up. "I should take this to everyone else. Don't want anyone to accuse us of having an unfair advantage or anything."

He nods. "Sounds good. I'll work on this, and we can talk about my ideas when we get to the park." When he looks up from the map, his eyes twinkle with excitement. "I hope we can find the tokens quickly because this park has a wing coaster like the one at Cedar Point we didn't have time to ride, and I don't want to miss out again."

I give him a wave as I head off in the direction of the guys' room. "Don't worry. We'll find them."

***

When it's time to leave the motel, Wylla plops herself in the back of the van between Dustin and Chloe, so she heads off with them the minute Ernie drops us at the park. He calls after them as they race for the entrance. "We've got a three-and-a-half-hour drive to Charlotte tonight, so when I say be back to the van by seven o'clock, I mean it."

Dustin throws a dismissive wave over his shoulder. I'm still watching them, pondering another way to get my sister to like me, when Seamus grabs my hand, dodging and weaving between other cars in the drop-off zone.

"I think I know where the tokens are, but on the off chance I'm wrong, I've got a few other places we should check. None of them open for another hour, though, so how about if we try to hit a coaster or two first?"

I agree. "The Lightning Rod looks cool. I read it's the only launched wooden coaster in the world. And we should try to do the Wild Eagle, too, since today is our last chance to ride a wing coaster."

As I pass through ticketing, Mikal and Travis appear on my left. "Where you guys headed?" Mikal asks.

Seamus side eyes me. "Hitting a couple coasters. Wanna come with?"

Mikal and Travis exchange a conspiratorial look before agreeing. "Interesting clue today, huh?" Travis says nonchalantly. "Guess you two super sleuths have it all figured out already, though."

Seamus shrugs. "We've got a couple different ideas, but the clues seem to be getting harder."

We discuss the King's Island clue, and they ask how I liked the Titanic Museum. I tell them about the exhibits but leave out the parts about Wylla. The guys have no interest in hearing the gritty details of our turbulent relationship, and since she still refuses to hang out with me, they've probably already made assumptions about our estrangement. Still, I keep checking over my shoulder for her, but along with Dustin and Chloe, she seems to have disappeared.

Seamus notices me searching for them while we wait in line for Wild Eagle. "You think they know something we don't?"

"I dunno. Maybe." I take a step as the line inches forward.

Mikal scoffs. "Those guys don't know anything. They were ahead of us when we came in. Headed right when we headed left."

"Maybe they're riding Lightning Rod," Seamus says.

"Or maybe they were going to find a quiet corner to make out." Travis pulls a stash of licorice from his fanny pack and offers the bag to the rest of us. "Want some?"

I pass, of course, because only an idiot would put food in his stomach three minutes before getting on one of the most intense roller coasters in the country.

And also, licorice is gross.

Approaching the loading platform, Travis and Seamus end up on one half of the row and Mikal and I end up on the other.

The seats of the wing coaster are divided—two seats on the right side of the track and two seats on the left—with the wheels and the rail in the middle.

After spending so much time alone with Seamus, being alongside Mikal feels strange, and I'm taken aback when he starts whispering to me the second the brakes engage at the end of the ride. "You and Seamus seem pretty tight," he says as we're waiting to unload.

I glance over at him, grinning at me like a four-year-old with a secret. He and Travis obviously planned this whole thing—inviting us to ride with them so Mikal could get me alone and grill me for details about today's token location. He thinks he can break me. Or at least trick me into giving something away. But the joke's on him because Seamus hasn't had a chance to tell me anything.

"He's nice," I say. "We make a good team."

As the words come out, I'm struck by how honest I'm being. He is nice. And for whatever reason, we do make a good team.

"Just teammates, huh?" His voice rises an octave as he nudges my arm. "What you've got going on seems a little less platonic than teammates."

The conversation's personal turn catches me off guard as the train inches into the station. Has Seamus said something to Mikal about me? Does he think after five days I'm suddenly interested in being romantic?

Am I interested in being romantic?

"Yeah. I mean, no. We're just friends. That's it."

The train lurches to a stop, and as the shoulder restraints raise, he says, "Hmm. Good to know."

CHAPTER 17

Both the coaster and my conversation with Mikal have my stomach rolling as we continue on to the Lightning Rod. Along the way, I pretend to listen while the guys evaluate Wild Eagles' every twist and turn, but Mikal's words keep replaying in my head like a Taylor Swift song on a *Top 40* station.

What does he know that I don't?

After the second coaster, Seamus coughs conspicuously drawing everyone's attention. "I, uh, gotta use the bathroom and might be awhile. You guys should go on ahead." He flashes me a quick look to indicate he's trying to ditch them, but of course, Travis sees right through it.

"That's fine. Guess you've decided it's time to get serious about those tokens, huh?" He claps Mikal on the shoulder, and the two of them turn from us, back in the direction of the Wild Eagle. "Good luck in the bathroom," he calls over his shoulder. "Hope everything comes out all right."

We head off without them to a bench around the corner, where Seamus is not at all subtle watching them amble away. "I don't want them to see where we're going, so let's wait here until they're gone.

I nod but can't seem to find my voice, still contemplating the strange exchange with Mikal. Seamus doesn't appear to notice my hesitation, though, and the instant Mikal and Travis disappear into the crowd, he makes for a nearby food stand.

"The clue is burgers and fries, so we might as well check the obvious places."

I search the Dogs 'N' Taters stand with him but come up emptyhanded. Seamus is ready to head out, but on a whim, I approach a teenage girl at the counter. "Hey. This is going to be a stupid question, but I'm doing this scavenger hunt thing, and I was wondering if you might have a couple of gold tokens back there by any chance?"

She looks at me like I've sprouted a unicorn horn from the top of my head. I'm about to apologize for bothering her when the guy at the neighboring register throws me a wicked smile.

"I heard this manager in the employee locker room mention something about hiding tokens the other day. He wasn't from the food department, though. Entertainment, maybe?" He shrugs. "I dunno if it's any help, but that's what I heard."

I thank him for the information and set off with Seamus to the next location.

He checks his phone's lock screen for the time, barely sidestepping a stroller-wielding family as we pass. "We have a couple minutes to check out Red's Diner if you want."

I tell him what the cashier said about the entertainment manager.

"If he knows what he's talking about, the tokens should be hidden at the show, *Dreamland Drive-In*."

It makes sense, with a clue like burgers and fries, that the tokens wouldn't be hidden in an obvious place like a restaurant.

But I'm not sure where he thinks we should look at the show. Is he planning to search under every seat in the auditorium?

I glance in his direction. Probably so.

"Still, if we've got the time, it can't hurt to check," he says. "Unlike the hot dog kiosk, Red's is an actual restaurant so there'll be lots of places to check."

Unfortunately, by the time we hit the diner, lunch is in full swing, and the place is wall-to-wall people. He holds the door for a family with three toddlers, each whining louder than the next about their Threatcon-level hunger. Once inside, a quick scan of the situation confirms what we both know to be true.

If the tokens are hidden in the restaurant, there's no way either of us are finding them now. I look around for someone who appears to be a manager, hoping the confirm the cashier's story, but every employee is busy serving customers, so I decide not to bother them about my stupid quest. "We should head to the show. If we get there early, maybe we can search around a bit before it starts."

Seamus agrees, following me past a herd of hungry patrons back to the midway. Luckily, Pines Theater, where the production of *Dreamland Drive-In* begins in less than half-an-hour, is right around the corner.

Approaching the theater, however, it's obvious we aren't the only ones convinced the token's hidden inside. Dustin, Chloe, and my sister are already posted near the front of the line, and Travis and Mikal are at the back.

Travis throws us a nod as we join the end of the queue. "Dreamland, huh? They have a decent milkshake?"

I shake my head. "We didn't eat. Just checking it out for later."

Mikal smiles knowingly at Travis before turning to me. "We already gave it a once over. Didn't find anything." He thumbs over his shoulder at Wylla. "I'm a little worried about these guys, though. Wonder when they got here to be at the front of the line?"

The conversation turns to potential hiding spots in the auditorium, and the appeal of sitting for the next half hour in air-conditioned comfort. The guys place bets on how late Dustin and his harem will be getting to the van tonight, and all the while, Mikal keeps glancing between me and Seamus, like he's watching for one of us to make some kind of move on the other. His tentative looks have me breaking into a sweat, and I'm relieved when the doors to the auditorium finally open, and he turns his attention back to the tokens.

Inside, everyone who isn't searching for a stupid coin fills the rows from the center out. You'd think from the way they're shoving each other to the side for the best seats we're at an Ariana Grande concert instead of a musical homage to the hits of the 1950's and 60's. Those of us who aren't interested in the quality of our seats wander the perimeter, checking under unoccupied seats and the rims of trashcans. Wylla examines an alcove in the wall, turning when I come up beside her.

"Any luck?" I ask.

She rolls her eyes. "No. But I'm not really trying."

I slide my hand along the floor-to-ceiling curtain running the length of the wall but there's nothing but fabric. "Are you having fun at least? This is a pretty cool park."

"Yeah. We rode the Thunderhead, and I didn't get sick so I'll take the win."

"Do you…" Something inside one of the seat's cupholder catches my attention. Upon closer inspection, it's only an empty Snickers wrapper, but when I turn back to Wylla, there's an attendant standing beside her who I'm sure is here to encourage us into our seats.

Instead, she turns to me and says, "Can I help you? Have you lost something?"

I recoil, pulling my hand from the seat and jamming it in my pocket. "No. No, I'm fine." The guilt accompanying my response is reflexive, of course, as she hasn't officially accused me of doing anything wrong. I halfway expect her to, but instead, she leans toward me, lowering her voice.

"Maybe you're searching for something specific, then?"

I narrow my eyes, skeptical. The tone of her voice suggests she knows what I'm up to. I'm about to respond when Wylla takes a step closer, like she's trying to give me a way out. "You coming, sis? The show's about to start."

I glance between them, torn, but something in the expectant look on the woman's face compels me to inquire about the tokens.

I double take as she pulls a red pouch from her pocket and hands it to me. "Congratulations," she says. "Enjoy the show."

I turn to Wylla, dumbfounded. Talk about being in the right place at the right time. I'm scanning the theater for Seamus when it occurs to me that she was part of the whole interaction and is technically entitled to the second token.

I hold it out to her. "Here. You should have this one."

Instead of taking it, though, she turns on her heel and makes for the closest aisle. "No way. Give it to Seamus. He's your partner."

"Yeah, but you were with me the whole time." She doesn't acknowledge my attempts at objectivity, so I continue trailing after her down the aisle. "She could have just as easily offered them to you instead of me. It's only fair."

She slips into an isolated seat in the back of the theater, tossing her daypack to the side, and I plunk down beside her. "You and I both know I give no craps about those stupid tokens," she says. "But you and Seamus obviously do, so you should keep them, and maybe if you win the vouchers, you two can go to Drury Park together when we get home." She says it casually, like me going to the park with a guy is the most normal thing in the world. That I've been hanging out with Seamus every day for the past week notwithstanding, the idea of doing the same thing back at home seems unrealistic for some reason.

I tuck the tokens into my pocket and thank her. As the lights go down and the curtains rise, she leans her head against mine and whispers, "Did you see Dolly's old tour RV is here in the park? I thought maybe after this you might like to go see it with me." When I don't immediately respond, she gives my elbow a nudge. "I remember how you used to love hanging out in Uncle Chip and Aunt Sarah's Winnebago when we were kids and thought, I dunno, it might be cool to see together."

I don't dare look at her and instead focus my attention on the poodle skirt and argyle sock clad performers taking the stage. "Sounds good." My voices waivers slightly, and I hope she doesn't notice.

Because maybe Dolly Parton's luxury tour bus is the breakthrough I've been hoping for.

By the end of the first number, she's fidgeting in her seat, bored. "You really wanna stay and watch this thing or do you think we could just bolt?"

I cut my eyes to Seamus and the others who are seated together half-a-dozen rows ahead on the opposite side of the theater. There's no way to get his attention while the show's going on so I shoot him a quick text.

Great news. I got the tokens. Text me when the show's over. Smile emoji.

I motion toward the nearest exit. "Let's go."

CHAPTER 18

It takes several seconds for my eyes to adjust to from the dimness of the theater to the glaring sun. Wylla lowers dad's ballcap before thumbing over her shoulder to the left. "I saw a sign for the RV earlier. It's back this way, toward the entrance."

It's a short walk to Dolly's Home-on-Wheels, and we're able to load right on for our 'tour' with four other guests. One of the women is sporting an airbrushed "Dolly's Biggest Fan" t-shirt with nails the color of cotton candy and an expression of reverence like she's about to enter a sacred space. Wylla notices, too, and suppresses a grin as we climb the steps into the tour bus.

"You have five minutes to explore," the attendant calls out behind me. "You can take photos but please don't touch the display items."

Inside the door is the driver's seat, as plush as the nicest La-Z-Boy recliner I've ever seen.

"Ernie would love that chair, wouldn't he?" Wylla asks.

I agree he would, and it strikes me as strange she called Ernie by his name or even considered him at all. Especially since it took three years for her to learn our bus driver Gloria's name when we were kids.

She follows our touring companions into what appears to be Dolly's living quarters, outfitted with a sofa, recliner, and television mounted to the wall, exactly like the one in our cousin's Winnebago. Further on is a dinette table and fully-equipped kitchen with a cooktop, full-size oven, refrigerator, and dishwasher.

Wylla peeks under the dinette cushion. "This one doesn't convert to a bed like Kora's did."

"It doesn't have to." I point past the kitchen to a row of bunks lining the wall. Beyond them, Dolly's massive bed takes up nearly the entire bedroom. "This thing has enough beds to sleep our whole family."

Ahead of us, Dolly's biggest fan is taking selfies with every artifact in the place, so while we wait to get to the back of the bus, we busy ourselves near the bathroom.

Wylla brushes an embroidered angel wall hanging with her fingertips. "There sure is a lot of rose-colored stuff in here."

"Dolly's known for being a girl's girl," I agree. "I mean, look at the wallpaper. There's pink everywhere."

She peeks into the shower and releases a sigh. "Remember how we begged Uncle Chip to let us use the shower in the RV, but he never did because there was nowhere to dump the waste? What was that all about? I mean, what good is having a shower if you can't use it?"

Wylla, my cousin Kora, and I put up such a fight about the stupid shower. I don't know why we were so obsessed with the idea of bathing in the tiny fiberglass cube, too small for one of us, much less all three, but we'd begged and begged until he finally compromised by letting us run around the yard under the sprinkler instead.

"Take some soap along if you're all so hellbent on getting clean," he'd said.

Now, as Wylla and I stroll past Dolly's makeup mirror on the way to her bedroom, she continues to wax nostalgic over the times we spent together in our cousin's Winnebago. The Disney Pixar movie marathons. The facials. The time we gave all our Barbies' pixie haircuts and got grounded for a week.

"Why'd the three of us stop hanging out anyway? We used to have so much fun together." She turns to me, wide-eyed, as if her question isn't rhetorical. Like she's looking for a legitimate answer.

"You don't remember why we stopped having campouts?"

"No." She shakes her head, brows furrowed. "I mean, I guess we made other friends and started hanging out with other people, but that didn't have anything to do with the three of us."

Watching her give Dolly's room a once over, it's like she and I lived completely different childhoods. Like she somehow redacted all the painful parts, leaving only pleasant memories. She can't honestly have forgotten all the times she acted like hanging out in our cousin's backyard was beneath her. Made me feel unworthy to be in her presence. Teased me for my frizzy hair and my glasses and my lisp. And there's no way she doesn't remember how it ended the last night we camped out together.

"You said, and I quote: *Sitting around watching the same old movies together in our pajamas is stupid and boring.*"

"I said that?"

My jaw drops in disbelief. "Yes. And you said the camper was old and smelled like boy feet."

Faded photographs of Dolly's parents and grandparents are nailed to the wall on either side of her bed. Wylla runs a finger along one of the frames, but she's not looking at the picture. She's looking through it, like she's concentrating hard on some distant memory she can't quite place. I'm about to say something when she swallows hard, her expression softening as she composes herself. A small smile plays at her lips. "It sort of did smell like boy feet, though, didn't it?"

A bubble of offense rises in my chest, but before I can speak up in defense of the camper, my sister turns to me, and our eyes lock.

"I'm sorry I stopped coming to the campouts." Her voice is soft. She swallows, like she needs a second to compose herself before going on. I brace for the justification I'm certain is coming; some reason she couldn't stay. But her shoulders fall in resignation. "And I'm really sorry for making you feel bad about yourself."

I shrug, averting my gaze like it's no big deal.

But it is a big deal.

Both her abandonment all those years ago and her apology now.

Painful memories of suffering in silence—never speaking up for myself when I should have—come racing back, and a lump forms in my throat. Of course, I only agreed to accompany her on this ridiculous trip to mend our broken relationship, but inside my head that always looked like her forgiving me, not the other way around. Now that she's offered an actual apology, though, I'm like one of Mom's withered tomato plants on the back patio—soaking up her regret like rain from a brief summer shower.

"It's okay," I say at last. "We were all getting too big to fit on the dinette bed anyway."

The small smile playing at the corners of her mouth reflects back at me in Dolly's rose-tinted mirror. Like the neglected plant, I'm thirsty for more of her apologies and would love to mine for more of them by reminding her of all other times she hurt me.

I'm desperate to hear the words, *I'm sorry,* again.

But I know better than to press my luck, so in the interest of finding some common ground, I let it drop. "And you're right. That place did really stink like Uncle Chip's feet.

We spend the last minutes of our tour reminiscing about all the nights we spent camping with Kora in her backyard. All the junk food. All the dreadful makeup. All the daydreaming about our future selves. It's surprising to hear how fondly Wylla remembers our time together, especially considering how painful so much of it was for me.

Because if we recall our campout days so differently, what other distorted memories could be dividing us?

In the morning, Seamus isn't waiting outside my door to discuss the day's clue. He doesn't bring me a leftover donut from yesterday's stash. And he barely acknowledges me when we finally climb into the van.

Which is why my voice feels so forced when I eventually find it.

I turn around in my seat to face him, my expression buoyant. "Hey."

He doesn't look up from his map of Carowinds. "Hey."

I glance over at Mikal and Travis who are doing their best to ignore whatever is or isn't going on between us. Travis busies himself reorganizing his fanny pack, and Mikal keeps his eyes locked on his phone.

I push my glasses up the bridge of my nose, determined to act like everything's normal even though it clearly isn't. Seamus doesn't appear sick or worried about finding the tokens. So, what the hell's going on?

"Nobody's told me about today's clue yet," I say, hoping to engage him in some form of conversation.

Travis opens a bag of licorice, pulls one out, and takes a bite. "It's 'straddle the line.'"

"Oh." I venture a glance at Seamus, but he's still staring at his map, not giving me anything.

"We know what it means," Chloe chimes in from the back seat. "And we're gonna get to the tokens first."

I half expect her to add 'nanny nanny boo boo' at the end, but she doesn't. Instead, she nestles herself under Dustin's arm, smiling sweetly at me.

It's obvious Seamus isn't interested in discussing the clue, so I turn back around in my seat and gaze out the front window, determined to ignore what's really going on between us. He might be giving me the cold shoulder because I left the show early to see Dolly's RV without him. But I honestly didn't think he'd want to see it and thought I was doing him a favor.

I'm still mulling it all over when Wylla pops up beside me. She leans across the seat, wearing a concerned expression. "You should text him," she mouths.

I widen my eyes to express my frustration. What in the world would I type?

Hey Seamus. This is Elise. Why are you acting so weird all of a sudden?

"Just do it," she whispers.

It seems stupid to send him a text when I'm sitting two feet in front of him, but I follow Wylla's advice and slip my phone from my pocket. It sits heavy in my hand, the weight of my friendship with this quirky, awkward guy hanging in the balance. I begin typing, then delete what I've written and start again. All the while, Wylla watches over my shoulder.

Hey. Are you mad at me or something? If it's because I bailed on the show, I already said I was sorry about leaving without you at lunch yesterday, but again, I didn't think you'd care about seeing Dolly's tour bus.

I hit send and turn off the screen, lacking the strength to watch for reply dots.

A minute passes. Then a second. Finally, a response illuminates my screen.

It's fine.

I stare at those two words as Ernie pulls the van into the Carowinds parking lot. *It's fine* could mean so many things. Some of them good. Some of them not-so-good. How am I supposed to know which kind of fine he is?

I shoot off another text.

Are we cool?

This time the dots are almost immediate.

Sure.

We clearly are not cool, though, because after exiting the van, Seamus heads off with Mikal and Travis, leaving me alone in the drop off lot with Wylla. Concern pulls the lines of her face, and I can't believe pity is what's finally compelled her to abandon her post beside Chloe and Dustin after all these days.

I start across the blacktop with her, and Mikal glances apologetically over his shoulder before disappearing into the crowd.

"What happened between you two?" she asks.

I don't know quite what to tell her. His reaction seems a little severe for simply being left behind at a show, which leads me to believe his sullen demeanor is the result of something else.

But what?

Is Seamus acting aloof because of my conversation with Mikal yesterday? Did Mikal say something to him about our exchange?

I replay the words in my mind, trying desperately to remember. Did I make an offensive statement? A hurtful comment?

Then it hits me.

"I think he might like me as more than a friend."

She stops midstride, eyebrows raised in curiosity. Matchmaking is definitely in her wheelhouse, so if I didn't have her full attention before, I have it now. "How do you know? Did he say something specific?"

The Fury roars overhead on our way to the entrance, forcing me to wait until it's passed to continue. "Mikal did, actually. He said we 'seemed pretty tight' and wanted to know if there was something steamy going on between us."

"Is there?"

I narrow my eyes at her. "No. And even if there was, it's none of anyone's business. I told Mikal that Seamus and I are just friends."

"Hmmm." She nods as we approach the metal detectors. "Seems like maybe Mikal took that info back to Seamus, and he's disappointed his feelings for you are stronger than yours are for him."

The thing is, I don't even know if that's true because until this very minute, I hadn't given much thought to my feelings for Seamus. Still, even if I might be interested in being more than friends with him at some point, I certainly won't be entrusting Mikal with that information now that I know he's such a snitch.

The sympathetic look on Wylla's face almost has me confiding in her, though, but our conversation's interrupted by someone hollering behind us.

"See! I told you we knew where it was," Chloe squeals, holding the red token pouch above her head for everyone to see. "Now that we know how to solve these stupid riddles, it's over for you bitches."

Seamus, Travis, and Mikal have stopped milling around in front of the 'Carowinds—Where the Carolina's Come Together' billboard. I assume the sign's being colloquial until I notice I'm literally standing at the border where North Carolina meets South Carolina.

"Straddle the line," Wylla says, placing one foot in the northern state and one foot in the southern.

"Straddle the line," I repeat.

The first wave of an enormous group of teenagers in matching neon pink t-shirts walks between us, separating Wylla and I from the others, but in the moments before they break our sightline, my eyes lock with Seamus's. Regret colors his face, and it's obvious he's disappointed about more than just losing out on the tokens.

He's upset about me as well.

"You should go to him," Wylla says.

The way she says it, as if walking over to explain what I meant when I told Mikal we were 'just friends' is the easiest thing in the world almost sets my feet in motion. Then I remember the last time I let myself fall for someone who seemed like they were interested in me, and all the memories of my last hours with Logan in his basement come rushing back.

"I can't." I pause, studying her face. "Will you hang out with me today instead? Ride the coasters and stuff?"

She smiles, taking a bottle of Dramamine from her back pocket. "Sure. Why not?"

CHAPTER 20

Wylla and I stand together in line, waiting to ride the Hurler, one of the park's older wooden coasters which starkly contrasts its closest neighbor, The Fury 325. Only minutes before, we'd been lucky enough to secure front seats on the steel giga coaster, giving us unobstructed views of the ride's nearly ninety-degree first drop.

I don't know which one of us screamed louder on the way down.

Now, though, in the aftermath of our excitement, we stand in awkward silence, both scrolling through our Instagram feeds. When the familiar tone of her text alert chimes, I glance over in time to see Mom's message come in.

She groans before shooting off a reply.

"Is that Mom checking in?" I keep my tone neutral, but my chest is tight.

"You know it is." Her voice is laced with contempt, like something's happened.

The line shuffles forward, and I slip my phone into my pocket. "Everything okay at home?"

Another text pops up from Mom, and Wylla quickly replies. "Yeah. She's fine. Just can't go ten minutes without bothering me."

Three more texts come in.

My phone rests silently in my pocket.

"It's kind of nice, though, right? I mean, at least you know she cares about you." Now, there's no mistaking my jealous tone.

"Cares about me?" She rolls her eyes. "Hardly. All she cares about it keeping constant tabs on me like I'm five years old. I wish she trusted me the way she trusts you. I guess I've got you and Logan to thank for that."

We take two steps forward, and as the Hurler's train speeds past, I consider all the implications of her observation. Is she blaming me? Is she truly bothered by Mom's texts?

"You know, Mom hasn't texted me in days."

She glances up from her screen for the first time since Mom's initial message arrived. "Really?"

I shrug. "Yeah. Really. Not a peep."

Wylla shifts uncomfortably. "Well, she knows you're fine. I mean, I told her you are, so that probably explains it."

It's possible the reason Mom hasn't called or texted is because Wylla's already given her all the intel. Or it could be Mom just doesn't give two craps about what's going on with me.

Disappointment and rejection twist themselves into a woven ball of anguish below my ribcage. Resentment builds but the wounded look on my sister's face squelches the accompanying anger. "You should be glad Mom cares. If she's texting, at least you know she's thinking about you."

"Mom's thinking about you, too." She scrolls backward through her history before showing me the screen. "See, look. Right there."

Tell Elise I say hi.

"That text is from three days ago."

"I know, but she said to say hi."

Tell Elise I say hi.

"She could've said hi herself, Wylla. She could've texted me. But she didn't. She texted you. Because you are and always have been her favorite."

The second the words escape my lips I want to take them back. There's no reason to direct my frustration at her. It's not her fault Mom loves her more than she loves me.

At least not entirely.

The coaster rumbles on the track overhead, punctuating the silence between us.

"That's not true, Elise. Mom loves us the same."

I sigh and shake my head.

"Seriously. You're the smart one. The one who gets all the marching band awards. The one who never gets in trouble."

What she says might be true. Maybe I am the smart one. The accomplished one. The good one. But that doesn't mean I'm the loved one.

I brush a loose strand of hair from my face. "Did you know one of my first memories is of Logan and his mom bringing us a casserole after Grandma died? I was four and you were two, and I remember Mom telling Miss Ginny she was glad you weren't a horrible toddler like I was because she didn't know if she'd survive raising a second terror. That's what she said. She was glad you were nothing like me."

Wylla's shoulders slump, and it's clear this is the first time she's heard this story. "I'm sure she didn't mean it. And we were babies. All babies are tough."

"You weren't."

To hear Mom tell it, Wylla was an angel sent from heaven. I, on the other hand, gave her nothing but grief.

Wylla scuffs the ground with the toe of her sneaker. "Yeah, but that was then. You're not the tough one anymore."

It's true. I'm not. But it's only because once I realized Mom loved Wylla more than me, I began working twice as hard for her approval.

"When was the last time Mom said you needed to be more like me?" I ask.

She purses her lips, racking her brain. "When I got that D on my algebra midterm. She said I needed to study more, the way you do."

I roll my eyes. "Perfect. Be a tryhard like me. Name another time."

We're almost to the front of the line, and she turns her attention to the incoming train. "What about driving? You passed your road test on the first try, and my driver's ed instructor gave up trying to teach me to parallel park. Mom says if I don't become a better driver like you, I'll never even get my permit."

This is news. Beyond congratulating me when I got my license, Mom's never mentioned my driving, one way or the other.

At least not while I was around.

Still, even if she did notice some of the good stuff, it doesn't discount all the times she fixated on the bad.

"Well, I'm certain Mom would still prefer if I was more like you than the other way around. Do you remember that neighborhood pool party we went to with Logan back in middle school?"

"The end of the school year one where the principal got thrown into the deep end?"

"Yeah. That one."

"What about it?"

I swallow hard. Even thinking about Mom's words all these years later still gets me choked up, and not in a good way. "As we were leaving that day, she handed me a t-shirt to wear over my suit. Apparently, she thought the top was, and I quote, 'unflattering' because of the 'gaping cups.' Then she suggested I should give the suit to you since your boobs would be a 'much better fit.'"

She reaches out, brushing my arm with her fingertips. "She said that?"

Now that I've started confessing the truth, more comes spilling out, and I'm helpless to stop it, like a river cresting its banks. "Yeah. She did. And also, that I should ask you to help me put together a proper outfit so I don't look so frumpy all the time. And while I'm at it, maybe you could give me a few makeup tips. Boys might find me more attractive if my complexion wasn't so washed out."

She swallows. "Stop."

"Oh. And remember when I went to speech therapy for my R/W reversal in second grade, and Dad reminded me a thousand times that even at five-years-old, you could say rabbit instead of wabbit and I couldn't."

"I'd forgotten all about that." She's staring at her shoes now, clearly embarrassed for her part of what I've experience. It's not her fault, of course, and I would never ask her to be less than who she is. I would never ask for her to give up her Homecoming date because I didn't have one. Or for her to stop dressing fashionably or wearing makeup because I looked a mess standing beside her. But she rarely spoke up. Hardly ever came to my defense.

And it hurt.

Before she can respond, the attendant directs us to our queuing rows, and we board the train.

She's silent for the duration of the ride, but the moment the train comes to a stop, she turns to me. "I had no idea all this stuff upset you. It always seems like you don't even care. I mean, I figured you don't use makeup or wear your hair down because you're busy with other stuff. I've never thought any less of you because of it. And I had no idea about Mom and Dad." She pauses as we exit the platform. "If they said stuff like that to me, I'd be angry, too."

The sincerity in her eyes is strangely reassuring, so against my better judgement, I go on. "But they don't say stuff like that to you, which is the point. I'm always the one who's not living up to everyone's expectations. And you're always the one setting the perfect example." I glance at her, looking for an indication of whether I should continue. Her expression is soft, attentive even. "It comes easy for you. Everything does. And honestly, that makes it hard being your sister sometimes."

At the bottom of the exit ramp, a large herd of middle schoolers shuffle past. As I wait for them to reach the Fury, I spot Seamus exiting a nearby restaurant, water cup in hand. He must feel my gaze because before I have a chance to turn away, our eyes meet. For a millisecond, I forget he's upset, and I raise my hand to wave him over. But when he turns away without even acknowledging my existence, a broken piece inside of me fractures into an even smaller shard.

Everything is easy for Wylla.

Everything is complicated for me.

"You could go talk to him, or go ride with him—act like nothing happened." Wylla pauses, like she's choosing her words carefully. "Not that you need advice from me, but that's what I'd do if I was you."

She would, of course. And she'd figure out a way to smooth things over, effortlessly.

Seamus, Travis, and Mikal head toward the Drop Tower, so I take off in the opposite direction, past Ricochet and the carousel. I have no idea where I'm going, but Wylla tags along by my side.

"The other night when I gave you a hard time about always falling for unattainable guys… I didn't mean to upset you, and I'm sorry." She swallows. "I don't know what your deal with Seamus is, but it seems like you two have hit it off this week, so if your nervous about where your friendship might be headed, you shouldn't be. Trust yourself and trust him."

In all honesty, there's some truth to her observations. Pinning my sights on unattainable guys has always taken the pressure off. If I convince myself it'll never happen, I don't need to worry about eventually having my heart broken.

Until now, my strategy's been pretty effective.

But that's only because no one's ever liked me first.

And now Seamus is complicating everything.

I scoff. I'm not ready to unpack all this now in the middle of an amusement park, so I throw the conversation back to her. "Like you know anything about rejection."

We've stepped into the shade of a vine covered trellis, and she stops dead, removing her sunglasses to level a glare at me. "You can't be serious."

"You've never been rejected in your life."

"I've been rejected plenty."

Now it's my turn to glare at her. "Name one time."

She smiles satisfactorily. "Ha," she says. "I didn't get the lead I tried out for in the fifth-grade play."

She must think I've got marbles for brains. "Of course not. It was a production of Jason Reynold's *Ghost*, and the reason you didn't get it is because the main female character is black. That's not rejection, Wylla. It's just good casting."

"Fine." After playing the only ace in her pocket, now she's wracking her memory for another example. "Oh, I know. Remember when you got picked to hold the American flag for our Girl Scout troop at the Veteran's Day parade that one time? I didn't even get to hold the state flag. Or the troop banner. I was stuck in the back marching along like a doofus with everyone else."

I suppress a snicker. "You didn't get to post the colors because you were six-years-old, and the flag weighed more than you did."

"So?"

I can't help but smile at her indignance. "Listen, I'm not begrudging you all the times things have gone your way. Like when you mentioned to Nia's mom about wanting to teach swim lessons at the Y, and the next week, she pulled some strings and got you the job. I mean, seriously, you didn't even interview for the position. That's the kind of stuff I'm talking about. And it's not your fault. You don't ask for special treatment, but you get it. You see that, right?"

When she doesn't immediately respond, it takes me a minute to realize my misstep.

The job at the YMCA.

She got it to be near Jackson.

She turns away, sliding her sunglasses off the top of her head back onto her face to cover her eyes.

"Wylla, I'm sorry. I forgot. That was a stupid thing to say."

She shrugs and steps further into the tunnel as a crowd of people leaving the *Seasons of Cirque* show push past. "It's okay. And you're right. Most of the time, I do get what I want." Her voice cracks, and I worry she's going to break down. "But it might be better for me if things didn't come so easily. Because I'm not the best judge when it comes to knowing what's good for me, and there's something to be said for not always getting what you want. Cuz when you lose it…" She trails off, welling up beneath her sunglasses.

It's been a long time since either of us has confided in the other, but as she stands before me, on the verge of bursting into tears, it's obvious she needs a safe place to fall.

Will she let me be that safe place now the way I was when we were kids?

Is she finally going to confess the truth about why we're even on this stupid trip?

I step toward her. "Hey. Do you wanna talk about it? What happened with Jackson?" She glances up, her mouth pressed into a thin line, considering me. "Whatever it is, I promise not to judge."

There's an open bench behind us, and when she heads for it, I follow. A refreshing mist sprays from above—welcome respite from the blazing southern sun. Droplets speckle our arms and my glasses, but I don't wipe them away. Instead, I sit attentively as she adjusts the brim of Dad's ballcap across her forehead, stalling while she composes herself. "Jackson cheated on me. With Brenda-freaking-Lauer. Can you believe that? I mean, probably you can, because she's gorgeous and everyone loves her, but still…"

An image of Brenda pops into my head. Wylla's not wrong. Brenda is gorgeous. And beloved. But, of course, beauty and popularity don't excuse Jackson's infidelity. I want to say something supportive, but everything I come up with sounds shallow, like a second-rate greeting card.

I'm sure he doesn't love her like he loved you.

She's not as pretty as you are.

He's a jerk. Forget about him.

"How'd you find out?" I say instead.

She turns her face toward the mister—lets the water run off her chin onto her shorts. "I caught them together. At that stupid lacrosse party he didn't think I was going to."

I vaguely remember something about Wylla not being able to go to the first lacrosse party of the season because she was supposed to be babysitting for the Vance's down the street.

"Yeah. But Collin got sick with the stomach bug, so when Mrs. Vance called and said they didn't need me to sit for them anymore, I headed to the party instead." She removes her sunglasses, wiping the water droplets off the lenses with her t-shirt, and it's obvious the pain of what happened next still stings. "The way everyone looked at me when I got there should've been a good indication something was up, but you know me—Little Miss Naïve. I just grabbed a drink and took off for the backyard with some of the girls, figuring Jackson and I would run into each other eventually." She swallows hard. "And we did."

I don't need her to explain what came next. It's unnecessary to rehash those painful memories.

"You could've come to me, you know. To rant or cry or whatever. I know I wasn't always a big fan of Jackson's, but I've always been a big fan of yours. You didn't need to keep the truth bottled up."

A June bug lands on the seat between us, and she shoos it away. It flies off, but she keeps staring at the spot like she can't force herself to make eye contact with me. "I told Mom, but couldn't go to you. We hadn't spoken in months, and after Logan, I didn't know if I could even trust you anymore. I was still really mad at you about him."

The day the police apprehended Logan, she and I stood together peering through the curtains covering the bay window at the front of our house as they took him away in handcuffs. I didn't plan on telling her the role I played in his arrest, but when the story leaked to the media, it didn't take long for her to realize I was the 'secret informant.'

But truthfully, it didn't take anyone long.

"Are you still mad?"

She looks up, meeting my gaze, and there's something in her eyes I've never seen before.

Understanding.

"Sad, yes. But mad? No. Not anymore. I shouldn't have done what I did for him. It was stupid of me. At the end of the day, Logan got what he deserved, I guess." She hesitates just a beat and looks away, hiding something. "Anyway, I'm grateful you were there to protect me."

I don't immediately respond, too stunned by her admission to speak. In the resulting silence, two tiny sisters race hand-in-hand beneath the trellis, turning their sunburned cheeks toward the overhead misters. As I watch them, Wylla's words replay in my head, and I wait for the relief I was certain would accompany her understanding. This is the turning point I've been waiting for, when she realizes there's no need to be angry anymore, and it's time to forgive me.

The entire trip has led to this defining moment.

And yet, the release never comes.

Instead, the emptiness and confusion remain, like a plague without a cure.

It obvious she's still holding something back—some key piece of information about Logan or a secret about Jackson she still doesn't trust me to keep.

Maybe there's a hidden pregnancy after all.

Or something worse. Did he hurt her? Take advantage of her?

The sisters toddle off, and as I turn my attention back to Wylla it becomes abundantly clear—when it comes to our story, there are still chapters she doesn't trust me to read.

And there are mysteries yet to be solved.

CHAPTER 21

After a full day in the park, I'm physically and emotionally spent, so instead of heading out to dinner with the others, Wylla and I turn in early. Despite our encouraging conversation earlier in the day, it's all I can do to hold back tears as the shower steam clings to the surface of the bathroom mirror, blurring my face. There's got to be a reason Wylla's understanding didn't bring the relief I expected, and as I stare at my hazy reflection pondering an explanation, the only thing I'm one hundred percent certain of is that she's hiding something important from me.

In addition to the confusion surrounding Wylla, the strained situation with Seamus also weighs heavily on my heart. After running into the guys three times today, he never invited me to join them, and all I got from Travis and Mikal were sympathetic glances from across the midway.

I step into the shower, and as the water washes over me, I wait for it to carry the day's disappointments down the drain. When the melancholy remains, however, I work to lather my hands with the minuscule bar of motel soap and scrub furiously at the sun-kissed skin on my shoulders and the back of my neck. This morning, I was certain reconciling with Wylla would be the singular answer to my prayers, and that Seamus and I would continue our friendship even after we got back home.

Now, I'm not convinced either one of those things is true.

The water starts to go cold, so I turn it off, saving some heat for Wylla and Chloe. I towel dry and slip on my pajamas—an old band t-shirt and cotton shorts—before leaving the bathroom.

"It's all yours," I say to Wylla, who's arranging her beauty products on the dresser the way she has every night.

"Thanks." She zips her toiletry bag shut and glances over at me, nose scrunching when she sees my face. "Have you been crying?"

I open my mouth to deny it, but the softness of her voice is strangely reassuring. "Yeah. It's nothing, though, really. Just me being stupid."

"You're upset about Seamus, aren't you?"

I consider her, wondering how much I should confess. The truth is, over the past couple of days, I'd begun imagining a future where the two of us spent time together back home. Maybe we would use our season passes to meet up at Drury Park a couple of times. Or catch a movie together. Or go for coffee. But I wasn't willing to let myself entertain the idea of anything more than that.

But spending today without him, knowing he was out there riding the Fury and the Intimidator and the Nighthawk without me, changed everything. I didn't like the thought of him being without me.

Because I didn't like being without him.

Unfortunately, now that I'm open to the idea of exploring something more with him, he's probably never going to speak to me again, much less want to hold my hand.

I shrug. "Do you think he's ever gonna talk to me again?"

She takes a step forward like she's coming in for a hug, but we've never been a particularly touchy family, so I'm disappointed but not surprised when she stops short. "He'd be a fool not to be friends with you." She smiles, and the space between us fills with unspoken understanding.

I settle under the threadbare floral comforter as she pads off to the bathroom. The water groans inside the pipes, and I say a silent prayer she won't run out of hot water before she's done. There's not much on television, so I flip to a rerun of *Keeping Up with the Kardashians* and turn off the light.

The glow from a nearby streetlamp cuts a strip across my face, but I don't know if it's the glare or a gentle rapping that wakes me hours later. I bolt upright, listening for the sound again, not sure if I'm imagining it or if there's a rat skittering about in the rafters. I don't need to wait long because less than ten seconds later, the tapping begins again, and it's definitely someone knocking on the door. Given what I've seen of the motel's clientele, it's probably some drunk dude trying to get into the wrong room, but on the off chance it isn't, I lean across the bed and pull the curtain to the side, just far enough to see who it is.

Seamus stares at his hands which are folded at his chest like he's praying to a god neither of us can see. His feet are bare, and there's something vulnerable about the way his pajama pants pool at his ankles—part child, part man. In a daze, he turns, abandoning whatever notion brought him here. I tumble off the bed, trying not to wake Wylla in the process, before struggling to disengage the chain and deadbolt in my haste.

He turns, blinking, as the door swings open. "Elise?" His voice is a whisper.

"Yeah?"

Even in the dimness, there's no mistaking the crimson spreading across his cheeks. "I, uh… can I come in?"

I glance over my shoulder and notice, for the first time, Chloe's not sleeping in the second bed. I'm about to ask if he's seen her when he goes on.

"It's just that Chloe's sleeping in my room with Dustin, and it's super awkward. They're being gross. Mikal left hours ago to stay with Ernie and Travis, and I thought I could ignore them, but when the moaning started, I had to get outta there." He hesitates, looking past me into the room where Wylla's gentle snoring permeates the darkness. "Would it be okay if I slept in the empty bed?"

I've never slept in the same room with a guy before, and just thinking about it causes heat to rise off my skin. He's staring at me now, and I'm fairly certain he can hear my heart racing inside my chest.

I take a step back and usher him inside with a wave of my hand. He mumbles a word of thanks and slips past, feeling his way across the room, arms outstretched.

"Ouch." He curses under his breath, bumping into the corner of the dresser before settling himself flat on his back on the far side of the bed. He doesn't slip between the covers or adjust the pillow under his head. He just lays there, arms folded across his chest like a mummy in a sarcophagus.

I want to say something. I want to tell him I'm sorry about hurting his feelings. But now isn't the time or the place, so I turn back to my bed only to discover Wylla has now sprawled herself across both sides. I edge gently into her, hoping she'll slide over and give me some room, but instead she throws her arm across my pillow with a loud sigh.

She's officially taken over the entire mattress.

At this point, my options are limited. I could give her a two-handed shove and force her to give me some space, but she sleeps like the dead so there's a good chance it'll get me nowhere. On the other hand, there's plenty of room on the bed next to Seamus, and he might not mind sharing with me.

I take a tentative step forward. He doesn't open his eyes, and without my glasses, I can barely make out the gentle rise and fall of his chest. At the edge of the bed, I bend down, bringing my face close to his. His breath smells of toothpaste; his skin of Neutrogena.

There's a wooden chair in the corner beside the dresser and for a second, I consider sleeping upright.

Then Seamus opens his eyes. "You okay? Is something wrong?"

I clear my throat, forcing the words from my mouth. "I was wondering if you would mind if I slept here with you tonight. I promise not to take up too much space."

His face softens, and he slides over less than an inch before patting the space beside him. "Sure," he whispers. "I don't mind."

I pull back the comforter and slide between the sheets. Wylla's got the air conditioner cranking, and the cotton is cool and crisp against my bare skin. I stop short of the tight edge where Seamus weighs down the blankets from the top. It feels nice having him there, only a few layers of fabric away.

His breaths are slow and measured, and it isn't long before I've matched the rhythm of my breathing to his. I want to let him know I might like the opportunity to be more than friends, but I'm afraid of getting it wrong, so I trace the watermark pattern on the ceiling with my eyes, trying to come up with the right thing to say.

Finally, I open my mouth to speak, and at the same time he clears his throat and says, "Elise, I'm sorry for ignoring you today. I was being a real dick."

My own apology catches in my throat, and I let out a long, slow sigh. "It's… yeah, I mean, it's okay. And I didn't mean to hurt your feelings or anything either. It's just, I didn't realize when Mikal was asking about us that he was, you know, *asking about us.*"

He shifts against the pillow, turning his face toward me. "I didn't tell him to say anything to you. He did that all on his own."

"I kinda figured."

"But in a way, I'm sort of glad he did. I'm not great at this kind of stuff, and at least this way it's all out in the open. I know it's only been a week, but I like you, Elise. I like you a lot. You're funny and smart, and I can't stop smiling when we're together."

There was a time when I would've given anything to hear these words come out of Logan's mouth. Logan, the guy with the perfect skin and the perfect hair and the perfect body, telling me he liked me, not only as childhood buddies, but as someone he wanted to make out with in his basement. But he didn't see me as the make-out-in-the-basement type. He saw me as the friend he could count on to help him with his geometry homework. The friend who would drive him to Taco Bell at two in the morning when no one else was around.

The friend he would take advantage of given the right circumstances.

In all the years we lived across the street from one another, I never made his heart race. Never made his palms sweat. But now, it seems, that's exactly what I'm doing to Seamus.

And maybe I'm sort of okay with it.

The covers are still tight against my body so it takes some maneuvering to pull my right arm from beneath them. Once I've freed my hand, I slide it along the length of my body to where Seamus's hand rests beside his hip. Slowly, I reach out my pinky finger until it grazes his palm, and when he doesn't pull away, I slip my fingers between his. An unexpected snap of electricity runs through my body, warming me from the inside out.

I'm glad it's dark so he can't see the flush of my face.

"I like hanging out with you," I say. "And if it makes you feel any better, I pretty much suck at this stuff, too." I don't add it's probably the reason I didn't realize why Mikal was probing to begin with.

He tightens his fingers around mine and slides a bit closer until the length of our arms are pressed against one another. His warmth melts away all the anxiety of our separation, and for the first time in a long time, it feels almost as if everything might finally be okay.

Then Wylla's gentle snoring breaks through the contented silence of my heart, forcing me to acknowledge the nagging suspicion that the full scope of our reconciliation has not yet been realized, and it won't be until she comes clean about the secret still keeping us apart.

CHAPTER 22

If Wylla's surprised to see Seamus sleeping soundly in the bed beside me the next morning, she doesn't show it. Instead, she makes heart hands and gives me her best puppy-dog eyes on the way to brush her teeth, which I take as an indication of her approval.

With the bathroom occupied, there's nothing to do but lay as still as possible to keep from waking him. He must've gotten cold at some point during the night because instead of being on top the comforter like he was when we finally fell asleep, he's now curled against me—skin against skin—his arm draped casually across my ribs. His face is so close, like I'm looking at him through a microscope—the curl of his eyelashes, the pattern of the freckles across his nose, and the slightest indication of stubble on his cheeks. His isn't the sort of face that would have me doing double takes across the lunchroom. Heck, it might not have gotten my attention at all. But the more time I spend getting to know the person behind the face, the more intrigued I become.

The sound of the hot water clanking through the pipes finally rouses him, and as he comes to, I'm encouraged by the intensity of his smile when he realizes where he is and who's beside him.

"Hey." He pulls his arm from my torso, and I immediately miss his warmth.

"Hey."

"Did you sleep okay?"

I grin at him. "Yeah, actually. Really well."

He sits up, throws his legs off the edge of the bed, and runs his hands through his hair. "I guess I better head back to my room. All my clothes are there. And my toothbrush." He sighs. "But I don't want to go back. God only knows what I'm gonna find."

"Just knock really loud on the door then wait a minute before you go in," I say. "That way you won't end up witnessing anything you'll never be able to unsee."

He sticks out his tongue like he's gagging. "Gross."

"Gross." I pluck my glasses off the nightstand nonchalantly. "I bet Chloe's gonna end up in your room again tonight, so you're welcome to stay with me if you want. But bring your stuff this time or whatever so you don't need to go back."

He thanks me for the offer and starts for the door with a wave of his hand. As he passes the foot of the bed, though, he hesitates, like he's reconsidering his trajectory. Before I realize what's happening, he's beside me, inches away and face to face.

"Would it be okay if I kissed you goodbye? I mean, I know I'm gonna see you in like twenty minutes for breakfast, but I just…"

I don't wait for him to finish. For the first time since Logan, I feel like kissing someone, so instead of overthinking it, I lean forward and press my lips against his. They're surprisingly soft, and there's no mistaking the longing in his touch as he presses his palm into the small of my back.

When we eventually come up for air, he hoists himself off the bed and makes an awkward beeline for the door.

My stomach drops.

Am I a terrible kisser?

Does my breath stink?

Has he suddenly changed his mind about liking me?

By the time he gets to the door, I'm certain he's bolting, and that I'll never be able to face him again. My heart beats uncontrollably inside my chest, but beneath it, a tiny sliver of something that resembles courage calls out from deep below my ribs.

Go after him, it says.

He crosses the threshold, and on shaky legs, I rise from the bed.

Then he leans back into the room.

"Why type of bagel do you want this morning?" he asks with goofy grin.

Relief washes over me, and I let out a breath, collapsing back onto the mattress. "Surprise me," I say.

***

It's more than a five-hour drive from Charlotte to Busch Gardens in Williamsburg, Virginia and for the first time ever, Seamus abandons his seat beside Travis to sit up front with me. Wylla takes the window seat, of course, so she doesn't get carsick, leaving me squashed between them. I don't mind, though. She falls asleep almost immediately, doesn't take up much room, and her presence gives me an excuse for invading Seamus's personal space when we change lanes. Her lips are full and slightly parted, head tucked against her arm, and as I watch the gentle rise and fall of her chest, I can't help but wonder if she could be suffering from prenatal exhaustion. Her oversized shirt bunches across her midsection, and it's impossible to tell if there's any sort of baby bump hiding beneath.

Every once in a while, muffled giggles emerge from the back of the van, but for the most part, it's almost like Dustin and Chloe aren't even here. Travis and Mikal, on the other hand, are cracking the rest of us up with their seemingly endless knowledge of commercial jingles.

Travis sings in a ridiculous falsetto. "Call 1-800-Steemer…"

"Stanley Steemer makes your home cleaner," the rest of us reply.

"Five. Five dollar."

"Five dollar footlongsssss…"

"Eight hundred, five, eight, eight, two, three-hundred…"

"Empire!" we all sing.

Mikal thinks for a second before singing, "The snack that smiles back…"

"Goldfish," Seamus replies.

"Gimme a break, gimme a break…"

"Break me off a piece of that Kit Kat bar."

"Like a good neighbor…"

"State Farm is there."

I'm laughing at Mikal's baritone reenactment of the Chile's baby back rib commercial when the squeal of brakes and a sudden lurch redirects my attention out the front window. Down the highway, not a hundred feet ahead, an eighteen-wheeler careens off the side of the road, spewing shredded pieces of tire into the air across all four lanes of traffic. Ernie deftly maneuvers the van onto the shoulder, barely avoiding a collision with the car in front of us. To the left, traffic comes to a complete halt as smoke billows from several of the cars ahead. Ernie reaches for his phone to call 9-1-1, but Seamus beats him to it.

"Yes, I'd like to report a serious accident on I-95. Yes, ma'am. A little south of Richmond. I dunno," He cranes his neck to look further down the road. "Yeah, I think we're somewhere around mile marker eighty-two. Okay. Yeah, definitely injuries. Okay. Okay, thanks."

Their conversation continues, and as our van creeps forward, the full scope of destruction comes into view. Outside the window, six cars in various states of ruin litter the highway, and the world around me begins to spin. Several waylaid drivers have abandoned their vehicles to assist other motorists struggling to escape the smoke and fire, and a middle-aged woman in shorts and flip flops tries desperately to wrench open the door of a nearby sedan. The nose of the car is folded like an accordion, and the dashboard is crushed almost to the trunk.

Blood coats what's left of the front windshield.

There's no way anyone in the front seat is still alive.

Still, the woman braces herself against the asphalt and pulls at the handle. The boy beside her has his chin tucked to his chest like he's praying.

Bile rises from the pit of my stomach as the memories of my own brush with death floods my system. The searing pain in my shoulder. The blood covering my hands and my face and the dashboard.

So. Much. Blood.

Recalling the crimson liquid releases another memory, nagging like a tiny pebble in the bottom of my shoe I can't seem to find despite the excruciating pain. There's something traumatic about the blood which has nothing to do with the amount or the color or the way it's splattered around like a discarded cherry slushy. For the first time since the accident, I force myself to recall the moment I first pried my eyes open.

Why was I so scared of the blood?

Sirens wail in the distance as we pass the semi that initiated the pile up. My head throbs, and I close my eyes, tucking my knees to my chest. My lungs are full of sand, and my breathing sounds labored even to my own ears. I'm still hugging myself, gasping for air—rocking back and forth, back and forth—when a gentle hand rests on my shoulder.

"Elise, you okay?" Seamus whispers.

In the aftermath of the accident, the van has gone silent—only the steady thump, thump of the tires over the cracks in the pavement. Somehow Wylla's managed to sleep through all the chaos, and I wish like hell I'd missed the whole thing, too. I'm afraid I might throw up if I respond, but I don't want Seamus to think I'm ignoring him, so I work to steady my breathing before willing myself to speak.

I shudder. "I'm fine. It's… accidents are hard for me."

"That was gruesome." He's trying to make me feel better by acknowledging how dreadful the scene was for everyone, but he doesn't understand how personal it is for me.

I don't want to tell him. Talking about the accident has never been easy. Not with my therapist. Not with Mom. And especially not with Wylla. I haven't felt safe enough with any of them to take off the protective armor shielding me from the painful memories.

But the compassion in Seamus's eyes is so undeniable, the words bubble out of me like a kettle full of boiling water—the pressure releasing like someone who's been on the verge of exploding for a very long time.

"Back in March, I was in this horrible accident, and until now, most of my memories have been faint sounds and smells. The doctors said I was unconscious for most of it, and that I didn't really wake up until much later in the hospital, but now I'm remembering blood. Lots of blood. I've still got the scars on my shoulder." I turn my torso and slide up the sleeve of my t-shirt so he can see where the broken glass embedded itself in my skin. "Anyway, physically I healed pretty quickly. Mentally, though, not so much."

Concern pulls the corners of his mouth into a worried frown. "Are you seeing someone? Like, a professional, I mean. Are you in therapy, or whatever?"

I nod, glancing around the van to make sure my confession won't be overheard, but Mikal's headphones are on, Travis is engrossed in his Sudoku, and Wylla's still racked out against the window.

I keep my voice low, though, just in case. I'm not ready for everyone else to know my business. "Yeah. I go to counseling once a week, and it's definitely helped. There's still certain stuff, though, like driving and seeing other wrecks that triggers the PTSD."

He nods like nothing's shocking. "What about meds?"

It's a super intimate question, but when you have a full-blown panic attack in front of someone, I guess it's sort of an invitation into your personal space. Part of me doesn't want him knowing the truth, though. Because what if he judges me or decides I have too many issues?

But my mouth starts explaining before my brain can shut it down. "I'm supposed to be taking anti-anxiety meds, but they upset my stomach and keep me from eating, so I stopped taking them a while back."

"And you're doctor's cool with that?" His voice sounds alarmed by my admission, and I avert my gaze to keep from looking him in the eye. This is exactly the judgement I could've avoided by keeping my mouth shut. Instead of seeming sketched out, though, he almost sounds parental.

"Yeah. I've been fine."

The truth is, I'm not fine, evidenced by the fact that the accident didn't cause any of the van's other passengers to have a panic attack. But instead of pointing out this obvious detail, he hands me a leftover napkin from lunch. "You're sweating," he says. "And white as a sheet. Do you want me to ask Ernie if we can stop and get you something to drink?"

I shake my head. I couldn't stand on my own two feet if I tried.

He reaches over and takes my hand in his, a silent show of solidarity, and I squeeze back in appreciation. "Listen," he says, "you're not the only one in the world who has mental health issues, and you shouldn't be embarrassed or ashamed to talk about it. When my mom was first diagnosed with bi-polar disorder, she tried to hide it from my brother and me. Looking back now, it would've been so much better for us if we'd known what was actually going on. Instead, we both sort of assumed *we* were responsible for her erratic behavior." He looks at our hands, still woven together in my lap like he can't believe he's telling me all of this.

And I almost can't believe it either.

But I'm glad he is.

"Anyway," he says, "you don't need to hide stuff from me if you don't want to. I mean, you don't need to share everything, of course, but if you ever need a friend…" He looks up, and there's so much empathy behind his eyes I almost forget to breathe. "I've got a bit of experience in the listening department."

At this point, my heart and my head are both swimming with so many emotions, I'm gonna lose it if I try to speak. I don't want to cry, so instead, I squeeze his palm a little tighter against mine and lay my head on his shoulder.

When I glance up a moment later, I catch a glimpse of my haggard expression in Ernie's rearview mirror, and it occurs to me that I've been lying to myself for a long time about the state of my mental health.

And now I might be so far gone I'll never feel normal again.

CHAPTER 23

Seamus sleeps in my room again, and in the morning, I'm awoken by a frazzled Ernie.

"Is Seamus here?" he asks when I open the motel room door.

I thumb over my shoulder to where he's still racked out across the room. "Yeah. Whatcha need?"

He holds out a sheet of paper. "I've got the token clue for him, but I might as well give it to you. Same difference, I guess."

I take the clue. "Thanks. I'll make sure he gets it."

"No problem." He grins over his shoulder as he turns to walk away. "But you two better be good if you know what I'm saying."

I shut the door behind him with a shake of my head. If he's worried about a Drury Park pregnancy resulting from this adventure, he's lecturing the wrong couple.

I throw myself across the bed onto Seamus's back. "Wake up, sleepyhead. Ernie brought you the clue."

He rolls over, taking the paper from my hands before reading it aloud. "Six countries."

Even I know Busch Gardens is divided into six different European countries. What I don't understand is how this stupid piece of trivia is going to help us find the tokens.

Seamus stares at the ceiling, counting on his fingers. "Germany, France, Ireland, Scotland, Italy, England. Those are the six. So, I guess we can eliminate a few sections: Octoberfest, New France, and Festa Italia." He sighs. "So only thirty rides to consider instead of forty. Fabulous."

"What if they grouped Scotland, Ireland, and England together as Great Britain? Does that help at all?"

He shakes his head, leveling an authoritative glare at me. "Ireland is *not* part of Great Britain. And with a name like Seamus, I should know."

He has points on both counts. "Okay. And grouping Scotland and England together wouldn't help either, would it?"

"No. It's got to mean something else." He throws back the covers and climbs out of bed as Wylla emerges from the bathroom, fresh as a spring day. I smile at her, and she moves coyly past.

"I guess I'll head in there now." He reaches for his duffle, fishing out a clean outfit, his toiletry bag, and a small stack of papers. "It'll only take me a couple minutes to finish, then I'll work on figuring out this clue while you get ready, unless you want to take a stab at it first."

I hold out my hand to take the papers. "Yeah. Sure. No promises, though."

"Don't sell yourself short." He pulls his white cotton t-shirt over his head, and I throw a hand over my mouth, barely suppressing an audible gasp at the sight of his bare chest.

Because who knew he was hiding those abs beneath his clothes all this time.

"I'll do my best," I say, but there's no way I'll be able to concentrate now.

The second he disappears into the bathroom Wylla gives me a sly grin. "I was gonna tag along with Travis and Mikal today if you think they'd have me."

I cock my head to the side, confused. "I'm sure they won't mind, but why don't you stay with me and Seamus?"

"Please." She raises an eyebrow. "You lovebirds don't need me tagging along all day, do you?"

"That's stupid," I tell her. "You wouldn't be tagging along. You'd be part of the group. We're not like Dustin and Chloe."

She lifts one hand to silence me and slips on her sunglasses with the other. "My mind's made up. I'm heading over to their room right now to ask." She opens the door, and I suppress a grin, secretly relieved she won't be hanging out with me and Seamus after all. Since he started staying in the room with us, she's been driving me bananas with all her hair flipping and lash batting. I'm trying not to let it bother me too much because when it comes to guys, Wylla's communication repertoire is limited to giggling and flirting. She can't help it. It's who she is. Still, the less time he spends around her the better since there's absolutely no way I can compete with her sultry ways.

"See you at breakfast," I call after her.

***

The van is exceptionally quiet on the way to the park. Everyone knows if Seamus and I find the tokens today, we'll only need to find one more to win the passes. It's do or die for them, and no one's willing to give anything away. I'm on my phone, reading everything I can think of on the park's website to help figure out the clue. I don't find much, until—in a burst of inspiration—I Google *six countries* and *Europe* together.

The first couple pages of results are full of useless information about the G6 and the six countries in the world with the most equal rights for women and the most convinced atheists. On the bottom of page three, however, I spot an advertisement for a river cruise which takes its passengers through six European countries.

Along the Rhine River.

I elbow Seamus in the ribs and point at the entry on my screen. A knowing smile spreads across his lips. "We've got this," he mouths.

The van barely comes to a stop before he wrenches open the sliding door, nearly tumbling onto the drop off lot. "Come on," he calls over his shoulder to me, his sneakers pounding across the pavement toward the main entrance.

The lines at the front gate are long so we split up to double our chances of finding the fastest way in. Unfortunately, neither of our lines moves as quickly as the one Travis, Mikal, and Wylla chose.

Travis gives a little wave at us as they pass through ticketing. "See you inside."

"You think they're heading to the same place we are?" I ask.

The family in front of us has misplaced their season passes, and Seamus chews at his thumbnail impatiently as they dump out the contents of their backpack, a diaper bag, and a double-stroller searching for them. "We better hope not," he says.

After racing past the Globe Theater in England and under the Loch Ness Monster in Scotland, we arrive at the Rhine River Cruise in time to see Mikal, Travis, Wylla, Chloe, and Dustin getting on the boat. Luckily, the line ahead of us moves quickly we make it aboard just before the attendant cuts off the queue behind us, sliding across the metal gate.

With a toot of the whistle, the leisure boat sets sail, and Seamus and I head in opposite directions—him to search under the benches while I feel under the handrails.

"Remind me again why we're wasting time on this?" Chloe says, with a longing look at the Griffin as we depart.

"The sooner we find the tokens the sooner we can get off this stupid boat and head to the good rides," Dustin tells her.

"Actually," Travis says, a stick of licorice hanging from his lips, "unless you wanna swim, you're stuck on this *stupid* boat 'til we get back, whether you find the tokens or not."

Dustin rolls his eyes, but Travis's unsolicited wisdom makes me smile. He catches me watching and gives a wink as he helps himself to another licorice from his fanny pack.

At the boat's stern, Seamus searches under the rim of a trashcan, but before I get a chance to tell him I've already checked there, Mikal cries out that he's found them, tucked beneath a hanging life buoy.

"That a way," Travis cries out, patting Mikal on the back with the gusto normally reserved for a father and son. Mikal holds them aloft for the rest of us to see, and Seamus responds with a respectful slow-clap.

"That's two for us." Mikal tosses the second token to Travis. "So, you better watch out, Elise and Seamus, because we're coming for you."

CHAPTER 24

At the end of the river cruise, Dustin and Chloe set off for Alpengeist, Wylla and the guys head across the park to Apollo's Chariot, and a disappointed Seamus and I turn back toward Ireland and the Finnegan's Flyer swings. Along the way, he points out Gaelic symbols and historic landmarks from a seemingly endless supply of Irish trivia.

"With a name like Seamus, your mom and dad must've wanted to make sure people knew you were Irish, huh?" I ask.

"Yeah. I mean, I guess there was no way for them to have known for certain when I was born that I was gonna end up with red hair, freckles, and transparent skin, especially since my older brother Kaelan has brown hair and a complexion that's actually pigmented with melanin." He sighs, rolling his eyes at the unfairness of it all. "But since both my grandparents immigrated from Ireland, it was a safe bet one of us was going to be a ginger."

The indignant tone he uses to describe his brother indicates we might both have complicated relationships with our siblings. "I like your freckles," I say, taking his hand in mine.

"Well, that makes one of us." He chuckles like he's just now remembering something. "When I was in elementary school, I hated them so much, I spent an entire summer coating my skin in lemon juice and buttermilk, hoping they would fade."

I motion toward his face. "It doesn't seem to have worked."

"Sadly, no. All it did was piss off my grandma who couldn't figure out why groceries kept disappearing from the fridge."

"Did you get in trouble?"

"Yeah. But not for taking the food. I got grounded for not 'embracing my ethnicity,' which is bullshit when my brother gets to embrace his Irish heritage without suffering from blistering sunburns."

"That sucks." I hesitate, considering whether to confess the truth about my own sibling insecurities. Nia's the only person I've ever confided in, but she's an only child so she's never been able to relate to my situation. It feels like Seamus might be someone who finally gets it, though.

"It's the same with me and Wylla. I got the poor eyesight, so I'm the one stuck wearing these awful transitional lenses, and she doesn't wear glasses at all. I'm also the one with the crooked teeth who had to endure not one—but two—rounds of braces while she was blessed with a perfectly straight smile from the day her permanent teeth came in."

I'm on a roll now and can't stop myself from continuing if I tried.

"You know what else has always pissed me off? The way she can buy something off the rack, and it looks as good on her as it does on the mannequin. We'll try on the same outfit and she looks classy and I look trashy. What even is that?"

I join the end of the Finnegan's Flyer line, and after boosting himself onto the railing beside me, Seamus glances over, his eyebrows knitted together in concern. "It seems like you might be harboring a little resentment toward your sister."

I blink. Twice.

Am I?

"Am I?"

He stares at me, like he's afraid to respond.

"I mean, I don't blame her for any of that stuff. It's not her fault she has perfect vision any more than it's Kaelan's fault he tans in the sun." I adjust my position on the rail to face him properly. "It's just hard, you know, having this other person around who I know people are always comparing me to."

"How do you know people are always comparing the two of you?"

"How do I know they're not?"

He gazes at me like he's searching for the answer to some mystery hidden in the lines of my face. "So, what if they are?"

I scoff. "Then I wish they'd stop because it's frustrating, you know, that people like my parents are constantly setting expectations for us. Like, I can't be the pretty one because Wylla's already the pretty one, so all that's left for me to be is the smart one. It's been like that since the day she was born."

"You so sure about that?"

"Sure about what?"

"That you can't be the smart one *and* the pretty one."

The line begins moving, and I'm grateful for the opportunity to turn my back as we hop off the rail. Wylla never gets embarrassed when people say nice things to her. She just thanks them like she can't believe how long it took them to notice how amazing she is. But compliments like Seamus's rarely come my way, so I'm glad he can't see the blush spreading across my cheeks as I shuffle forward.

"I get what you're saying, though," he admits. The line's stopped again, and the ride's enormous cars lift the passengers high into the air above our heads like two giant pendulums. "My parents compare us, too, sometimes, and it used to get on my nerves. But it's like these swings, right? The whole thing is a balancing act. If both swings shifted to the left at the same time, this whole contraption would collapse. The ride only works because the weight of the cars is evenly distributed to the left and the right at any given time. It's the same with parenting, I think. It might seem like when your folks compare you and Wylla, the pendulum is always leaning in her favor, but I'm willing to bet it leans in your direction sometimes, too."

I don't know if any of what he's saying is true, but it's enough that he's trying to make me feel better. And I do have to admit, there've been a few times when my folks acknowledged my good decisions, like when I kept Wylla from being arrested by the cops.

Then again, they might have only stood behind me because I was protecting Wylla, not because it was the right thing to do.

For all its symbolic gesturing, Finnegan's Flyers turns out to be something of a bust, leaving us at a loss about what to choose for our next ride.

"A coaster? Or how about the virtual reality one?" Sweat pools at my bra and hairline. I fan my face with my hand. "It's probably air-conditioned."

"I'm hot, too," he says, pulling the map from his back pocket. "How about if we head over to the Roman Rapids or Escape from Pompeii to cool off? They're in the same area, and we could hit both before lunch."

A water ride sounds like heaven, so after checking our bearings, we set off for the far side of the park.

"Don't walk under the skyride." His eyes dart between the family in front of us and the gondola above my head like he's calculating a circuitous route.

"You afraid it's gonna fall on us?"

He shakes his head. "Nah. I'm afraid of getting spit on."

I peer up at the row of gondolas stretching from one side of the park to the other. "Do people do that?"

"I saw a guy get an entire Coke spilled on him on time at…"

Commotion from behind draws my attention, and he stops midsentence. Three paramedics maneuver a stretcher, weaving between patrons strolling along the midway.

"Move to the side, please. Coming through."

Their heavy footfalls are enough to encourage most people out of their way, but one oblivious teenage boy steps into their path, causing the medics to stop abruptly. The defibrillator perched atop the stretcher nearly topples to the ground at the same moment a text alert rings in my pocket.

Beside me, Seamus's phone is already in his hand. "Oh, crap," he says.

I scan the text from Mikal.

Something about Da Vinci's Cradle.

Something about an emergency on the ride.

Something about Travis being unresponsive.

CHAPTER 25

I've chewed my thumbnail to a nub watching helplessly as the medics load Travis's lifeless body onto the stretcher. While two of them strap him down, the third, a petite woman wearing crisp black slacks and a determined expression, straddles his legs to administer chest compressions.

"Jesus Christ," Mikal whispers.

To my left, the ride's been shut down, and the initial crowd of rubbernecking onlookers has

dispersed, leaving the four of us—me, Seamus, Mikal, and Wylla—in silent contemplation. The head of the paramedic team keeps relaying messages into a walkie on his shoulder, but the ambient noise of the surrounding rides makes it impossible to hear what's being said.

"It was so weird," Mikal says. "He seemed fine on Apollo's Chariot, but on the walk over here, I had to slow my pace so he could keep up. Then, while we were waiting in line for this, it was almost like he was in a daze. Kept saying 'huh' and asking me to repeat myself like he couldn't follow the conversation."

Wylla remains motionless beside me, strangely introspective. She hasn't taken her eyes off Travis, like her connection to him is somehow keeping him alive.

"Come on, buddy," Mikal says. "Don't die on us now. Not when we're so close to taking the passes away from these morons."

Until this moment, I'd successfully kept my tears at bay, but hearing Mikal begging Travis to stay alive is too much. Lord knows, if gifting him our tokens was all it took, Seamus and I would've already done it. But I'm afraid whatever's wrong with our friend can't be cured with a bribe.

As the medics wheel the stretcher away, Seamus pulls all of us into his embrace, and Mikal shudders against me. Of all the parings in our strange little group, theirs is by far the most unexpected. But somehow, in the time we've been together, the gay kid in the short shorts and the biker dude with the leather fanny pack have become the best of friends.

"We need to go with him," Mikal says. "And we need to call his daughter. She lives in Tampa, I think. And, what about the principal at his school? Should we call the secretary or something?"

I slip his hand into mine, trying to calm him down.

"We can do all of that." Seamus places a gentle hand on his shoulder. "But Ernie should be the first call. Drury Park's management needs to know what's happened, and without him, the rest of us are stranded here."

Seamus searches online for the closest hospital, and I volunteer to call Ernie, who picks up on the third ring.

"Hey. It's Elise." My voice shakes, and I take a breath to steady myself. "We need you to come get us. Something happened to Travis. Paramedics came and took him to the hospital."

My declaration is met with silence on the other end of the line. When Ernie finally responds, the fear in his voice is unmistakable. "Did the medics give you any indication of what's going on?"

"No." My voice is a whisper. "They wouldn't tell us anything. But they were doing chest compressions like his heart had stopped."

Another pause. The sound of shoes against pavement. "Meet me at the front gate in fifteen minutes."

"Okay. A few of us are together, but I don't have any way to get in touch with Dustin or Chloe to let them know."

"Leave them. I'll pick them up after we know what's going on with Travis." Keys jingle and a car door slams. "See you in a few."

The call disconnects, and I relay Ernie's message to the others. In the time we've been walking, our pace has slowed dramatically as Seamus attempts to navigate the crowd and search Google maps at the same time. It's taking forever to get back to the entrance, and Mikal's growing impatient.

"Come on, Seamus," he calls over his shoulder, dodging a couple of hand-holding teenagers and a stroller-wielding dad.

"We're never going to find him if we don't know where the closest hospitals are."

"You can search once we're in the van. You're wasting time."

Seamus powers off his phone with an exasperated sigh, and with everyone now focused on getting to the entrance, we hit the parking lot as Ernie pulls to the curb.

"Where'd they take him?" he asks as we pile into the back.

"They wouldn't tell us because we're not family."

"Christ," Ernie mumbles under his breath. "Well, give me something. Anything."

Seamus, back on his phone, climbs over the center console into the passenger's seat. "According to the map, there are two hospitals close by. Eastern State is on the other side of town, but Riverside Doctors' is pretty close."

"Which one looks bigger?" Ernie asks.

"Probably Riverside."

Ernie shifts the van into drive. "Then let's head there first."

No one speaks on the eight-minute drive from Busch Gardens to the hospital, like mentioning Travis's name might jinx something. There's an urgency to Ernie's driving I haven't witnessed in the thousands of miles he's chauffeured us—speeding through two yellow lights and making an incomplete stop at a four-way blinker.

My own heart races inside my chest—there's no way I could operate a motor vehicle with the way my hands are trembling in my lap. Ernie's clearly as upset about the situation as I am, if not more. Somehow, Travis has found a way to bond with nearly all of us.

A cool uncle to Seamus and Mikal.

A good friend to Ernie.

And a weird sort of father figure to me.

The van turns sharply into the emergency room parking lot, and the motion catches me off balance, tossing Mikal and I into one another. Mikal rests against me for a beat too long, as if relishing the reassurance of our contact, before straightening himself. He turns away, like he's embarrassed to look me in the eye, so I take his hand. If there are times not to apologize for being vulnerable, this is one of them.

Ernie maneuvers the van into a super tight spot, but the lot is surprisingly full and beggars can't be choosers. The guys throw their doors wide open and tumble out like they're racing after the stupid tokens, now long since forgotten. Mikal turns back, offering his hand to assist me, but my body's suddenly made of rocks.

The hospital looms in front of me—a two story monstrosity of brick and glass and uncertainty. To the left, the red emergency entrance is a beacon, beckoning me inside, and yet, the more I stare at it, the more my chest compresses in on itself. I try taking in air, but my lungs resist, and all that comes out is a wheeze.

"Elise? You coming?" Mikal's voice plays at the periphery of my consciousness, but it's too late to lure me out of my own head.

The smell of burning gasoline and rubber tires and asphalt overwhelms me, but when I close my eyes I'm not at the scene of my accident. I'm in the ambulance, on the way to the hospital. Medics work to stabilize me on all sides. There's an oxygen mask covering my nose and mouth, but my hearing is sharp—heightened even.

"What's her pressure?"

"One fifteen over eighty-three and holding steady."

"That's good news." A pause. "I've got the bleeding stopped over here, for now, but Lord, this is gonna leave a scar."

"Better her arm than her face."

"Mhmm."

The quiet rhythm of the heartrate monitor grounded me in space and time. If I allowed myself to worry about everything that had already happened or was about to happen, my blood pressure wouldn't remain steady for long.

"Did you get a look at her car?"

"Oh, yeah. What a mangled mess. Didn't stand a chance against that moving truck."

"Shouldn't be legal for people without class B licenses to drive big vans like that. They're heavy. They take twice as long to stop. But Joe Homeowner trying to move on the cheap doesn't realize it, and this is the result." He applied pressure to my shoulder which was no longer throbbing with the same intensity as before.

I was cognizant enough to realized they'd administered morphine or some other pain medication, and I was grateful.

"Well, regardless, our girl Elise here might be the only one to come outta this thing in one piece. Sharice and Nick have their hands full with the woman from the truck. If she'd been wearing her seatbelt, she might not have gone through the windshield."

"Yeah, the others are definitely in rough shape."

"Elise. Elise, what's wrong?"

I open my eyes to find Seamus sitting beside me in the van, holding my shoulders at arm's length. He's shaking me gently, and as I come around, he folds me into his embrace. I stay there for a long moment, breathing him in to push the memories out. They're getting crisper, and with each new recollection my anxiety grows.

When I finally unwind myself from Seamus, his hair is disheveled, sticking out in every direction, and for some reason it makes me smile. He lets out a relieved sigh. "Hey. You okay?

I nod slowly.

"Were you having another panic attack or something?"

"Yeah. I…"

His gaze is desperate, like he's willing me to confide in him. But I'm not certain I can make enough sense of what just happened to explain it to myself, much less to him.

Wylla lays a reassuring hand on my arm as I slide to the edge of the seat. "Another flashback, that's all. After the accident, I spent a few days in the hospital, and… I dunno. It was scary."

"You need another minute before we go inside to see Travis?"

Oh, God. I'd forgotten all about him.

"Is he here?"

He shrugs before helping me out of the van. My knees buckle, and he wraps an arm around me for support. Wylla takes my other hand, giving it a gentle squeeze.

"Ernie and Mikal went inside, but no news yet. You okay to walk?"

My strength is returning, and by the time the three of us reach the sliding glass doors, I'm fully mobile and in a much better headspace. It's chaotic inside—children running wild, CNN blaring on the television, and people in wheelchairs scattered about—so I shouldn't be surprised there are still two people waiting in line ahead of Ernie and Mikal at registration.

We manage to find three seats together in the waiting area, keeping close watch on the others. The second they make it to the front of the line, we hurry to the desk where Ernie is already inquiring about Travis's condition, introducing himself as his brother. After a quick call to a nearby nurses' station, the desk clerk tells him there's no update to report, but that we're welcome to take a seat in the waiting room for now.

"Can you tell me anything about his status?" Ernie asks.

"Only that he was brought in as a possible coronary patient and was taken into immediate surgery."

"So, he's alive?"

Beside me, Mikal's breath hitches, and he reaches out, holding onto my arm for support.

"I'm sorry, sir, but I can't say for certain one way or another."

CHAPTER 26

I wake with a start, my head jerking off Seamus's shoulder.

"They just called Ernie over." He grimaces, stretching his lower back, and I wonder how long he's been held hostage beneath me while I slept. "Maybe we'll finally get some answers."

But instead of the immediate response I'm hoping for, Ernie throws us a shrug before following a nurse through a set of coded double doors into the hospital.

"Well, that's gotta be a good sign, right?" Mikal's voice is buoyant. "I mean, they're not gonna take Ernie back there just to tell him Travis is dead."

Seamus cocks an eyebrow. "You think they're gonna tell him his brother died here in the waiting room?"

"I guess you're right." Mikal's shoulders slump, and he glances at me. "While you were sleeping, I managed to track down all three of Travis's kids on Facebook. I left them messages but haven't heard anything back." He clicks off his phone and sets it on his lap. "It doesn't matter, though, since I still don't have anything definite to tell them."

He explains what he discovered about Travis's daughter, Tracy, and his two sons. Where they live. What they're like.

Ten minutes pass.

Fifteen.

When Mikal eventually goes back to checking for messages on his phone, Seamus stands up like he's been cattle prodded out of the seat. "I gotta stretch my legs, guys. Do something. Any of you want a snack from the vending machine?"

Wylla shakes her head. "I'm good."

"I'll take a Snickers," Mikal says without looking up from his screen.

"How about you?" His eyes cut to where I'm still curled up in my plastic seat, legs tucked beneath me. He obviously wants me to go with him, but I'm not convinced it's a good idea to leave the relative security of the waiting room. The last thing I want is to have to explain away another panic attack, and who knows what triggers might be lurking around the next corner?

"Grab me something salty and cheese-flavored." I smile. "And hurry back."

The minute he's out of earshot around the nearest corner, Mikal slips into the newly vacated seat beside me. "Hey, listen. I wanted to apologize for the other day, when I asked about you and Seamus. Your friendship is none of my business, and even though things seem okay between you now, I feel bad I might've messed things up." His voice is heavy with remorse, and it washes away any lingering resentment I may or may not have been harboring against him.

"It's okay," I say. "Actually, it probably turned out to be a good thing. Neither one of us is good with any of this stuff, so it sort of forced us to come clean to each other about, you know, everything."

"I'm glad," he says, relieved. "One less thing to worry about, I guess. All that's left now is Travis." He opens his mouth to go on as his phone chimes, alerting him to a new message. "It's her. His daughter." He scans the text, his eyes ricocheting back and forth across the screen. "Oh, crap." He rises to his feet. "We gotta tell someone. A doctor. A nurse. Somebody."

"What?" Wylla and I say together.

"It's the damn licorice he's always eating. There's some compound inside that lowers potassium levels and interferes with the diuretics he takes for high blood pressure. I guess his daughter's been on him for years to stop eating so much because it's known to cause heart problems, but he's an addict."

I widen my eyes at Wylla, remembering our conversation about the evils of black licorice from the first night. "You go tell the woman at registration, and I'll call Ernie."

By the time Seamus returns from the vending machine with our snacks, Wylla, Mikal, and I have convinced the receptionist to send out the triage nurse who's now assuring us she'll pass on what we've learned about Travis's condition.

"It's suuuuuuper important," Mikal tells her. "Please let his doctors know right away."

She disappears through the same doors as Ernie, and beside me, Mikal deflates like a three-day-old balloon.

"He's gonna be fine," Wylla says. "Have faith. You'll see."

But Mikal doesn't look like he believes it.

An hour later, Ernie returns to the waiting room, and the smile on his face tells me everything I need to know before he ever opens his mouth. "He's okay. I mean, he's sort of a mess now, but he's going to be okay in a few days."

He takes an empty seat beside me in the waiting room and explains how the medics initially thought, when they couldn't find a heartbeat, he was having a heart attack. The hospital prepared him for possible bypass surgery, but when they didn't see any blockage on his echocardiogram, they started looking for another explanation for why his heart seemed to stop for no reason. "When you provided the clue about the licorice and the diuretics, they realized it was this thing called hyperkalemia which is basically too much potassium in the blood. Sometimes it can cause a person's heartbeat to significantly decrease. In Travis's case, it stopped altogether."

"So, what now?" I ask. "We can't leave him here, can we?"

Ernie glances at his watch, a gold-plated relic with hands and a face from the last century. "It's getting late, and honestly, we don't have much of a choice. He's stuck here in the ER until a bed opens up in the cardiac wing upstairs, and it could be hours until that happens. By then, visiting hours will be over."

"It's not fair the rest of us don't get to see him." The whine in Mikal's voice reminds me of Wylla any time she doesn't get her way. "You told him we're here though, right?"

"He knows," Ernie says with a nod. "But he needs his rest, so maybe the best thing we can do now is let him get it."

I pile back into the van with the others, and after a stop for dinner, Ernie picks up Chloe and Dustin at the park. We check into our motel for the night—a modest two-star halfway between Busch Gardens and Kings Dominion, along Rt 64. Ernie checks in, and the minute he distributes our keys, Dustin and Chloe disappear into their room.

Stale, muggy air raises a sheen on my skin, and the glass-like surface of the motel pool glimmers in the lamplight, drawing my attention. It sucked being cooped up in the hospital all afternoon, which is probably why I'm not quite ready be locked inside my room for the rest of the night.

I gather my bag from the back of the van. "Anyone wanna go for a swim?"

A grin spreads across Wylla's face as she glances sideways between Mikal and Ernie. Seamus hands Mikal his bag and considers me. "D'you bring a suit?"

"Yeah, of course. Didn't you?"

Seamus shakes his head. "Didn't think about it." He points to his athletic shorts. "But I guess I could wear these."

Mikal frowns. "All I've got are chinos, and I'm not about the chafing."

"You can borrow a pair of mine," Seamus says. "What about you, Ernie?"

"I'll see what I can dig up," he says with a wink.

Ten minutes later, Wylla and I hug the wall while the guys impress us with their best cannon balls. I'm trying to ignore how great she looks in her suit, with her killer curves and bronze goddess skin. I'm also trying to ignore Seamus noticing how great she looks in her suit, but it's a struggle. Still, he doesn't say anything outright and even tickles my toes under the water each time he surfaces.

"Are those your sleep shorts, Ernie?" he asks, flipping droplets from his hair as he climbs the ladder out of the deep end. Wylla kicks me in the shin under the surface, throwing me a look that implies if I'm going to stare after him, I should try being more subtle about it. I slide my focus across the pool deck to where Ernie is adjusting his waistband, and quickly return to Seamus.

"Best I could do in a pinch," Ernie says.

Mikal throws him an incredulous look. "Then what're you gonna sleep in?"

He shrugs. "Probably nothing."

The rest of us groan as he throws himself into the pool—butt first, knees pulled to his chest. An enormous plume of water shoots into the air after him, sending circular ripples outward toward the perimeter of the pool.

"Ten out of ten," Wylla and I call in unison when he surfaces.

The guys take turns trying to outdo Ernie's perfection, but eventually give up, joining Wylla and I in the shallow end.

Seamus bobs beside me, and the circulation of water from the jets keeps bumping his thigh into mine. I run my hands across the pool's surface as a distraction, focusing on the exact spot where the air meets water. I imagine those molecules, pressed against one another. Are they as curious about one another as I am about Seamus?

"Can you believe how upset Chloe and Dustin were about having to leave the park early tonight?" he asks with a roll of his eyes.

"Yes." Mikal hoists himself out of the pool, water cascading down his skin in tiny rivulets. He grabs a towel from a nearby table and wraps it around his shoulders before returning to the pool deck, dangling his legs beside Wylla's shoulders.

"You know, the thing about people is, some are wired for compassion and some aren't," Ernie says. "Can't see beyond their own needs to anyone else's. Those of us who get it, we really get it. But those of us who don't…"

In the silence that follows Ernie's declaration, Wylla clasps my hand beneath the water, taking me by surprise. When I glance up to meet her gaze, I'm shocked to see tears pooling in her eyes.

Is this her way of telling me she really gets it? That she fully accepts I wasn't trying to ruin her life when I turned Logan in—I was trying to save it.

Does she finally forgive me for what happened? Not only with her head, but with her heart?

I squeeze her hand in mine. If it is an apology, I want to let her know I accept it.

Around me, the others pack their shoes and towels, ready to turn in for the night. Seamus sets my flip flops beside the pool before turning to Ernie. "So, what's the plan for tomorrow? Will you take us back to the hospital to see Travis?"

Ernie ruffles his hair with a towel and what little he has sticks up in every direction. "You don't want to go to King's Dominion?"

I glance around the group at the others. A silent look of understanding passes between us.

"No. We wanna see Travis," Mikal confirms.

"Hmm." Ernie slips his feet into his unlaced sneakers and considers us. "Well, I gotta take Chloe and Dustin over there, one way or the other. I'm contractually obligated. You understand. The park doesn't open 'til 10:30, but we're only about half-an-hour away, so I suppose if you don't mind waiting a couple hours, we could head to the hospital together after I take them to the park. Could probably make it by lunchtime."

Mikal looks to the rest of us. "I don't mind waiting."

"Me neither," Wylla says.

"Same," I say.

Ernie nods. "Then it's decided. I'll take Dustin and Chloe to the park, then the rest of us will go see Travis." He hesitates, attempting to wrap a too-small towel around his ample waist. "You guys know what this means, though?"

"No. What?" Seamus says.

"It means as long as they can find them, Chloe and Dustin get tomorrow's tokens by default."

Mikal fishes his room key from his pocket and scoffs. "As far as I'm concerned, they can have them. Travis is the only thing that matters to me now."

CHAPTER 27

After dropping Dustin and Chloe off at Kings Dominion, Ernie drives me, Wylla, Seamus, and Mikal to the hospital the next morning. On the way, Mikal calls admissions to confirm Travis has been moved to a room and will be allowed to have visitors. I listen to his half of the conversation from the back seat, trying to piece together what's going on.

"Okay, thank you. I appreciate all the information," he says before disconnecting. He slips his phone into his pocket and turns to Ernie in the seat beside him. Seamus leans forward, elbows on his knees. "Well, he's awake and apparently a bit more lucid than he was yesterday. The nurse said he's been trying to call us, but his cell's dead, and no one has a charger to fit his stupid phone."

It's not a surprise. Travis might be the only person I've ever met who still carries a flip phone.

"Did she say what he wanted to tell us?" Seamus asks.

"No, but knowing him, he probably wanted to make sure I find the tokens." Mikal chuckles. "Or for us to bring him some licorice."

Breakfast was hours ago, and at the mention of food, my

stomach grumbles. "Should we take him a sandwich, at least?"

Mikal shakes his head. "The nurse said he's on dietary restrictions because of the whole potassium situation. Maybe we should have lunch before we get there. It'll be rude to eat in front of him if he's stuck eating gross hospital food."

I agree, and a few miles outside of Williamsburg Ernie pulls into a KFC drive-thru for a couple buckets of chicken. The closer we get to the hospital, the quieter everyone gets—just the occasional crunch of extra crispy. Knowing how close to death he looked on the stretcher yesterday, I'm a little nervous about what we'll find when we finally get to the hospital.

I'm also more than a little worried about embarrassing myself in front of everyone with another panic attack, but when Seamus takes my hand in the parking lot and whispers for me to breathe, I somehow manage to stay present all the way to Travis's room.

"Ernie, Mikal—oh my God, all of you!" Travis exclaims from his adjustable bed as I slip through the door. A young woman sits in the chair beside him wearing sweatpants, a threadbare t-shirt, and an exhausted-looking smirk. Dark circles shadow Travis's eyes and even though it's been less than twenty-four hours since I last saw him, he looks frailer now than he did yesterday, draped beneath the crisp white hospital sheet. There are tubes taped to both of his hands, tethering him to various IV bags hanging from a nearby stand. And on the wall behind him, illuminated monitors beep and click, a constant reminder of how thin the veil between life and death actually is.

My mind wanders back to when my own body teetered between those two worlds. Back to the rush of the emergency room and the agony of my own voice. But as my legs give way, Seamus places his hand on the small of my back like he can somehow sense he's about to lose me again, and I'm able to refocus my attention on Travis.

"What in the world are you guys doing here? It's King's Dominion day. The Dominator. Twisted Timbers. And what about the tokens?"

Mikal hurries across the room, the rubber soles of his Vans squeaking on the linoleum. He barely slows as he approaches the bed, gathering Travis into an awkward embrace. "No. No way. Nothing at the park was more important than seeing you today."

"Good Lord. What's with you all? Between Tracy here flying in all the way from Florida for no good reason and you guys missing out on a day at the park, it's like you think I'm dying or something."

At the mention of Tracy's name, the family resemblance between she and Travis becomes obvious. The wide-set of their eyes. Their ruddy complexions. Their laid-back demeanors and broad smiles.

"You literally died yesterday, Dad," Tracy says, her voice taking the tone of a protective parent. "Your heart stopped. You were dead."

He waves a dismissive hand in the air. "I was simply resting for a bit. Needed to get off my feet was all."

Tracy scoffs. "You and that damn licorice. All these years, the family's always assumed you'd die in some fiery motorcycle crash, but we never expected candy would be the thing to take you out. Maybe you'll listen to your doctor about all the junk food you eat now that it almost did you in."

"I'm not switching to Twizzlers if that's what you're thinking."

Their banter continues as the rest of us seek out various places to relax around the room. Tracy occupies the only legitimate chair, so Wylla and I perch on top the air conditioning unit under the window. Seamus hoists himself up on the nightstand, Ernie leans against the wardrobe, and Mikal plops himself at the end of the bed beside Travis's feet.

Once everyone's settled, Travis takes a long glance around the room, giving us all a once over. "I appreciate you all giving up your park day to visit me. It means a lot. But I gotta say, I'm a little disappointed you couldn't convince Dustin and Chloe to come along." Although his tone is facetious, the slouch of his shoulders suggests at least a tiny part of him isn't joking.

"Yeah, that wasn't happening. You should've heard them on the way to the park this morning, though," Ernie says with a shake of his head. "You don't know how bad I wanted to give them the wrong clue."

"Something about a 'flushing good time' would've been fun," Seamus says. "Could've had them checking bathroom stalls all day."

Everyone laughs, including Tracy, who seems to already have some background on the dynamics of our little group.

The dynamics of his actual family seem to be less straightforward.

"Did you call Mom, yet?" Tracy asks as the room falls silent.

"And tell her what? I almost died, but I didn't. Sorry to disappoint you."

She shakes her head, staring at her hands. It seems like this should be a private conversation, but maybe it's one of those topics that's easier to broach if strangers are around to help keep everyone's emotions in check. "No, Dad. You should tell her what happened. She deserves to know. And don't ask me to make the call because I won't do it. And neither will Garrett or Rusty, so don't even ask."

Travis adjusts his position in the bed to give Mikal more room, wincing as the wires attached to his chest pull at his skin. "Your mother doesn't care what happens to me, one way or the other."

"That's not true, and you know it."

"She hasn't spoken to me in over six years. If I was on a slab in the morgue right now it wouldn't make any difference to her."

The beeping of the heartrate monitor intensifies, and Seamus throws me a look like if he could climb under the nightstand he would.

"Dad, for the hundredth time, if you call her, she will happily speak with you. And I know you conveniently chose to forget that you were the one who stopped talking to her, not the other way around."

"I stopped talking to her because of the money, and you know it."

Tracy takes a deep breath and holds it like she's counting to ten to keep from chucking his IV stand at his head. "It's been long established, the only reason she took Sam's advice to put her pension into a trust was to protect the money for us kids. It didn't have anything to do with keeping the money from you."

Travis gazes out the window past me and Wylla, releasing a heavy sigh fraught with the pain of misunderstanding. There's no way of knowing the truth about his marriage, but it's probably not a stretch to assume a messy history still keeps him from appreciating his ex-wife's point of view.

Something tightens in my chest as Wylla picks at her thumbnail beside me. Travis and his ex-wife aren't the only ones who have lost time to disagreement.

Tracy holds out her phone. "Just call her. Imagine how

horrible she'd feel if something had happened to you and she didn't get to talk to you one last time." She hesitates as he takes the cell from her hand. "Imagine how horrible you would feel if something happened to her and you didn't get to say goodbye."

If Travis is going to call his ex, he deserves a little privacy. Ernie makes some excuse about getting his parking validated, and I follow him out the door along with everyone else like it takes five people to stamp a ticket.

CHAPTER 28

"That was intense," Seamus says as we stroll along the hallway. "I guess everyone's got family baggage, huh?"

I glance beside me at Wylla who raises an eyebrow. "Yeah, I guess so."

Seamus wanders off to find a bathroom, Ernie legitimately goes to get his parking validated, and even though we've just finished lunch, Mikal can't resist a trip to the snack machine.

"They've got those little chocolate ho-ho things I love." He throws a flamboyant wave over his shoulder. "Tootles."

Alone in the hallway together, Wylla clears her throat like she's prepared a speech. My jaw clenches involuntarily, fearing whatever's about to come out of her mouth. Our truce is in its infancy, and there's no telling where this conversation might be headed.

Maybe she's finally ready to tell me what's really going on with her, though.

"I, uh, I'm really glad we decided to go on this trip together," she says.

My muscles relax. It's not the secret reveal I was hoping for, but at least she hasn't changed her mind about forgiving me. Yet. I elbow her gently and roll my eyes. "It's not like you gave me a choice. What Wylla wants, Wylla gets." The second I say it I want to take it back. I'm so grateful for her understanding, the last thing I want is to piss her off.

"You're not wrong," she says with a shrug. "But seriously, I'm glad we've had a chance to talk things through, you know?"

"Like Travis and his ex-wife are doing right now?"

"Yeah. I guess." A nurse carrying a clipboard rushes past and after moving aside, Wylla falls into step beside me again. "I mean, if we hadn't both won that stupid contest and come on this trip, we'd still be at home not talking."

She's right, of course. No one at home was forcing us to hash things out. There was no Tracy in our family hosting a sister intervention, even if there should've been.

Why didn't Mom force us to listen to one another? Why didn't she lock us in a room until we straightened things out?

Probably because she knew it wouldn't work. That we were already too far gone.

It breaks my heart thinking about how hard our estrangement's been on her.

I tuck a loose tendril of hair behind my ear. "Not to change the subject, but have you heard from Mom recently?"

"Yeah. She called me this morning while you were in the shower."

"And?"

We've wandered outside into a courtyard. The brittle corpses of spring blossoms need deadheading—the harsh summer sun and near drought conditions exacerbating their shriveled remains. Weeds and thistles have taken over the once flourishing flower beds, and instead of a place of serenity, the garden is now a depressing reminder of what used to be.

We sit on a bench together in the shade of a willow tree,

and Wylla slides off her flip flops. "And nothing. She asked how it was going. I told her fine. Same old, same old."

"Did you tell her we're, you know, speaking again?"

She takes her sunglasses off her head and slides them onto her face. Is she hiding something or merely avoiding the sun's glare? "No. I haven't said anything specific."

The last text I got from Mom two days ago was similarly vague. She did mention something about running into Nia and her mother at the grocery store. But, of course, Nia had already given me the update right after it happened, telling me Mom looked as good as can be expected, considering…"

Considering both of her daughters abandoned her.

I clear my throat. "Do you think it's weird Mom didn't try to patch things up between us the way Tracy is with Travis and his ex-wife?"

She doesn't answer immediately, and I follow her gaze to a family pushing their son in a wheelchair. His arms are in casts, his neck is encased in a brace, but despite the difficulties they've obviously been through, they're laughing and smiling together as they pass. "She did try with me. At least in the beginning."

This is news to me. "She did?"

"Yeah. After she got over being mad about my part in everything, she kept dropping all these hints about reasons I shouldn't shut you out."

If there was ever a time in my life for the mind-blown emoji, this was it. Why didn't Mom ever say anything to me? "You didn't listen, though."

The family goes back inside, and Wylla turns to me, sliding her sunglasses from her face onto her head. When I look into her eyes, I see every fight we've ever had. Every misunderstanding. Every difference between us—magnified by a hundred—wedging us apart.

"Tell me what happened with Logan that night," she says. "Tell me what I don't know."

At the time, Logan's arrest was the worst day of my life, and not just because I was responsible for the set up and execution of my childhood best friend's arrest. There was more.

More I'd never been able to tell Wylla.

More I'd never been able to tell anyone.

But maybe it's time.

My therapist's voice rattles around the back of my mind as Wylla gazes at me. After the accident, when I struggled to recount even the smallest detail, the doctor encouraged me to pretend I was a reporter delivering a news story—objectively and without emotion. After several weeks, I was able to describe a few memories, and the more I shared, the better I felt.

So, maybe now, if I can trick myself into believing I'm simply relating a news story to Wylla instead of something terrible that happened to me, I might get it out.

"Where should I start?"

She leans back on her arms, getting comfortable. "At the beginning."

My airway closes involuntarily—my body fighting to protect my soul from potential pain—but I force air into my lungs and explain about Nia's dad, and how the department was looking to arrest everyone involved.

"I know that part," Wylla says. "Tell me about that night."

I clear my throat, buying myself precious seconds to collect my thoughts. I've spent so many months blocking that night from my memory—retrieving all the details takes time. "The police fit me with a wire at the station, and Nia's dad dropped me off at home. I walked across the street and let myself in the basement door around back. Logan was there, headphones on, playing Xbox."

The lingering sweetness of his vape pen permeated the stale basement air, underscoring the carefree tone of his voice. He was so engrossed in his game, strategizing about how to corner his opponent with whoever he was playing with online, he barely acknowledged my arrival when I appeared beside him on the sofa.

"Hey, Logan," I said, sitting closer than necessary on the worn sectional.

He didn't look away from the screen. "Hey."

My throat went dry with worry that I wouldn't be able to accomplish what I'd come to do. But protecting my sister's future required getting the words out.

"I was wondering if you could sell me some of your stuff."

This got his attention. "Gimme a sec, Sam," he said into his mic before pausing the game and turning to me. "You want what now?"

I swallowed hard. "I, uh, wanted to get a couple hits from you. I've got a bunch of assignments due. Some tests and stuff coming up, and I want to be sharp, you know?" My voice trembled, and I chuckled like it was no big deal, praying he won't see right through my pathetic excuse.

Apparently, he did, though, and I wasn't surprised when he started laughing—not with me—but at me. "You've got to be kidding. Little Miss Goodie-Two-Shoes Elise is finally succumbing to the pressures of junior year? I don't believe it."

In the moment, the only thing I could think to do was bat my eyelashes like I was some kind of Disney bad girl, trying to sell the illusion. "I'm no goodie goodie, Logan. I do what I need to do."

He set down his controller and took off his headphones before turning to me. "You do, do you? Anything?"

"There's not a lot of money for college. I need as many academic scholarships as I can get, and I'll do whatever it takes to get them. If that means taking Adderall to give me an advantage, it means taking Adderall."

He leaned forward, eyebrow raised, breath hot. "This is really unlike you. Honestly, you're the last person I'd expect to come begging for a hit." His eyes dropped, taking me in like I was a puzzle to be solved. "Now your sister, yeah. I mean, she's a hot piece of ass and all, but she could honestly use some help with the school stuff, am I right?" He chuckled, and my stomach lurched. "But you. You've always been such a good girl. Not as pretty as Wylla, obviously, but you're so smart, looks probably don't even matter to you." Bile bubbled in my throat as he slid over, filling the space between us until his hip pressed against mine. "You spend so much time being good, I bet you've never even kissed a guy."

There was a time I would've been thrilled by his proximity. Every nerve in my body would've sparked like fireworks on the Fourth of July.

Now, I wanted to throw up.

"I've kissed lots of boys." My voice cracked as I spoke, but I bent toward him, pressing my lips against his. I waited for the electricity to surge through my veins. For my heart to skip a beat. But there was nothing.

He was already dead to me.

I pulled away as he reached for my chest. One kiss and he was already trying to cop a feel. "There's a lot you don't know about me. But maybe I'll let you find out more if you sell me what I came for."

Now, as the splintered edge of the bench digs into the back of my thighs, I exhale sharply, grateful for the release. "After that, he sold me the Adderall, I got the hell outta there, and you know the rest."

A single tear trickles down Wylla's cheek.

"Oh my god, Elise. I'm so sorry. I had no idea he treated you that way. I'm sorry I got angry about him. I'm sorry I blamed you. I'm sorry we didn't talk or hang out all those months." She hesitates. "Honestly, I'm sorry we didn't talk more or hang out more before the whole Logan thing. Maybe if we'd spent more time together over the past few years…"

An enormous lump takes up residency in my throat. I'm powerless to swallow it as tears spill down my cheeks. There's nothing I can do to stop them. I open my mouth to speak, to tell her I accept her apology and offer my own, but at that exact moment, Seamus appears in the courtyard doorway.

"Jesus Christ, Elise, are you alright?"

I turn to him, hastily rubbing at my face with the back of my hands. I'm not ready to explain all of this to him, especially not in front of Wylla.

And especially when I'm still sorting all of it out myself.

I spring off the bench and throw a quick glance at Wylla, hoping to convey my embarrassment and desire to continue our conversation later. "I'm fine. Just, uh, a little emotional about everything, I guess."

He crosses the courtyard and is to me before I have a chance to fully compose myself. He looks me up and down—once—before gathering me into his arms.

For a second, I remain rigid, unaccustomed to this sort of unbridled physical contact. But when he pulls me a little closer, instead of pushing back, I relax into him, folding myself into the hollow space against his chest.

"It's okay to be emotional," he says. "A friend of ours almost died yesterday. Only soulless bastards wouldn't be at least a little shaken up about it."

"Like Chloe and Dustin?" Wylla says.

I chuckle and sniffle into his chest. "Yeah. Like Chloe and Dustin."

We stand together for a few more seconds soaking each other in. There's something grounding about being physically tethered to another person when everything going on around you is out of your control.

Finally, I take a deep breath and step back, turning to Wylla. "We should check in with Travis to see if he needs back up in the ex-wife department."

Seamus nods. "Mikal might need us, too. When I was searching for you, I saw him at the vending machine loading up on chocolate cupcakes like he's stockpiling for the apocalypse. Dude might need an intervention."

Back in Travis's room, he and Mikal announce they've decided to spend the afternoon binge-watching Buffy the Vampire Slayer on Hulu. A nurse brings a few folding chairs into the room, and after Tracy draws the blinds across the window, I settle into a seat between Seamus and Wylla.

"Things go okay with your ex-wife," Mikal whispers over the backbeat and guitar solo of the opening credits.

Travis nods. "We're not moving back in together or anything, but let's just say she seemed glad I was still alive. And she's still entitled to some of my life insurance policy, so that's saying something."

Seamus casually drapes his arm across the back of my chair, and I scoot over a bit, close enough to rest my head on his shoulder. Together, we watch Buffy slay vampires with

Xander, Willow, and Giles, and when I catch Mikal sneaking a ho-ho under the bed tray to Travis, it occurs to me that families take lots of different forms. Sometimes you share blood, like me and Wylla, and sometimes you're sort of slung together by the whims of the universe and a stupid amusement park promotion like Travis and Mikal.

Either way, we're all pretty lucky to have each other.

CHAPTER 29

Leaving Travis behind is hard. Harder than I thought it would be, even knowing his daughter's staying with him. The doctor said if he keeps improving, she could take him back to Pennsylvania as early as the next couple of days, but who knows? Hopefully, he'll be waiting at home when I get there next week.

Since losing Travis, my mood has gone from light-hearted pop single to funeral dirge, and the rest of the van seems similarly affected. On the five-hour drive from Virginia to New Jersey, the good-natured smack talk between the guys has been replaced by solemn faces and grave introspection. Mikal's moved from the back of the van to the front passenger's seat, and I'm now sandwiched between Wylla and Seamus right behind him.

The only two who seem unfazed by Travis's departure are Chloe and Dustin, of course. They're still watching movies together in the back seat like the rest of us aren't even in the van.

"Listen. I know you're all upset about Travis," Ernie scolds as the Baltimore skyline passes by out my window. "But do you think he wants you all sulking like a bunch of sad saps for the next four days, or would he want you to enjoy the rest of your time together?"

Knowing Travis, I'm certain he wouldn't want me moping around. But I can't help it. Traveling without him is like eating a plain cake donut. Without the frosting, what's even the point?

Ernie takes his eyes off the road, glancing into the rearview mirror at me. "What if you could still involve him, huh? I mean, he's not dead, right? He's gonna live to ride coasters another day." He hesitates, changing lanes like he's considering whether to go on. "What if I give you all tomorrow's token clue today so he can help you all figure it out."

Mikal narrows his eyes at Ernie before turning around in his seat. "I doubt Elise and Seamus need our help. Honestly, we need them more than they need us. But there's no way they'll partner up, especially since they only have one more token than we do. They'd be stupid to help us."

I raise my eyebrows at Seamus and give a shrug. I don't mind collaborating if it means I get to spend a couple hours talking with Travis, but I'm not as hellbent on winning the vouchers as he is.

He studies me briefly, pursing his lips as if to say: *You really want to risk losing the tokens to these two?*

I smile, willing him to read my mind. *Absolutely.*

A beat passes before Seamus turns to Mikal. "If we help you and Travis figure out the clue, you're still on your own finding the tokens. If Elise or I get to them first, they're ours." He throws me a grin, and I almost can't believe he's going to help them.

Almost.

Mikal looks at Seamus over the top of his purple-hued sunglasses. "I wouldn't have it any other way. But what about those two." He glances toward the back of the van at Chloe and Dustin. "They're gonna hear everything."

On my knees, I peer over the seat to where the lovebirds are nestled against one another under Dustin's baseball hoodie. They're sharing a set of headphones, deeply entrenched in whatever they're watching on Dustin's phone.

And I'm pretty sure Dustin's hands are on her boobs.

I slip back into the seat with a shake of my head. "We don't need to worry about them. They seem pretty… busy."

Less than five minutes later, Mikal's got his phone on speaker with Travis on the line.

"I'm ready," he says from his hospital bed. "What's the clue?"

Ernie instructs Mikal to retrieve the manila envelope from his duffle on the floor between them. "Just the page on top," he warns. "No peeking at the other clues."

Mikal pulls out the top sheet, returns the envelope to the bag, and with a flourish only a man wearing a floral scarf could achieve, reads the clue in a faux British accent. "Not all heroes wear capes."

Travis groans over the phone. "Say what?"

Seamus sighs, taking Mikal's phone from his hand so he can speak directly to Travis. "It's gotta be a superhero reference. Six Flags holds a licensing agreement with DC Comics so lots of their rides are based on DC characters." He checks his printout of Great Adventure, scanning the rides list. "Yeah, there are like a dozen or so. This could be tricky."

"The Batman roller coaster is there, right?" Mikal asks. "And correct me if I'm wrong, but he wears a cape."

I've already pulled up an image search for all the DC superheroes. "Affirmative," I say. "Against Edna's better judgement, a lot of them do."

"Should we keep the caped rides or eliminate them?" Mikal asks. "Because the clue is '*not* all heroes wear capes,' so maybe we should concentrate on the ones who don't."

Even Wylla, who has zero skin in the game and couldn't care less about the tokens, gets sucked into the conversation. "That makes sense," she says. "It's like a double negative or something."

"Can we cross reference the caped crusaders with the park rides to make a list of potential token locations?" Travis asks, his voice buoyant.

"Absolutely," Seamus says.

Ernie's plan to get us out of the doldrums works, as evidenced by the perma-grin on my face helping Mikal and Travis solve the clue. Of the dozen or so possible rides, I immediately dismiss Batman, Superman Ultimate Flight, The Dark Knight Coaster, and Wonder Woman Lasso of Truth because they all wear capes. I also eventually convince the others to scratch Bizzaro, The Joker, and Harley Quinn Crazy Train for being villains.

"What rides are left?" Travis asks.

Seamus scans his sheet. "Green Lantern and Justice League: Battle for Metropolis."

While they've been narrowing down the list, I've been Googling official Six Flags' ride trailers. We've never had this much time to research and watching the videos feels like a luxury. When I come across one for the Justice League ride, I know I've hit the jackpot.

"Hey guys, listen to this."

I play the video. A deep movie trailer voice fills the van.

"There is only one person who can save Metropolis, and that person is you."

"Oh, God, that's it," Mikal says. "That's gotta be the ride."

"Yeah, but look." I turn my phone screen for the others to see. "It's one of those interactive, shoot-the-target rides. Finding tokens on a ride like that isn't going to be easy."

"Not only that," Mikal says with an impish smirk, pointing to an image of himself dressed as Morpheus from *The Matrix* on his phone. "I've been known to wear a cape on occasion."

I'm momentarily distracted, scrolling through some of the other amazing costumes Mikal's crafted for his cosplay Instagram feed. "Here I am as Agent J from *MIB*. Oh, and here's my Into the Spider-Verse Spidey."

"Hey now," Travis pipes up. "I can't see what you all are looking at, so can we get back to finding those tokens?"

"Gimme a sec." I open another browser tab on my phone. "Maybe someone's uploaded a video of the ride. If the queue is the type I think it is, we'll find the tokens waiting in line, not on the ride itself."

Sure enough, there are several Justice League videos on YouTube. The first couple don't show anything useful, but the third is absolutely perfect.

"Look at that." Seamus peers over my shoulder, clearly impressed by my investigative prowess. "There are all kinds of animatronics and props, like you're actually walking through the Hall of Justice. There'll be lots of great hiding places along the way."

"I still can't see what you people are talking about," Travis whines.

"Sorry, dude," Seamus says. "You *could* see if you entered the twenty-first century and got a smart phone like the rest of us. But those who choose to live in the past..."

Mikal rolls his eyes. "Don't listen to him. I'm here, so you don't need to see. Trust me. I'll find the tokens." He takes the phone off speaker and puts it to his ear. "And when we win the passes, you're gonna need to be well enough to use them, so get some rest and feel better." A pause. "Yeah. Yeah, I'll get it." Another pause. "Okay. You, too. Everyone says bye, and we love you."

He holds up the phone, and I yell my goodbyes with the others.

"Jesus, any chance you morons could keep it down? We're trying to watch a movie back here."

Wylla and I giggle as Seamus throws his hand over his head to flip Dustin the bird.

"Right back atcha, dork," he replies.

Despite the bumper-to-bumper traffic, miles of construction, and severe lack of rest stops for the duration of the trip, I'm in a ridiculously good mood when Ernie pulls the van into the motel parking lot off the New Jersey turnpike.

While he checks in with registration, I gather my bags from the back of the van with the others. Even without Travis, our new sleeping arrangements seem established: Dustin and Chloe in the first room, Mikal and Ernie in the second, and me, Wylla, and Seamus in the third.

"Hey, so, I was thinking," Seamus says, crossing the parking lot on the way to drop off our bags in the room before dinner. "What if we invite Mikal to hang with us tomorrow." He's walking between me and Wylla, and I can't help but notice how he keeps glancing in her direction.

"Sure." Wylla gazes up at him, doe-eyed, the way she used to with Logan, batting her lashes.

I shake my head at her behavior, wishing she had an off button, and return my attention to Seamus. "Yeah, of course. Mikal should definitely come with us."

He turns to me with a nod. "And also, you should ride with him some. It doesn't seem right for the two of us to sit together all the time, you know what I mean?"

I nod in agreement even though I'm not entirely sure I understand why. Maybe he thinks it's not fair to stick Mikal with Wylla on every ride since they haven't really bonded the way the rest of us have.

Or maybe it's something else.

I swallow the acrid burn of jealousy, already angry with myself for even considering what's in my head. "You can ride with him, too." My voice wavers, and I hope he doesn't notice. "I don't mind."

We reach the room, and as he holds the door open, the broadness of his smile indicates he blissfully unaware of the ridiculous battle going on inside my head. I set down my things, and he prattles on about which rides we should hit first after finding the tokens, and whether he should hold back on getting a milkshake *and* fries with dinner tonight after sitting in the van all day. Wylla offers her suggestions to both the rides and the meal selections in her sweetest voice, stoking the nagging sensation in the pit of my stomach.

I think back to all her innocent flirting over the past couple days. Giggling with him on the bed watching cartoons while I was in the bathroom brushing my teeth. Leaning against him like a pillow in the hospital waiting room. And while I'm perfectly aware that her outgoing disposition is just part of her nature, I'm starting to wonder if Seamus might be taking all of her unsolicited attention a bit too seriously. Maybe he's starting to believe she's really into him. If that's the case, I don't stand a chance. It'll be game over just like it was with Logan.

Honestly, what else am I supposed to think when he tells me outright that I should ride with Mikal instead of him tomorrow?

I wish I was the type of girl who was confident enough in myself to believe his only concern is Mikal's well-being, but here I am what if'ing every worst-case scenario like a maniac. What if he only wants me to ride with Mikal so he can ride with Wylla? What if I'm no longer enough to distract him from my sister's charms, and he's officially sick of hanging out with me?

I don't want to believe it, but it's possible he's decided Wylla's a better option after all.

CHAPTER 30

I don't sleep all night. Not when Seamus reaches for my hand under the covers after we finally turn off the light. Not even when he whispers my name in his sleep at three o'clock in the morning.

The self-doubt that began creeping in the moment he suggested splitting up yesterday has now fully embedded itself in my psyche, effectively silencing any rational thoughts working to quiet it. Given the right circumstances and enough time, everyone eventually chooses Wylla over me.

Mom.

Our cousin, Kora.

Logan.

And now Seamus.

If he notices how quiet I am as we pass the bagel bag around the back of the van, he doesn't say anything. If he's aware of the wordless tension building between me and Wylla, he doesn't comment about that either. Instead, he and Mikal urge us to keep up as they take off for the park entrance once we arrive.

"Who are they trying to beat?" Wylla asks breathlessly over

the clapping of our flip flops against the pavement. "Aren't you two giving the tokens to Mikal and Travis today anyway?"

"No. We only agreed to help them solve the clue, remember?" My tone is harsh—harsher than it should be—but even responding is a struggle. I don't want to be mad at her for something that's not even her fault—she hasn't thrown herself at Seamus or anything—but knowing how I should behave and actually following through are two different things. "Plus, Dustin and Chloe are unpredictable. There's no telling what they might do."

I slow approaching the admission gates, falling into line behind the guys. To my left, Dustin and Chloe wiggle their way through a disorganized mob of middle schoolers and slip into a line significantly closer to the turnstiles.

"They have two tokens now, too, so they've got as good a chance as any of winning the vouchers," Wylla whispers, following my gaze. "I bet they weren't really watching movies back there yesterday. They were probably eavesdropping on our conversation with Travis the whole time."

Although I know she's not accusing me of anything outright, the truth of Wylla's realization feels like a kick to the gut. After all, I was the one who convinced everyone else they weren't listening. "I won't make the mistake of trusting them again."

I pass through bag check and ticketing, and once I'm inside, sprint with the others to Justice League. Not surprisingly, Dustin and Chloe are already thirty people ahead of us in line.

"Guess we should've been a bit quieter on the phone with Travis yesterday." Mikal cranes his neck to see down the hall. "It felt so good strategizing with him, though…"

Seamus gives him a commiserate pat on the shoulder.

"Don't worry about it, dude. They have no idea where to look."

As the line inches forward, we divide the task. Wylla and I search all the usual places—under handrails, around trash cans, and inside wall niches—while Seamus and Mikal check the props, statues, and animatronics as best they can without drawing too much attention to themselves. All the while, I keep glancing ahead to Chloe and Dustin as they check the same areas ahead of us in line.

Wylla follows my gaze to where Chloe's nonchalantly ogling a marble-like statue of Batman, Superman, and Wonder Woman, stretching her neck as far as she can to see behind them without getting out of line. "Think they've found anything, yet?"

I shake my head. "You better believe when they do, though, they'll make sure their celebration is loud enough for all of us to hear."

I'm still feeling my way along the railing when Mikal cries out a moment later. "I've got them. Here behind this wall hanging." He slips his hand around the back of the frame, but comes out empty. "My arm's too thick, though. I can't reach."

I throw him my most innocent smile. Seamus won't be able to reach them either, which leaves the task to me or Wylla.

I push past Seamus and slide my arm behind the sign describing all the villains we'll be encountering on the ride. My fingers graze the token bag, but I can't grab it properly. I pull my arm back out.

"Gotta come at it from the other side," I explain, brushing into Seamus on my way around. From this angle, the bag is closer. I pull it out and hand it to Mikal. "You're welcome," I say.

He stands frozen, gaping at me. "For real?"

Seamus glares a hole through the side of my head, but I don't care. Mikal found the tokens fair and square, so who am I to take them?

In a burst of unexpected fervor, Mikal throws his arms around my shoulders, wrapping me in an enormous hug. "Thank you," he says. "Travis is gonna be stoked."

I return his embrace with a squeeze of my own, and when we finally release one another, I'm pretty sure there are tears in his eyes. "Well, go ahead then," I say. "Call him to let him know. But don't expect this type of concierge service again. If your arm's too big tomorrow, it'll be too bad, so sad."

He thanks me again and tries calling Travis, but there's no reception inside the giant metal building. Ahead, Dustin and Chloe are still aimlessly searching around an animatronic Cyborg while the people behind them glance sidelong at each other like they've lost their minds.

Beside me, Seamus appears to have conceded. "Those tokens could've been ours if you weren't such a softy."

"You'll find tomorrow's." I cut my eyes to Chloe, who's pissing off a whole line of strangers with her aggressive searching technique. "Should we tell her she can stop looking?"

We consider one another and laugh.

"This way's more fun," Seamus says. "The two of them can search all day for all I care."

In the loading area, a visibly disappointed Chloe and Dustin climb aboard their RTV along with several other guests. But as their transport departs, Mikal can't contain himself—waving the token bag over his head to draw their attention. "Better luck next time," he calls in his most theatrical voice.

Seamus and I are still laughing about it when our RTV arrives, and my chest feels like it's about to burst when he follows me into the front row, leaving Mikal and Wylla in the back.

He pulls his weapon from its holster, holds in front of his chest like a movie cop, and turns to me. "Let's fight some bad guys."

***

After Justice League, we head next door to The Dark Knight. I let my hand swing casually by my side on the walk over, hoping Seamus will take the hint, but he seems oblivious. I hoped, once the tokens were found, his attention would return to me, but even without the tokens occupying his time, he's still more focused on the others. Especially Wylla, who he keeps glancing at when he thinks I'm not looking.

As we enter the queue, Mikal opens a charades' app on his phone. "Travis and I have been playing this to pass the time," he says. "We've done pretty much all of the blockbuster flicks. And famous people. And a bunch of the Hits of the 70s." He grins up at me. "You can image which of us did better at that." He continues scrolling through the list of topics before landing on dance moves. "Travis refused to dance in line, but I know you guys don't embarrass easy."

I actually do embarrass easy, but I can't admit to it now that he's called me out. Even still, he doesn't give me time to object, holding his phone to his forehead as the first clue appears on the screen.

Seamus and Wylla dance in place, much to the amusement of everyone around them.

"Moonwalk," Mikal cries, tapping the screen to bring up the next dance.

Following the game's instructions, they do the Double Dab followed by the Floss. Mikal guesses both correctly, and I swallow hard as the fourth move appears on the screen—

watching Seamus and Wylla cracking up as they attempt the Milly Rock knots my stomach.

I pull out my phone to distract myself when Wylla's voice draws my attention.

"Come on, Elise. You gotta let loose a little and dance with us. Stop being so uptight."

Of course, guys have always loved when Wylla lets loose.

Logan did.

And Jackson.

Hell, her first boyfriend Declan all the way back in kindergarten was probably drawn to her lack of inhibition.

Yet another difference between us.

Until now.

I take a deep breath and shake out my arms. Because I'll be damned if I'm gonna watch from the sidelines as she 'lets loose' all over Seamus right now.

With a bevy of other riders watching, I perform the Shimmy, the Nae Nae, Single Ladies, and the Shoot while Mikal looks on. The family to my right cheers, and with each correct guess, their enthusiasm grows. When the timer buzzes, applause erupts around me, and I take a well-deserved bow.

My insecurities are all but forgotten as we near the front of the line. I glance over at Seamus, and when he gives me a wink, I realize I'm probably overreacting to his simple request to switch riders.

Maybe it doesn't have to do with Wylla at all.

I ride this wave of confidence all the way to the platform where the attendant instructs us to board.

Seamus turns to Mikal. "You and Elise take this one together," he says, sliding into the front of the car.

Mikal shrugs and extends an arm—an invitation to board first. I take the seat behind Wylla, Mikal sits behind Seamus, and before there's a chance to get my bearings, the train takes off down the track.

The car is pitched into immediate darkness, and I can just make out the shadow of Wylla's head leaning toward Seamus. She shrieks as the ride plummets down the first steep drop and lurches side to side, nearly landing her in his lap. Blood pulses in my ears and along my neck as my pressure rises. Unlike Wylla, I find a way to remain in my seat, but of course she's smaller than me, and lighter, so I suppose there's always a chance she's legitimately having difficulty staying on her side of the car.

But as the ride slows and comes to an end, she giggles.

The same giggle she used on Logan to get his attention while we were growing up.

The same giggle that won over Jackson after Logan was arrested.

Now, my mind conjures images of her curled against Seamus, giggling into his ear like she's the one he's been sleeping beside all these nights.

It doesn't make sense.

Or maybe it does. Because maybe I'm not moving fast enough for him. Maybe riding coasters and solving riddles and playing dance charades feels too much like friendship and not enough like romance. And maybe holding hands under the covers and feeling the whisper of my breath on his cheek isn't enough for him.

Maybe he thinks bubbly, sultry Wylla will give him all the things I haven't.

But of course, it's too dark to see what she's giggling about up there. It's too dark to know if she's giving him more right now. Wrapping her hand around his bicep. Running a finger across his chest.

Kissing him on the cheek.

As the lap restraint releases, I push the thought from my mind. Wylla's my sister, not some stranger. She would never intentionally hurt me, and she knows how I feel about Seamus.

Then again, she also knew how I felt about Logan, but it didn't stop her from competing for his attention at every turn

CHAPTER 31

"What's next?" Seamus shields his eyes with his hand as I step into the glaring sun.

"The other Batman coaster's right here," Mikal says, nodding across the midway. "Can you all handle two coasters back-to-back, or do you want to pass for now and come back to it?"

A week ago, Wylla would've gladly opted out. But the determined expression on her face leads me to believe she may have finally gotten over her fear of coasters.

Or the Dramamine's been working.

Or perhaps, she's simply succumbed to her predisposition for doing whatever it takes to please a guy. Like when she distributed prescription drugs for Logan and rode a coaster at Drury to win a trip for Jackson.

And now it seems, although she may not be consciously aware of it, she's trying to impress Seamus.

Images of her pressed against him on another coaster give me the courage to speak. "I'd actually like a little break. It's scorching out here." I fan the hem of my t-shirt for dramatic effect. "Maybe we could find some air-conditioning for a few minutes."

Seamus scans our surroundings before pointing to a nearby arcade. "Wanna blow some quarters together?" His eyes are bright, sparkling with the childlike wonder I've grown more than accustom to since we started hanging out. "How much you want to bet I can win more tickets than you in the next fifteen minutes?"

Mikal pulls a five-dollar bill from his Velcro whale wallet. "I want in on this action. And how about if the winner gets everyone else's tickets."

"Agreed," Wylla says, turning toward the arcade.

"Fine." I level a glare a Seamus. "But no cheating. Lord knows you've probably got some fancy trigonometric formula for the exact angle to toss the ski-ball up the ramp."

He brushes off my accusation with a wave of his hand. "You give me too much credit. And I'm more of a Whack-A-Mole man myself."

After dodging a large group of people wearing matching family reunion t-shirts, we make a dash for the only change converter in the arcade.

"No one starts until we all have our tokens," Mikal says. "If I'm gonna beat you guys, I'm gonna beat you fair and square."

Seamus goes first, followed by me and Mikal. They scan the game selections as Wylla retrieves her tokens from the slot. Around me, half-a-dozen pre-teen boys crowd around the latest Call of Duty iteration, and the rhythmic sound of a puck being knocked across an air hockey table fills the air. Two little girls in matching pigtails are practically vibrating, bouncing up and down as their dad attempts to snag a Wonder Woman doll from the nearby claw machine.

An obvious lesson in futility.

I set the timer on my phone for fifteen minutes. "Okay. On your marks. Get set. Go."

Seamus and I take off in the same direction while Wylla meanders to the left, and Mikal races to the right. For a second, it seems as though we're both heading for the basketball nets, but before we get there, he veers off toward the Whack-A-Mole. "Good luck," he calls over his shoulder.

If I didn't already know about his mile-wide competitive streak, I might almost think he was being sincere. "Back atcha," I say, slipping my first two tokens into the machine.

Three balls drop from the chute, and the timer counts down—three, two, one. At the sound of the buzzer, I start taking shots, one after the other. The first two miss, bouncing off the rim to the right, but by the third shot I find my rhythm, and the ball goes in.

"Yes." I pump my fist and hit three more shots in quick succession, glancing briefly over at Seamus to see if he's noticed my mad skills.

But, of course, he's singularly focused on whacking his moles, his mallet pounding head after head. Talk about being in the zone.

I turn back to the net, sinking six more shots before the buzzer sounds.

Below the token slot, the first ticket pops out, followed by another and another until I'm holding eleven in my hand. Not bad for a first attempt.

I chance another glance at Seamus to see if he's gotten any tickets and am shocked to see a trail of them sticking out of his game. I obviously need to spend more time sinking baskets and less time watching Seamus to have any chance at winning this thing. Either that or I need to find a more profitable game.

I slip two more tokens into the slot, pick up the first ball, and wait for the buzzer. The second it sounds, I sink the first basket, followed by the second and the third. Now I'm in the zone, almost like I'm back in Logan's driveway when we were kids, playing H-O-R-S-E on summer evenings until our moms called us in for bed. Back then, I didn't practice shooting layups by myself on the school court at recess so I could impress him at home. I practiced so I could legitimately beat him at his own game. What I didn't realize is guys like Logan don't like losing, especially to girls. What they like is for girls to cheer them on from the sidelines, the way Wylla did.

But I was never the sort of girl to sit on the sidelines.

And I'm never gonna be.

My second attempt earns me sixteen tickets, so instead of searching for a more lucrative game, I go all in with my free-throw abilities. I stop peeking over at Seamus. I stop taking time to count my tickets between rounds. I just put in the tokens and make the shots.

When the tokens are gone, I've amassed a small mountain—two-hundred-seventeen to be exact. I have no idea what I'll be able to buy with my stash, but I'm pretty sure no one's gonna beat my total. I'm still preparing my victory speech in my head as I turn my attention back to Seamus.

Across the arcade, a group of teenagers and adults cluster around the Whack-A-Mole game where Seamus is still beating the poor vermin like he's Mr. McGregor defending his vegetable patch. He pounds one after another and as his final score is revealed, a cheer erupts from the crowd.

The loudest of which belongs to Wylla who's now standing directly beside him, watching intently.

"Dude, that was a perfect score," someone calls from the crowd.

"Do it again," says another.

He's got to be getting low on tokens, but he pulls two more from his pocket and slips them into the machine. The happy little Whack-A-Mole jingle plays, and as I inch my way through the crowd, the game begins. Every time his mallet connects with a mole, they chant his name—Seamus! Seamus! Seamus!—with my sister serving as the pastor to his ad hoc congregation. Finally, the GAME OVER sign illuminates, and when he turns to Wylla for her approval, I half expect her to leap into his open arms.

"I'm all outta tokens," he says to his adoring fans, turning out the front pockets of his cargo shorts to prove it. "Thanks for stopping by, though. I'll be here all week. Try the veal."

His attempt at humor falls flat with his fair-weather fans who disperse quickly now that the show's officially over. Of course, Wylla lingers by his side, gushing to him about his mole whacking abilities like she's some sort of arcade groupie.

"That was soooo amazing. You're an absolute master." She bats her eyelashes coyly, taking a step closer to him before reaching out to touch his forearm. I can't tell if it's a simple congratulatory gesture or something more, but I'm not about to stand around and find out.

"You've got a mighty big stack of tickets there," I say to Seamus, interrupting Wylla outright.

He turns to me, joy raising the freckled apples of his cheeks. "Not too bad." He eyes my stash. "But maybe not as good as you. Damn, girl. You didn't mention you had a side gig playing for the WNBA."

There's nothing for me to do but stare at my shoes. I'm not great at taking a compliment. Never have been. And on the rare occasion someone does congratulate me, I usually end up saying something stupid, like the time my chemistry teacher told me I did well on my lab assignment and I said, "You, too."

"Not Elise," Wylla says, when I don't respond. "She's more band geek than jock."

I'm about to call off our truce and blurt out something cruel about her paltry stack of tickets when my fifteen-minute alarm goes off, and Mikal shows up out of nowhere, still counting his haul.

"I've got one-hundred-sixty-five. How many do you guys have?" he asks.

"Two seventeen," I say.

Mikal's eyes widen.

"Seventy-nine," Wylla says with a shrug.

Seamus continues gathering his pile off the floor. "I just finished," he says. "Let's take these to the machine to count them."

On the other side of the arcade near the prizes, Seamus spots the ticket counting machine. I feed my tickets into the slot first, and once the machine's eaten them all, it spits out a slip of paper with my total.

"Two-hundred-seventeen," I read. "Like I told you."

"Mad free-throw skills and mad math skills." Seamus gives me a nod as he inserts his first ticket into the machine. A minute later, his total is revealed, and he reads it off the slip. "Two-eleven," he says, with only the slightest air of disappointment in his voice. "Major props." He gives me his slip, and after inserting their tickets in the machine, Mikal and Wylla hand me their winnings as well.

"Fair is fair," Mikal says. "Now go pick out something fabulous."

Unfortunately, I'd need to sink about $500 worth of free throws to afford anything fabulous in the arcade store. With my measly earnings, I purchase a taco plushy and a bunch of

Laffy Taffy to share with the others.

"You're a good sport," Mikal says, ripping open a strawberry one.

"The best," Seamus agrees with a gentle elbow to the rib. "So, are we ready for another coaster now? Batman, perhaps?"

"I'm ready, unless one of you needs a longer break," I say smugly, cutting my eyes to Wylla. If she thinks she's gonna sit next to Seamus again anytime soon, she's got another thing coming.

"I'm fine," she says.

"I'm good," Mikal adds.

"Then it's decided." Seamus takes off through a crowd of moms and preschoolers while I dodge and weave my way between the minefield of strollers attempting to keep up.

As we wait in line, the guys have a philosophical discussion about which Batman was the best Batman, canonically speaking. For her part, Wylla hangs on Seamus's every word, nodding and agreeing with him every time he opposes Mikal.

I suppress the urge to strangle her.

When they begin discussing the merits of Michael Keaton, I pull out my phone to send a quick text to Nia.

Do you think Logan ever liked me as much as he liked Wylla?

Nia's never out-of-pocket, typically replying in less than two seconds, but this time my screen remains blank. I leave it open, watching for the reply bubble, but after a minute passes without a response, I start to worry something's happened to her.

I'm still imagining worse case scenarios, making it all the way to number eleven—death-by-brain freeze at the fro-yo shop—when the first dots appear.

But two minutes later, there's still no message and even the reply bubble is gone.

She's deleting. Retyping. Choosing her words.

What doesn't she want to tell me?

Finally, a response.

What's this about Elise?

It's about Wylla seducing Seamus the same way she seduced Logan.

My finger hovers over the send button, but I don't tap it. Now it's my time to delete. To retype. To choose my words.

Why am I never enough?

Quick dots. Quick response.

You're always enough. You just have to believe it. And be yourself.

I take a deep breath, let her words fill me up. I send her two heart emojis and a kissy face before returning my phone to my pocket.

I take a step closer to Seamus and at the first break in his conversation with Mikal whisper, "You wanna ride with me this time?"

He smiles. "Yeah. Sure. I mean, the ride sits four to a row, but I'll sit next to you." He hesitates a beat, like something's dawned on him, before gazing coyly at me. "You must've missed me on the last ride, huh?"

If I had Wylla's self-confidence, I'd tell him the truth. I'd tell him I do miss him when he's not around, and I don't like sharing him with my sister or anyone else for that matter. But, of course, I sidestep his question by asking a question of my own.

"I heard a lot of giggling on Dark Knight. What was that all about?"

He looks dubious. "Giggling? Really? I didn't hear anything."

I raise an eyebrow, unconvinced, but decide to let it drop. If I press him for info, and he tells me Wylla was laughing at something funny he said, I could handle it. But if he breaks down and tells me the truth about how she was nibbling on his ear or some BS like that, I'd die right here on the spot.

On the ground.

In the middle of the Batman line.

Nia's words replay in my head.

You're always enough.

It's hard to believe in yourself when no one else does either. Not Mom. Not Wylla. Sometimes, not even Nia. Which is probably why I always assumed the reason I'd never had a boyfriend was because unlike Wylla, I was simply unlovable.

"You two gonna get a room or are you coming?" Mikal asks. A quick glance in his direction confirms the line has snaked all the way around the next corner without me. I hurry to catch up, and when Seamus reaches back to take my hand, I don't hesitate to grab it.

Because maybe I'm not so unlovable after all.

CHAPTER 32

The next-to-last park of the trip is Dorney, back in good old Pennsylvania. It feels weird crossing the state line, like I'm returning home a little different than I left. Beside me, Wylla's curled up alongside the window, listening to the Spotify playlist Nia made. I catch her gaze, and she offers me a sweet smile, nodding at Seamus who's racked out against my shoulder. The weight of him is still sort of surreal—a wonderful and unexpected gift from the universe—and my chest feels like it could explode when I think of it.

Of course, whatever's going on with Seamus isn't nearly as important as my relationship with Wylla. This whole trip was supposed to be about making amends, and looking at her now, it feels like we've definitely made some progress. She's still hiding something from me, though. I'm certain of it. I've known my sister her entire life—was there in the hospital the day she was born—so it doesn't take a genius to figure out she's keeping a secret.

And I'm still determined to figure out what it is.

She hands me one of her headphones, and we listen to Nia's playlist together until after our breakfast stop, when the topic of conversation turns to the location of the ninth tokens.

"Do or die, huh, Seamus?" Dustin teases from the back seat. "You know, if Chloe and I find the tokens today and tomorrow, we'll be taking those vouchers for ourselves."

Seamus relocated to the middle row behind me and Wylla after breakfast, and now he's stretched out with paperwork spread around him like he's planning a government coup. Unlike yesterday, when he and I openly shared what we knew with the others, now our lips are sealed. "It'll never happen." The dismissive edge to his voice is enough to deceive Dustin, but I still catch a touch of trepidation buried inside.

Dustin scoffs. "If you say so. You gotta be running a little scared, though, considering I almost got them yesterday."

Mikal rolls his eyes from the passenger's seat. "If by 'almost' you mean 'passed them right by without noticing' than sure, dude, you almost had them."

The guys continue bickering, and I peer over the back of my seat at Seamus, feigning interest in his research. It's a ruse, though, since increasing my proximity to him is less about strategizing and more about taking in the crisp fragrance of his bodywash.

It was hard not taking it personally when he opted to sit in the open second row without me, but looking at the paraphernalia spread around him now, his reason for wanting a seat to himself is obvious. Still, our separation is keeping us from talking strategy, so I text him instead.

What're you thinking?

He shakes his head and texts back. It's almost too easy.

Like how?

The clue is Greek mythology and the only ones that fit are Apollo and Hydra.

I scan the list of rides printed on his sheet. What about the

Zephyr? Isn't it some mythological being?

He pulls up Google on his phone to check, and gives me a thumbs up before sending another text. Good catch. In Greek mythology, Zephyr is the west wind or messenger of spring. Guess we better add it to our list.

His jaw clenches as he adjusts his route on the map to account for the third ride. He hesitates, chewing on his pen cap, and I worry he's going to invite Wylla into the fold now that there are three possible hiding locations. I struggle against an overwhelming urge to talk him out of it before he suggests it on his own, and distract myself by plotting a route of my own—tracing the freckles on his cheek, past his ear, and across his neck with my fingertip. All these days in the sun have caused even more freckles to appear, but they've also given his skin rosy glow I'm finding hard to resist. I'm about to lift a hand to his face when my phone chimes with a text alert.

We've got a coaster, a carnival ride, and a train to check. Where should we head first? He gazes up at me, leaning a tiny bit closer as the van bounces along down the highway. "Wait. Why are you smiling like that?"

I arrange my face into a more serious expression. There's no way I can tell him what I was about to do. "Like what?"

"I don't know. Like you have a secret or something."

I shrug, trying desperately to imagine what Wylla would do if she was in my position. Would she tell him the truth? Flirt? Lean in for a kiss?

All three?

It doesn't matter what she would do because I don't have the chutzpah for any of it. Instead, I look past him out the back window and wrack my brain for something innocuous to say. "I was just wondering if there's a bathroom close to the entrance because I've really gotta go."

He raises both eyebrows, taken aback. "Okay. We can make time for that, I guess."

Of all the stupid things to say, the state of my bladder was the best my brain could come up with. Now I've got to change the subject quickly before he wastes time checking the map for restrooms. "So, uh, which ride should we hit first?"

His eyes shift slowly from my face to his map and back to my face before sending me another text. I was going to say we should split up when we get there. Like, maybe you should check the Zephyr, and I can check the Hydra, and we can meet up at Apollo? Or the other way around is fine, too. It doesn't matter to me.

I'm relieved he doesn't ask Wylla to search the third ride, which I take as a sign that her charms might not be working on him quite the way I thought they were. Or maybe he just doesn't trust her not to give the tokens to Dustin and Chloe or even Mikal.

Either way, the prospect of splitting up is disappointing. Logically, it makes sense—two birds with one stone and all—but part of me hoped spending time together was more important than finding tokens. Obviously, that's not the case.

My fingers return to the screen. Okay. Yeah. I don't mind searching whichever ride you think is best.

The thing is, the clue didn't give us a number, so if it's in one of the seats, we might need to ride a few times to check multiple locations.

You think you'll need to ride the Hydra more than once?

He shrugs. It's a definite possibility on Apollo. And I don't know what the deal is with the train—whether you'll be able to move around the car to check different areas or if you'll be stuck in one seat. Either way, we might both need to ride a few times. If we split up, we'll get through them faster and increase our chances of finding the tokens.

He glances over his shoulder at Dustin and Chloe who are conspiring in the back before composing another text.

This clue is even simple enough for those two, but you know they'll never split up, so checking two rides at once will give us an advantage. Not to mention, they don't look nearly as thoroughly as we do, and Mikal's on his own so he'll have to do one ride at a time.

It's hard to argue with his reasoning. Still, I'm not wild about the idea of searching on my own. Okay, I reply at last.

With the plan established, I hunker down in my seat beside Wylla to research the Zephyr. Halfway through my second YouTube video, I'm distracted by the sound of Dustin ripping open a cellophane wrapper in the back of the van. It takes less than ten seconds for the scent of strawberry Pop Tart to overwhelm me, but when it does, I'm back in the kitchen with Mom on the morning of my accident, sun streaming through the window, dust dancing in the space between us.

"It's supposed to be a beautiful afternoon. Mid-seventies. Plenty of sun." She turned off the TV as the weather report ended. "I was thinking, it'd be nice to host a cookout to thank some of the neighbors for their help shoveling the snow off our path this winter. Nothing big. Just some burgers and hot dogs. A couple bags of chips." She sipped her coffee and turned to me. "What do you think?"

I took a bite of Pop Tart, remembering all the times our neighbors pitched in to clear our sidewalk when Wylla and I weren't able. "That'd be nice. Do you have all the food?"

The rickety stool creaked beneath her as she stood. "I think so." She opened the refrigerator and peered inside. "Couple pounds of ground chuck. Some lettuce. Ketchup. And there should be a few tomatoes and an onion in the pantry. Will you check for me?"

'The pantry' was a set of small plastic shelves wedged beside the washing machine in the mudroom so it didn't take long to spot the tomatoes and the onion. Or at least what was left of it.

I returned to the kitchen. "The tomatoes look fine, but I'm pretty sure the onion's gone bad."

Mom glanced the black, moldy sphere in my hand. "Yeah. Definitely not fit for consumption. I should run to the store and get a fresh one and maybe some paper plates and a bag of hot dog buns."

I threw my Pop Tart wrapper and the onion into the trash and pulled the bag from the can to take out. "Why don't you make a list of the stuff you need, and I'll run into town so you can get ready." My offer elicited one of her rare smiles, warming something deep inside of me.

"Oh, would you? That would be so sweet. And if you're heading out, would you mind dropping Wylla off at Jackson's on the way? She said something about needing to go over there to talk to him." Her voice took a strange, contemptuous tone, but instead of questioning the origin of her sudden dislike for Jackson, my only thoughts were of being locked inside a car with my sister and the awkward silence which would accompany us. But Jackson's wasn't far, and I could drop Wylla off first, so taking her was the least I could do to help.

"Sure, Mom. No problem," I said, tossing the trash bag onto the porch.

Now, I glance at Wylla seated beside me in the van, wishing I'd paid more attention to Mom's tone that day. Did she know about Jackson and Brenda at the party? Would she have confided in me if I'd asked?

"I took you to Jackson's the day I had my accident," I say.

She pulls out her earbuds and raises an eyebrow at me. "Um, duh."

"I'd forgotten all about it. Or I had, until just now."

She stares at me. "Okay."

"So why did you need me to take you to his house? Were you going to confront him about hooking up with Brenda?"

She wraps her earbud cord between her fingers, looping it from her thumb to her pinky and back again.

Outside the window, the roaring engine of an eighteen-wheeler rolling past isn't enough to mask the sound of my own heart thudding inside my chest. In the stillness that follows, waiting for her to respond, I get the sense that if we weren't speeding along the highway at sixty-five miles per hour, she would jump from the van to avoid this conversation.

"That night at the party, I went inside, looking for a bathroom—just opening random doors, you know—when I found them making out in the pantry."

"That's horrible."

Her lips curl into a grimace. "You don't know the half of it. They were licking chocolate syrup off each other's chests."

Inside my own chest, my heart breaks for my baby sister. Despite his obvious lack of moral character, Jackson was integral to helping her recover from the pain of losing Logan. He was there when her pride and her heart needed mending. He gave her hope there were other people in the world who loved her and losing Logan didn't mean losing faith.

But truthfully, stuff like this doesn't happen to Wylla. Her life's been devoid of disappointment, so this blow must've shaken her to the core.

And all this time, I could've helped carry the burden of her grief.

Maybe this is the painful secret she's been keeping from

me all this time.

A long pause stretches between us, full of all sorts of unspoken things. "I wish you would've said something to me that day in the car. Maybe instead of dropping you off, I could've gone in with you for support." I glance at her staring blankly across the highway at cars speeding by. "I'm sorry I wasn't a better big sister when you needed me. I should've been there to support you when all this happened." I offer a tentative smile. "Maybe you'll let me support you now."

She straightens against the seatback and pulls a loose strand of hair from between her parted lips. "I was going to break up with him. I was going to tell him all the apologies in the world wouldn't make up for the trust he broke. But then everything got crazy that day, and there never seemed to be a good time. Not that it's your fault or anything. I lost my courage and fell back into old habits. That's on me. Not you." She lets out a little shudder. "I guess what I'm trying to say is, it's okay you didn't help then because you're helping right now by being on this trip with me. I needed time and space away to figure stuff out, and you made it happen. You helped me get away from him, at least for a little while." Her voice is laced with dread, and with only a couple days until the end of our journey, it's obvious I'm not the only one who's worried about what life's going to be like once we get back.

"Yeah, but what happens at home?"

She sighs, blotting the corners of her eyes with the hem of her T-shirt. "I'm gonna finally do what I was supposed to do that day. I'm gonna break up with Jackson, take back my dignity, and keep going."

"You need a wingman?"

She shakes her head. "Nah. I can do it on my own. Might need someone to take me out for ice cream afterwards, though."

"With extra sprinkles?" I ask, remembering how much she loved them as a kid.

"All the sprinkles," she says, taking my hand. "And what about you and Seamus? Are the two of you gonna hang out after all of this?"

I shrug like I'm indifferent, but I'm definitely concerned things might be weird for us once all the tokens are found. Like on those reality TV shows when the couples fall madly in love on screen but can't seem to keep it together when the cameras stop rolling. "I hope so. But it's been super easy here. Come Monday, we'll need to make an effort to see each other."

She scoffs. "You won't make the effort?"

Something prickles the back of my neck, like a spider creeping along on tiny legs, leaving a web of uncertainty trailing behind. I've been ignoring the sensation for the past few days, but under Wylla's perceptive gaze, I'm forced to acknowledge its presence. "It's not me I'm worried about."

CHAPTER 33

By the time we finally make it to the front entrance of the park, I've pushed aside thoughts of my future with Seamus and mentally prepared myself for the task at hand—get to the train, search for the tokens, meet up with him at Apollo. I'm in the zone, imagining all the places the tokens might be hidden inside a tiny locomotive, when Seamus grabs my arm.

"I thought you had to go," he says, pointing to the nearest restroom.

"Oh, yeah. I did. I mean, I do." I turn toward the building, calling over my shoulder before crossing the threshold. "You go ahead. I'll text you if I find anything on the train."

Wylla follows me into the ladies' room, which is full of women slathering on sunscreen and primping in front of the mirrors. It's a lesson in futility, though, because as any seasoned amusement park veteran will tell you, there's no hairspray on the planet that will hold up against one trip on a decent coaster.

I use the bathroom—at this point I actually need to go—and when I emerge from the stall, Wylla's waiting for me by the sink.

She tucks a wisp of hair under Dad's ball cap. "I could go check Apollo for you, if you want."

The water from the faucet trickles down the drain, and I squeeze soap from the pump on the wall, working a foamy lather between my hands before considering her. "Do you even know where to look?"

She shrugs, handing me a paper towel after I rinse. "I mean, I've watched you guys do it every day, so I'm pretty sure I can handle it." She pulls a tube of Chapstick from her back pocket to apply a second coat of gloss to her lips in the mirror. "I'll check the handrails and the trash cans, then ride a few times to check inside the seats. How hard can it be?"

I side-eye her in the mirror, wanting to protest. But she's right. How hard *can* it be?

"Okay. That would actually be a big help." A satisfied smile brightens her face, but instead of putting me at ease, I worry Seamus might be upset about this change of plans. I'm inclined to trust her, especially after all we've been through together on this trip, but I can't forget about our past and her long history of selling me out when it was in her best interest. If something were to happen now—if she were to miss finding them or lose them or God forbid, give them to Dustin—it would ruin everything, and I'm worried about taking the chance.

I should keep my mouth shut, but it engages before my brain can stop it. "You'll give the tokens to me and Seamus if you find them, right?"

She slips her Chapstick back in her pocket. "Of course. Who else would I give them to?"

"I dunno. Mikal. Chloe and Dustin. I just—"

"Don't trust me?"

"I do."

"You don't." She levels a glare at me before turning from the mirror.

"Wylla, wait," I call after her as she heads through the door. "I'm sorry."

She throws a dismissive hand over her shoulder and disappears into the throng of patrons entering the park. I elbow my way through a group of teenage girls taking selfies in front of the nearest coaster, but by the time I pass them, Wylla's nowhere to be found.

I pull up the park map on my phone, determined to follow after her. If she's heading to Apollo, that's where I'll go, too. A quick check confirms the ride's on my way to the Zephyr, so I squeeze past a line of people waiting for the carousel and set a course for the west side of the park.

When I get there, though, I don't see her anywhere. Not in line. Not scanning the perimeter. Not even on the ride.

I step into the shade of a nearby tree and pull out my phone to text her only to discover a new message. My heart quickens involuntarily, hoping it's from Mom, but instead it's Nia checking in.

Hey girl. Haven't heard from you in a while. Just wanted to make sure everything's okay. Same old same old here. Crusty Carl's excited for you to come home (and me too!)

Kiss emoji. Smile emoji. Heart emoji.

Her message serves as a reminder of my real life, tethering me to the world I'll return to once this trip comes to an end. It's been days—I don't know how many—since we've had a proper conversation, but as much as I'd like to talk to her about everything now, there's too much going on to waste time giving her a thorough response. I send a generic reply to placate her until I can give our friendship the attention it deserves.

All is well. Having fun. Lots to fill you in on. More later.

Miss you too.

Heart emoji. Heart emoji. Heart emoji.

I close out Nia's thread and open Wylla's. It's buried deep since the last message I got from her was months ago.

Jesus I said I was coming. Hold on.

I reread the text, remembering that part of the morning for the very first time.

Wylla was dragging her feet the day of the accident, as usual. Mom told her I was leaving at eleven, but fifteen minutes later, I was still waiting in the front seat of my car for her, sending stupid Snapchats to Nia. My impatience grew, thinking about all the stuff I had to do and all the time I was wasting, so I fired off an angry text, the first in months. I was done dealing with her crap.

I'm leaving now, with or without you.

She returned my text and appeared thirty seconds later, the gravel driveway crunching beneath her sneakers as she ran to the passenger's side. She slid into the seat, but I ignored her sidelong glare and threw the car into reverse, rocks flying as I backed out of the drive.

Concentrating on the road should've been a challenge with all the heavy sighing and groaning going on beside me, but as her loyal chauffer, my car practically drove itself to Jackson's. Her pursed lips and crossed arms begged for attention, but instead of giving in, I ignored her, slipping inside my own head to create a mental list of all the ways she took advantage of me during the week.

It was an extensive list.

"Are you in line, Miss?"

"I, uh, no." I step to the side, allowing a family to join Apollo's queue as I reflect on my time in the car with Wylla that day. How had I been so blind to her needs? How could I have been so self-centered? What kind of monster was I not to realize how much pain she was in? She needed me to reach out. To say something.

But I ignored her.

Is this what she's been hiding from me all along? Has she been suppressing her own disappointment for the way I treated her?

If she has been, it's more than I deserve.

Beside me, two preschoolers giggle together as they pull cotton candy from a shared cone. Their faces and fingers are sticky and blue. Their past obviously isn't as long or complicated as Wylla and mine, but maybe it doesn't matter. Maybe what's already happened isn't nearly as important as what comes next.

Despite all the things Wylla and I have said and done to each other through the years, I've got to do better now. Be better now.

For both of us.

I heave a sigh and begin typing.

I'm sorry I hurt your feelings. I do trust you. Please tell me where you are so we can look for the tokens together.

The glare from the noonday sun is bright, and I shield my screen with my hand, watching for a reply. I scan the ride again as I wait, hoping maybe I missed her, but she's definitely not here. When I glance back at the screen, it's still blank.

Disheartened, I move on to the Zephyr, where I'm encouraged to discover the first good news of the day: an empty queue. I check all the usual places for tokens along the way, and when the bright purple train arrives in the station, I scope out the first of the four passenger cars.

The train is tiny—like, child-sized—with five rows of seats per car. There are no doors, but the openings are so low, I'm forced to duck so as not to hit my head as I climb aboard. There are two other families behind me in line, both with small children, but they opt for cars in the back. This leaves me with the entire first car to explore on my own, as long as I can climb over the seat backs without drawing the attention of the conductors.

Of course, as the train pulls out of the station, a canned announcement reminding riders to remain seated throughout the entirety of the ride is played over the loudspeakers, but after a thorough check of the first row, I ignore the safety advice and slide myself over the seatback into the second row. I continue this process through the entire car all the way to the fifth and final row where I'm forced to admit there are no tokens to be found.

After a ten-minute ride through the overgrown and restricted areas of the park at a whopping two miles per hour, we return to the station where I queue up to ride again. This time, I wait for the other passengers to choose their seats first, and slide onto the only vacant car once the loading gate has closed. I follow the same search procedure as the first time, coming up emptyhanded yet again.

Same with the third trip.

And the fourth.

Once it's clear the tokens aren't hidden anywhere on or around the Zephyr, there's nothing left to do but text Seamus to see if he's had any luck.

You find them?

His reply is immediate.

Nope. You?

Nada. You heading to Apollo now?

Yeah. I'll head that way in a few.

Before closing my screen, I check Wylla's thread because maybe I missed her response.

But there's still no reply from her.

It's not far from the Zephyr to Apollo so I'm there in less than two minutes. The line's pretty long, but it seems stupid to jump in before Seamus has a chance to catch up. I do a little light searching around the perimeter while I wait, and as I work my way to the front of the ride, spot Chloe and Dustin near the entrance. I have no idea how many times they've ridden or how many cars they've already checked, but they wouldn't still be waiting in line for this stupid carnival ride if they'd already found them.

Which means the tokens are still out there.

Somewhere.

Just like Wylla.

CHAPTER 34

There's a raised flowerbed full of red zinnias and Gerber daisies on the far side of the ride where I brush some loose mulch off the bricks to sit and wait for Seamus. My phone sits in my lap, screen dark, anticipating a text from Wylla, but of course, all the wishing in the world doesn't make something so. People stroll past, some of them aimlessly, some with maps in hand, purposeful in their direction. Several guys who resemble Seamus pass by, causing my heart to skip. They're about the same height, wearing blue shirts and pasty complexions, but of course, none of them are him. I glance at my phone for the time—a minute later than the last time I checked—and try to figure out why I'm suddenly so nervous about his whereabouts. The Hydra's not far, but there are a couple different routes he could take to get here, so I don't know which way to watch.

Then Wylla's giggle, like sugary bubbles collecting at the top of root beer float, snags my attention. My eyes drift to the left, already knowing what I'm about to see, as a ball of tension tightens in my gut.

She's there, sandwiched between Seamus and Mikal, arm

draped casually around Seamus's neck. He's said something funny, I suppose, and her charm is on full blast like a hundred-watt bulb, with the same flirty head tilt and doe eyes she perfected vying against me for Logan's attention growing up. If there's one thing I know, it's most guys don't stand a chance against her effortless charisma, and if the look on Seamus's face is any indication, her magic is working.

As they approach, I lock eyes with her, and she makes a point to ruffle the back of his hair before pulling her hand away. She knows exactly how to get under my skin, and I'd be lying if I said she wasn't pissing me all the way off. I guess flirting with Seamus is her way of getting back at me for not trusting her, but this type of behavior is exactly why—when it comes to her—I'm never comfortable letting my guard down.

I'll need to try now, though, if I have any hopes of not losing all the progress we've made.

"So, hey. Uh, change of plans." Seamus clears his throat, his eyes scanning our surroundings, avoiding my face. I don't like the way he's got his hands stuffed in his pockets like he's a five-year-old, hiding something from his mom.

"Another adjustment to our seating arrangement?" My voice is sharp, and he recoils.

"No. I—" He pulls a bag out of his pocket and takes a step forward. "Hold out your hands."

I turn my palms face up, and he dumps out the bag, dropping two tokens into them. "You found them? But you said…"

"I know what I said." He runs his hand through his hair and shakes his head. "I didn't want to tell you over text. I figured I'd surprise you instead."

I glance at Mikal who gives me a 'what're ya gonna do' kind of shrug before turning to Wylla, who's obviously quite pleased with how well she manipulated my emotions.

"That's awesome," I say, wanting nothing more than to throw my arms around his neck in celebration. But now I'm confused. Confused about where I stand with him. Confused about where I stand with Wylla.

And frankly, confused about where they stand with each other.

"So, you guys wanna go hit a coaster or something?" The tone of Mikal's voice suggests he's acutely aware of the growing tension between us. "Thunderhawk and Steel Force are right around the corner."

We all agree a celebratory coaster ride is in order, and after a somewhat awkward wait, we make it to the front of Thunderhawk's line.

"After you," Seamus says, arm outstretched toward the open seat.

It appears Mikal and Wylla aren't coming with us. Instead, they're waiting for the front car on the next train. Apparently, Seamus is satisfied with our random offering here in the middle, so I slide in, lowering the lap bar across my hips as he settles in beside me.

The attendants walk the line, checking everyone's restraints. Once they've passed, he says, "We got lucky today."

"Yeah?"

"Yeah. I was super discouraged when I saw Mikal right ahead of me. There were only a dozen or so people between us, so I figured if the tokens were there, he would spot them first. When neither of us found them in line, though, and I saw Hydra is a floorless coaster, I assumed they were hidden at another ride. I mean, no way would they hide them in the seat, right?" He pauses as the attendants give the all clear, and the train jerks out of the station. "Anyway, I happened to get the front seat, and unlike the Dragster, Hydra has a really slow start, so I thought 'what the heck' and felt under my seat for the tokens. I almost died when I found them."

"That is lucky."

The lack of enthusiasm in my voice draws his attention as we climb to the top of the first hill. He turns to me, eyes narrowed. "Is something wrong? I thought you'd be happy. Or are you like pissed or something that I found them without you?"

Of course, my seeming indifference has nothing to do with the stupid tokens and everything to do with Wylla. It should be enough that he hasn't encouraged or frankly even acknowledged her flirtatious behavior, but I ignored her when she acted the same way with Logan and look where it got me.

The train speeds down the first drop and over a couple of smaller hills, and I use the time deciding how best to respond. Should I be honest with him about how her flirting makes me feel or just put on a happy face and let the whole thing drop? The ride isn't long so there won't be time to get into everything with him before reuniting with Wylla and Mikal.

And the last thing I want is to cause a scene.

But the moment I think this, the train slows, coming to a complete stop along an uphill bank.

"What the hell?" the guy behind us shouts.

A wave of confusion spreads along the train, with various degrees of annoyance. A woman in front of us tries to wiggle out from beneath her lap restraint as an announcement booms over the loudspeaker.

"Ladies and gentlemen, we apologize for the delay. We are experiencing temporary technical difficulties and are working to bring the ride back online as quickly as possible. For your safety, please remain seated and thank you for your cooperation."

As the chaos continues around me, I sit nestled against Seamus, shoulder to shoulder and thigh to thigh, in a cocoon of intimacy. It occurs to me that the two of us haven't been alone together since before Travis got sick which makes this opportunity feel strangely sacred. If there was ever a time to speak my mind, this is it.

"I'm not upset you found the tokens without me. I'm excited, actually."

"Then what's bothering you. And don't say nothing because I'm smart enough to know that's a lie."

I swallow hard. Part of me wishes the coaster would take off down the track this second so I could avoid this conversation altogether. But the other part knows I'm never going to feel safe moving forward in—whatever's going on with him—if I don't tell him the truth about Wylla.

CHAPTER 35

The sun bakes down. Out here, high on the track, there's no tree tall enough to provide shade, but the sun isn't the only reason sweat's pooling at my nape and along my bra line. I slide my glasses up my nose and try unsuccessfully to face Seamus, shifting under the bar.

"My sister and I have a complicated relationship."

He tilts his head to the side and runs his tongue along the front of his teeth, sizing me up. "And?"

He's staring at me now like I've just said the dumbest thing in the world, and it feels like the only way I'll be able to get him to understand my frustration is to give him the backstory. "And there was this guy we were both friends with for a long time growing up, but once we all became teenagers, she and I both starting liking him, as more than friends."

"Are you trying to tell me you and your sister fought over the same guy?" His tone is bemused, and I don't like that he's taking this so lightly.

I need him to understand the seriousness of the situation, especially as it applies to us. "It wasn't much of a fight. I mean, you know how she is… how she looks. I didn't stand a chance against her." If I was hoping to capture his attention with my tale of woe, I have it now.

He's gaping so wide I can see to his tonsils. "Wait. Have I met your sister?"

A stab of pain radiates across my forehead, and I close my eyes, hoping to subdue it. I don't know if it's the heat or the stress of being stuck eighty feet up on the top of a coaster, but I'm getting angry with him for being so dense. "Um, Wylla."

"Wylla?"

"Yes. Wylla. My sister, Wylla. The golden girl who's been tagging along after me and sharing a bedroom with us all week."

He leans away from me, against the side of the car. His expression is grave, like he's nervous about being stuck on this ride together. He takes in a long breath, and something inside my stomach rolls over. He's scared of me, and I have no idea why. "Elise, I don't know anyone named Wylla, and I've never met your sister."

Silence fills the space between us, and he stares at my face with such intensity, it's almost as if he's trying to see inside my thoughts. After a moment, the lines around his eyes shift slightly from confusion to concern. "Is everything okay with you?" He reaches for my hand, but I swat it away.

I don't know why he's being such a jerk about this, unless maybe he's got a crush on my sister after all. It's the only plausible explanation. Even the idea of it makes me want to puke. "This isn't funny," I say. "She was just with us, standing in line for this ride. And she was all chummy, chummy with you, draping her arm around your neck when we met up after you found the tokens. Not to mention you rode the Dark Knight and Kingda Ka and a bunch of other rides with her this week." I close my eyes and press my thumbs against my temples—anything to relieve this horrible headache. "Listen, I don't blame you for how she's been acting. I mean, maybe I did a little, at first, but I got over it. It's just that now, everyone sees how she's always smiling at you and laughing at all the funny stuff you say, and it might seem to you like she's flirting because she's got a thing for you, but she doesn't. It's just how she is. She's like that with all the guys." I open my eyes, expecting to see a hint of understanding somewhere on his face, but instead, he looks horrified. "I mean, that's not to say there aren't a ton of good reasons for her to be into you. There's nothing wrong with you or anything. It's just—you're not really her type, is all. And she's—"

"Elise." There's something painful in his expression preventing me from going on.

"Yeah?"

"Your sister isn't here with us. Not in the park. Not on this trip. She's. Not. Here." He punctuates each word like he's trying to explain to a police officer all the reasons he shouldn't be arrested. His voice is earnest but also a little scared.

Why is he looking so sheepish?

And why does he keep insisting Wylla isn't here?

I glance across the park, past the Ferris wheel and the drop tower and the water slides to the summer haze collected on the horizon, racking my brain for some plausible explanation.

But there isn't one. There's absolutely no logical rationale for his behavior. And there's no reason for him to lie to me.

Unless maybe he's playing a prank.

I turn to face him and level a glare. "What's going on right now? Are you teasing me? Is this some kind of joke?" My jaw clenches considering another possibility, and my hands ball into fists. "Wait, did Wylla put you up to this?" I glance over the side of the car, back toward the platform, hoping to catch a glimpse of her watching for my reaction, but my sightline is blocked by the loading platform roof. "I swear to God if you two are messing with me, I'm going to be so pissed."

I expect him to confess the truth—yes, they thought it would be funny to convince me I was going insane—but he doesn't. His jaw remains slack, his eyes bulging.

"Friends don't do stuff like this to each other." I'm yelling now. Unconcerned about upsetting the other stranded passengers. "And that goes double for friends with mental health issues. It's not funny. It's just mean."

"Elise, I don't know Wylla. I've never met Wylla. And I'm not conspiring with her behind your back to make you feel stupid. Something else is going on. It happened to my mom, too. She believed stuff that wasn't really there. But it's okay, Elise." He leans into me, his muscles tensing. "I'll help you figure this out. Because we are friends. More than friends."

A bead of sweat trickles along my hairline, past my ear, and under my jawline. I wipe it away with the back of my hand, trying to make sense of it all. The lap restraint rests heavily against my thighs, pressing tighter than it was a moment ago. I take a deep breath to calm my nerves, but the air is humid and thick with the scent of hydraulic fluid from the coaster's brakes. It lodges itself in my throat, and when I try swallowing it down, a small groan escapes my lips. Panic sets in as the pungent metallic odor shifts to burning gasoline.

All at once, my accident comes screaming back.

Pain laced through my shoulder—icy shards of glass burning like fire under my skin. It hurt like hell to move, but I didn't have a choice. My seatbelt strained across my chest, and my lungs stung, desperate for air. I reached to disconnect the buckle so I could take a proper breath, but the center console was crushed against my seat, blocking the release.

Tears pricked my eyes as I threw myself forward against the belt in a last-ditch effort to free myself.

The tension on the strap gave way, and as I took a gulp of fresh air, saw blood splattered across the dashboard clear to the passenger's side. It was too far to have sprayed from my shoulder.

Slowly, painfully, I twisted my torso from behind the steering wheel to check the passenger's seat beside me.

My body shuddered, spasming uncontrollably as I gazed upon my beautiful sister, crushed beneath the car's dashboard like a porcelain doll.

I reached out to her—running my finger across her cheek, through the blood oozing from a gaping wound on her temple. Despite the contorted angles of her body, her face was serene. Her eyes were closed; eyelashes curled upward, not a single one out of place.

She was sleeping.

She had to be.

I tried speaking her name, but my throat was swollen shut. I brushed her lips with my fingertip.

Waiting to feel the warmth of her breath against my skin.

Waiting…

Waiting…

"Wylla! Wylla, please! Open your eyes! Please open them! You're going to be fine. Everything's going to be fine."

Emergency vehicles arrived with flashing lights and too loud sirens. Men's voices deep and booming.

Help was here now.

They would make my sister breathe.

I screamed for them to come get her. To pull her out. To fix her.

But they didn't come.

And didn't come.

And didn't come.

My muscles ached beneath my skin, and after what felt like hours, I gave in to my exhaustion. My eyes closed, and my voice became a whisper.

"Wylla, I'm sorry."

"Wylla, I'm sorry."

"Wylla, I'm sorry."

I'm still murmuring her name when the motion of the coaster descending the next hill jostles me from my thoughts. My head throbs as round of applause erupts from the surrounding riders, and although Seamus must still be seated beside me, I can't see past the image of Wylla's bloody face as the train jerks and clatters its way back to the station. I ignore him through debarkation and stand awkwardly beyond the gate waiting for the next train to return with Mikal and Wylla.

I take in a breath as their car approaches.

She's vibrant, with sun-kissed cheeks and sparkling eyes. A wide smile splits her face, having obviously enjoyed the ride. But my lips are stuck together; my mouth dryer than the air swirling around us. "You don't see her?" My voice is trembles.

He shakes his head. "Just Mikal."

My stomach drops faster than it has on any coaster, because there she is, shrugging on her bag. When she notices me, though, her buoyant expression changes, like she's realized something for the first time.

I take a step back. Then another, nearly tripping over a crack in the sidewalk. Tears threaten to spill over.

I can't. I just can't.

What the actual hell is going on?

Seamus reaches out his hand, eyes wide and confused as he glances between my face and the platform. "You okay?"

I shake my head and take another step toward the exit before turning my back on all of them to take off at a run.

CHAPTER 36

Dark storm clouds billow in the western sky, lifting like great sentinels high into the upper atmosphere. Thunder rumbles in the distance, barely audible over the echoes of the surrounding rides as I race across the park.

I have no map or idea where I'm going. Not that it matters. I'm so stuck inside my own head, Dorney Park might as well be the moon.

The pounding of my feet against the concrete slows as my legs threaten to give way beneath me. My calves seize, and I nearly collapse to the ground, chest heaving. There's something satisfying about the way my lungs burn, and for a minute, there's only pain.

Not Wylla's face.

Or the blood.

Or her lifeless body beside me in the car.

A warm breeze plays with my hair, and I tuck a tendril behind my ear, considering the one thought I've been avoiding since the top of the coaster.

If Wylla died in the accident back in March, why am I still seeing her?

The only logical explanation is I'm losing my mind.

A shiver raises goosebumps to my flesh, and I take off again, as fast as my legs will take me, like somehow if I keep moving, I'll be able to outrun the figurative storm building inside of me even if I can't avoid the literal one in the sky above.

Families and teenagers, couples and employees pass without incident. Some pause to look after me, probably wondering what I'm running from. Others see me coming and step out of the way to let me pass. I'm only vaguely aware of the disturbed looks on their faces and must be oblivious to any directional signs, which is probably why I'm completely shocked when the footpath ends abruptly at the Ferris wheel entrance.

My head throbs. My legs tremble. The Ferris wheel slows, beckoning me like an artist's muse.

Take a seat and rest your weary soul, it seems to say.

There's no line, so I take a step forward. Then another. Until I find myself at the gate.

The operator lets off two exhausted looking parents carrying sleepy toddlers, and I can't help but wonder if the two napping sisters will grow up to be friends or if they'll end up not speaking to one another the way Wylla and I did.

They walk away, and I'm trying desperately to keep my tears from spilling over when the attendant clears his throat, motioning for me to enter.

"Riding solo?" he asks.

I nod, a rush of realization washing over me.

I'm alone. Completely and utterly alone.

I slide into the car across the bench, and he latches the door behind me. A crack of thunder rolls in the distance as the gondola lifts into the air. Warm breezes kiss my cheeks, and as the world falls away beneath me, I'm struck by how peaceful this moment might have been if things were different.

If I'd never offered to drive to the market for Mom.

If she hadn't asked me to take Wylla along.

If there had been no accident. As the gondola lifts, the horizon falls, and I stare at the rolling clouds with unfocused eyes. My lids are heavy, and I shut them, inhaling through my nose and exhaling through my mouth, trying desperately to calm my nerves. In the stillness, I can almost feel Wylla's warmth beside me, hip to hip and shoulder to shoulder. I breathe her in, remembering the sweet smell of her peach-scented body lotion. Her powder deodorant. Her citrus shampoo.

I open my eyes.

She's there, sitting beside me, and I resist the urge to back away. I shouldn't be frightened—whatever psychotic break I'm experiencing now is no different than it was yesterday or the day before—but fear winds itself inside me like a snake ready to strike.

Our eyes lock, and my heart races, threatening to explode from my chest. Splinters dig into my palms as I press them against the wooden seat, trying to keep myself upright. She gives a tentative smile, but I don't return the gesture. My hands are made of lead, and I couldn't pry them from the seat if I tried.

"It's beautiful up here, isn't it?" Her voice is familiar. Soothing.

My body's flight or fight instinct takes over, and I can almost feel the adrenaline coursing through my veins. My pulse quickens, and my muscles tense, preparing to jump if it should come to that. But I don't move. I remain in the seat, frozen.

Because maybe if I can just convince myself she's not really here, she'll go away.

When I force myself to look closely into her eyes, though, the pain I see there is as real as the gondola beneath my feet. I don't know what else to do so I nod and swallow a lump, blinking back tears. Somehow, I find the strength go along with whatever's happening to me now.

Because this must be the truth she's been keeping. There is no secret pregnancy. No other incidents with Jackson.

Just this.

"You're not really here anymore, are you?" I ask.

She scans the horizon, taking it all in—the coasters, the parking lot, and the town of South Whitehall Township beyond. There's an unexpected serenity to her face I've never seen before. The look of someone who's purpose has been fulfilled. "The part of me you needed is still here."

I swallow hard, trying to reconcile what I see with what I know to be true. "But I killed you."

She shakes her head. "I died in the accident. But you need to stop blaming yourself. It wasn't your fault."

"Not talking to you all those months was my fault." I take a deep breath and release a quiet sob.

"It was my fault as much as yours. We were both stupid and selfish."

"Yeah, but I should've forced the issue. Been a better sister."

"We both could've been better sisters. This isn't just on you."

A bolt of lightning crosses the sky, illuminating her face and the sincerity of her smile. I want to ask if she's a ghost or a hallucination or some figment of my imagination I've conjured as a way of coping with my grief, but she speaks before I have the chance.

"Do you remember the year we both got new bikes for Christmas?"

I nod. "I hated you that Christmas. But now I realize, I wasn't really angry with you at all. I was pissed at Mom and Dad. But it was easier to be mad at you."

Her eyes cut to me, confused, as the gondola peaks and we begin our descent. "Mad at me? What was there to be mad at me for?"

Maybe it's her realistic appearance or some secret longing of my own heart, but I'm somehow able to suspend reality long enough to call upon the frustration I felt that day—begging for something for so long only to have it handed to my little sister at the same time. "I was angry they got you the bike I asked for. It didn't seem fair to me at the time, I guess."

She shrugs. "At least *you* got what you wanted that year." As she says it, it occurs to me for the first time that getting something she didn't want meant not getting something she did. She got a bike. That was it. And I never heard her complain or saw her throw a fit. She just got on the bike and rode it around like she was wholly satisfied.

"So, what did you ask for?" My voice breaks. I can't believe I'm sitting here, talking with my dead sister. I can't believe I never bothered to have this conversation with her while she was still alive.

"An American Girl doll, Felicity," she says without a moment's hesitation. "The one with the horse."

She never got that doll. Or any American Girl doll for that matter.

She got a bike, though.

A stupid bike she didn't even want.

Since the day she was born, I wasted a lot of time comparing my life to hers. Who had the nicer hair, the best skin, the coolest friends? Who had Mom and Dad's approval?

Who was the better sister?

When I faced adversity growing up, I never held myself responsible. Instead, I looked to her as someone to blame when things didn't work out. It was easier that way, I guess. Easier than having to be accountable for my own failings. To do that, I would've had to admit things weren't perfect for her either. But from my perspective, her life seemed utterly charmed. No matter what the storm, she always managed to walk between the raindrops while I got drenched.

Somehow, she was always, always in the right place at the right time.

Until the day she wasn't.

My breath hitches, remembering the accident now. How angry I was on the drive to Jackson's house. How oblivious to her needs. My stomach knots when I consider how easy it would've been to speak up. To have simply been her friend instead of her adversary. All those years spent in constant competition, vying for everyone's love and attention, it never dawned on me it didn't need to be that way. I could've backed away and said enough.

I should've done it a long, long time ago.

But she's gone now, and it's too late.

I glance at her—the blush of her cheeks, the intensity of her gaze—and realize maybe it isn't.

Inside, the last scraps of resentment and jealousy I've been carrying around my entire life dissipate like fog on a winter morning. It's time to stop blaming her for all the stuff she had no control over while we were growing up, to hold myself accountable for my own shortcomings, and to stop being upset about everything that wasn't her fault. All the stuff with Mom and Dad. My friends.

And especially my relationship with Logan.

"I'm sorry, Wylla. I'm sorry you didn't get your doll." I take a deep breath to center myself. The rest of the world falls away, and it's just the two of us now, face to face with the truth. Logan may have been the catalyst for our estrangement, but I was the one who allowed him to destroy us. To wedge himself between us until the crack split all the way to the foundation of my soul. Images of our lives together flicker across my memory—from him pushing her on the swings of our playset when we were in elementary school to the last time I saw her climbing into the front seat of his car. She never ostracized me. Never told me to go away. The only person responsible for keeping me out of the narrative was me.

The truth is an artist's palette, shading my gray memories with vibrant hues. Things were never as bad as I thought they were.

"I'm sorry for all the times growing up when I was angry and shouldn't have been. And I'm sorry for not trusting you."

"I forgive you." She smiles. "For everything."

Above me, the skies open. Rain deflects off the exposed sides of the gondola, sprinkling my arms and face, masking the tears running down my cheeks. I'm bawling now, gasping for air, my throat thick with remorse, and I can't stop. She isn't really here, but I'm not ready to be without her. All those years I wished she would go away and leave me alone, and now all I want is for her to stay.

I cough and sniffle, forcing myself to speak through my sobs. "Am I ever. Going to see. You again?"

"I don't know." She brushes a finger along the scars on my arm, soft as a whisper. "But I don't think I'll ever be far."

The storm intensifies, and she settles beside me the way she used to when the thunder scared her as a child. This will be my last memory of her—my baby sister, curled against my arm, seeking shelter from the storm. I let the feeling of our closeness soak in, all the way to my bones so it will be a part of me forever. Just the two of us and the rain and our forgiveness.

Below me, the attendants call out to the other passengers, hurrying to get everyone safely off the ride. As the car makes its final descent, I work to steady my breathing, a feeble attempt at composure. I pull away from Wylla, with shaky hands and snot running down my face, not caring how I might appear. "You're not coming, are you?"

She smiles at me—a splintered expression, heavy with the weight of all that could have been. All that should have been.

My heart breaks.

"I'm gonna take another spin. The view's nice from up there, don't you think?"

I swallow the enormous lump in my throat. "It is," I whisper.

The ride operator who let me on releases the bolt on the door and raises a confused eyebrow at me when I don't immediately disembark. He ushers me off, feigning concern for my safety, and I take a step toward the exit, ignoring the rain pelting my face. At the last second, I turn back, hand on the gate. "Love you, Wylla," I call into the wind.

"Love you, too," she replies.

I don't watch as the gondola returns her to the sky.

CHAPTER 37

The rain is torrential, and I duck under a nearby pavilion with a few dozen other people seeking shelter from the storm. The roof effectively blocks the rain, but there's nowhere to hide from the tempest raging inside my own heart.

My sister is gone.

Gone forever.

And I'm never, ever going to see her again.

In a deserted corner, I brace myself against one of the building's wooden posts and let the sadness overwhelm me. It comes in huge, surging waves, and my entire body trembles under the weight of my sorrow. My shoulders heave, my eyes swell shut, and my nose runs until eventually, I cry myself out.

The families on the far side of the pavilion stare as I swipe at my face with the back of my hands, attempting to pull myself together.

I won't make apologies, though. This is who I am now. An only child. A girl without a sister.

Alone.

Alone.

Alone.

But not quite.

An image of Seamus floats through my head. His kind heart. His thoughtful smile. The way he listened patiently when I confided in him about the accident and my PTSD. I want to be with him now. I *need* to be with him. And God knows he deserves some sort of explanation.

I pull out my phone to text him, only to discover a message from Mom.

Elise, please call me. Or at least respond to my texts. It's been days and I'm worried sick.

I can almost hear the frantic tone of her voice as I scroll upward, through every message she's sent me over the past two weeks.

There are dozens of them.

Are you taking your pills? Please make sure you are.

Why won't you answer your phone, Elise? Hope you're okay.

Please text when you get a chance. I'm worried about you.

A crack of thunder startles me, causing my legs to give out, but as I lower myself onto the concrete floor of the pavilion, my eyes remain locked on the screen.

Resting in my palm is proof Mom didn't always choose Wylla over me.

I reread the final text again, allowing the truth to sink in.

All this time, Mom hasn't been ignoring me.

I've been ignoring her.

And her messages to Wylla were all inside my head.

My breath hitches, and I nearly drop my phone, realizing those texts might not have been the only things I imagined. Maybe all this time, my perception of Mom and Wylla's relationship was skewed, too. Of course, there were times when Wylla took her attention—when her needs took precedence over mine. And there were times when Mom might've chosen poorly, not realizing I needed her more than I let on. But I was never neglected, and things might have been difference if I had simply spoken up.

My finger hovers over the screen to return her texts, but a text isn't what I need right now. Characters on a screen are no substitute for the caress of my mother's voice, so I touch her name, and the audio icon, without stopping to think about all the ramifications of the call I'm about to make. My eyes close as I wait for Mom to pick up.

"Elise?" She gasps out my name like she's been holding her breath for the last two weeks, waiting for me to respond.

"Mom." My voice is a whisper.

"Elise. Elise, honey, are you okay? Is everything all right there?"

A huge sob overtakes me, and my body spasms. I sniffle into the phone, trying to sufficiently compose myself to get the words out. "I'm so sorry, Mom. I'm so sorry I killed Wylla."

Thunder rolls overhead and between the storm and the people around me, it's nearly impossible to hear her response. I strain, pressing the receiver against my ear. "It wasn't your fault, baby. It was an accident. No one blames you."

Rain floods into the pavilion, and while the others squeal and climb onto nearby picnic tables to avoid getting their feet wet, I let the water lap against my legs as it rushes past. Mom's voice is muffled by the chaos, but I manage to catch the last little bit.

"It's time for you to stop blaming yourself."

The water is cold along my thighs, causing my skin to prickle despite the hot, muggy air. My clothes cling to me, heavy and wet, like some physical manifestation of my grief. Wylla's death rests twice as heavy on my soul, and I shift uncomfortably on the concrete, languishing in the intensity of the pain—fully accepting it as penance.

I deserve every ache. All the discomfort and distress. "It was all my fault, Mom. The not talking. The accident. All of it. I don't deserve anyone's forgiveness."

She's silent for a long moment, and I worry she's hung up until she sighs heavily across the line. "You know, Elise, the thing about forgiveness is, you don't get to choose whether you're worthy or not. The person offering gets to decide. So, if you need to hear it, I forgive you, and I know if she was here, Wylla would forgive you, too."

From the floor of the pavilion, the Ferris wheel is barely visible beyond a nearby grove of trees. It's frozen in place, completely deserted. If Wylla was there before, she's not anymore. Still, if I close my eyes, it's not hard to imagine her beside me.

"I forgive you," she'd said.

So, maybe Mom's right. Maybe forgiveness is what my extra time with Wylla was about after all.

And if Wylla stuck around longer than she had to so I could have peace, I should find a way to accept it.

A surge of energy courses through me. The need to move. To figure things out. To set things straight.

I hoist myself off the ground, water cascading in tiny rivulets along my arms and legs. "You might be right about Wylla," I say. "She wants me to stop blaming myself, too."

"Absolutely she does."

"Okay." My voice wavers slightly, thanks in no small part to the three months I spent living under the delusion my dead sister was still very much alive. It doesn't lessen my resolve, though, and in face of everything I've been through, the truth is strangely comforting. "I'm going to be okay now, and I hate to hang up, but I have somewhere I need to be. Can I call you back later and fill you in on everything?"

"I'd like that."

I disconnect and shoot a quick text to Seamus. *Where are you?*

He responds immediately. *We're camped out in the Chicken Shack with a hundred of our closest friends trying to stay dry. Are you okay?*

I check the park map on my phone. He's about as far away as he could possibly be, but I need to get to him now, storm or no storm.

I'm heading there now. Wait for me ok?

The reply dots appear, disappear, and appear again.

Just you?

There's a lot of subtext crammed into those two words. A lot to unpack when I have a chance.

Yeah. Just me.

The rain is blowing sideways now, and everyone huddled under the pavilion has moved to the center, away from the deluge. Except for me, of course.

I step out from under the eaves, relishing the first drops against my face—stinging a little—before spilling down my cheeks and off my chin. I take off at a run along the now desolate midway, past the carousel, the Kaleidoscope, and the Cinnabon. Wind howls around me, and I'm drenched to my underwear before hitting the halfway mark. None of it seems to matter, though. Not the hair plastered to my face. Not the squelch of my sneakers underfoot. Not the ache of my muscles.

Because I'm still here.

Still alive.

Still able to be the sister I should have been all along, even if Wylla's no longer with me.

I slow my pace as I approach the Chicken Shack, skirting past all the people wedged under the eaves, water pooling at their feet. Seamus must've been watching the door for me because I spot him waving as soon as I walk through. He and Mikal are squished beside one another in a booth, but they manage to slide even closer to make room for me on the edge.

"Hey," they say in unison.

It's clear from Mikal's lack of eye contact that Seamus mentioned something to him about my sister.

"Hey." My t-shirt and shorts hang heavily against my skin, dripping all over the seat, and for the first time since trekking across the park, it feels like waiting out the storm might've been a better idea. I'm here now, though, so I might as well start explaining.

But explaining is easier said than done.

I'm embarrassed about everything, the least of which is looking like a drowned rat. Beyond my haggard appearance, there's no way to adequately explain what's happened to me over the course of the past hour—or over the past three months for that matter. Anything I say will make them lose all respect for me.

They're going to think I've lost it and won't want to be friends anymore.

But I can't lie. They deserve the truth.

"So, uh, my sister Wylla isn't here." My knuckles blanch as I grip the edge of the bench, waiting for them to respond.

Seamus clears his throat, like he's worried about upsetting me. "Yeah. We know."

Mikal passes me a stack of napkins from the dispenser at the end of the table, and I wipe off my face as arms as best I can. I'm not quite sure how to go on. How to explain what's been happening when I honestly have no idea myself. Can I trust them not to laugh in my face?

Will I blame them if they do?

Beside me, Seamus lays a gentle hand on my arm—warm and dry— encouragement to go on. The lines of his face are soft and his eyes are full of compassion. Looking at him makes me want to burst into tears. How will I ever tell him the rest?

Do I even want to?

I glance across the restaurant to where another rain-soaked teenage girl shivers against her girlfriend in the too-cold air conditioning, and for a split second I consider lying to him. Making up some story about being part of improv acting troop or social experiment project. But there are no hidden cameras around. No one to corroborate whatever deceitful web I weave.

He must sense my trepidation, squeezing my arm reassuringly. "You can tell us whatever it is that's going on. We're friends, Elise. We won't think any less of you."

My eyes cut from Seamus to Mikal and back again. Once I tell them, they'll never look at me the same way again.

But maybe that's okay.

"The thing is, she's not here at all anymore. Like on the planet. She died a couple months ago," I say, and Seamus's eyes go wide like he knows what comes next. "She died in the car accident back in March, and I dunno, I must've blocked it out or something because somehow, I forgot. Or maybe I never knew. Or maybe I knew and was too angry with myself to face the truth. Either way, I know now."

"But you've been seeing her, walking around, interacting with the rest of us all this time?" Seamus asks.

The answer to his question is nothing short of ridiculous, and I have no idea how he'll respond to my confirmation.

My head bobs slowly up and down, unable to speak the words aloud.

"Do you think it was her ghost?" Mikal asks, side-eyeing Seamus like they've already discussed the possibility. There's no sarcasm in his tone. No mocking intonation. He's asking a serious question and expecting a serious reply.

Considering everything Wylla said and did in the months since the accident—from the cadence of our interactions to the way she made me feel—it occurs to me that she always acted exactly as I expected her to. So maybe I did dream her up out of the memories in my head, providing me with an excuse to come on this trip and avoid the truth of what was going on at home. If that's the case, her flirting with Seamus was the embodiment of all my insecurities and our reconciliation was nothing but wishful thinking.

But perhaps she wasn't imagined at all. Maybe the Wylla who's been by my side for the past two weeks was her ghost, a spirit guide shepherding me back to the life I should've been living all along.

If she was a ghost, she certainly wasn't here to haunt me.

I'll probably never know one way or the other. And it doesn't matter anyway. Because I forgive her, and I know she forgives me.

"It was a gift," I respond at last. "One I don't intend to squander."

CHAPTER 38

My key disengages the bolt, and the motel door swings open, releasing a damp, musty odor from within. It's not as bad as some of the other accommodations I've suffered through this trip, and at this point, I smell worse than the room. I've been dreaming for the last hour about peeling off my wet clothes and lingering under a hot shower, but when I flip on the wall switch to illuminate the overhead lamp, the reality of my situation crashes into me like a runaway coaster speeding down its tallest hill.

Furniture notwithstanding, the room is empty. Wylla's bags aren't scattered on the floor. Her lotion and makeup and hairdryer aren't lined up across the dresser. Her nightshirt isn't tossed onto the bed.

And, of course, she's no longer by my side.

Alone with my thoughts, I step across the threshold and exhale, letting my bag drop at my feet. Tears threaten to spill over for about the hundredth time, but something shifts inside of me when I catch a glimpse of my reflection in the mirror.

My eyes are red, lids swollen around them, and yet, there's

a hint of Wylla there, hidden behind my sorrow. Her need for acceptance. Her willful stubbornness. Her joyful energy.

We may have approached the world differently, but when it came to what we wanted from life, we weren't so different after all. We both wanted love and acceptance and a chance to make things right, and for now, as I close the door behind me, the hope of eventually fulfilling our shared desires will have to be enough to see me through until tomorrow.

***

It's not a shock when Seamus shows up in my room after dinner, but I am surprised to see Ernie and Mikal tagging along with a store-bought chocolate cake.

"It's Travis's birthday." Mikal sets the cake on the dresser next to the TV and pulls up Facetime on his phone. "His daughter called me about an hour ago. Said she drove him home from the hospital this afternoon, and on the way, he was complaining about not getting to celebrate with us."

"So, we decided the five of us could still celebrate together, virtually." Seamus pauses to search my face. "As long as you're feeling up to it." He's got to be wondering about my mental state, given everything that happened this afternoon.

I've already brushed my teeth, but the cake does look amazing, and there's no way I would miss out on a chance to wish Travis a happy birthday. "Yeah, of course. Call him."

Mikal scrolls through his recent calls for Travis's daughter's number and hits send. Seconds later, her face appears on the screen.

She waves at all of us. "It's so sweet of you guys to do this for Dad." She thumbs over her shoulder to somewhere off screen. "He's racked out in his La-Z-Boy in the den. Lemme go rouse him."

The image on the screen bounces along as she hurries from the kitchen and along a hallway into a wood-paneled room stacked with books and magazines. "Dad," she says softly. "I've got some folks here who have something they'd like to say."

He rubs sleep from his eyes as he comes to. "Wait, now." He takes the phone from her hand. "What's all this?"

Ernie belts out the first off-key, baritone note of the birthday song, and the rest of us join in. Mikal pans around the room, making sure to get each of us on screen before finishing on the cake.

"We were gonna get candles," Mikal says, fumbling to get everyone into the shot. "But we didn't know how many we needed, and we didn't have any way to light them, so we just got the cake."

"We'll save you a piece and bring it to you when we get home," Seamus says.

Travis's face may be small on the screen, but it's still large enough to see the emotion overtake him. I wait in silence for his reply as he wipes a tear from his cheek. "You guys are the best, you know that?"

Mikal curtsies. "We know."

Everyone settles around the room, and Ernie cuts the cake, passing out slices on paper napkins. Eating with my fingers, I help the others fill Travis in on the best coasters from the last several parks, the status of the tokens, and today's thunderstorm.

No one mentions the ghost tagging along with me the whole time.

"Tomorrow's the last park," Travis says. "If Elise and Seamus find the tokens, they win the passes."

"But if I find them, we tie," Mikal says. He turns to Ernie. "What happens then? We'll have four a piece."

Ernie licks chocolate frosting off his thumb and shrugs. "I dunno. It doesn't seem like Mr. Blankenship thought it all the way through."

Mikal, Seamus, and I glance at one another, obviously thinking the same thing.

Travis pipes up. "What you're saying is, he might give vouchers to all four of us."

Mikal hands the phone to Ernie for him to respond. "He could, I suppose, if he's feeling generous. Or—" A look of dismay washes over him.

"Or what?" Seamus asks.

"Or he could decide since no one won outright that none of you get them."

Travis lets out a muffled groan as Seamus and I lock eyes. Something inside him has changed over the last few days. Like he's not as worried about winning the vouchers anymore. I give him a nod to let him know I'm fine with whatever he wants to do.

"We're gonna help you find them tomorrow," he says to Mikal. "Then we'll confront Blankenship when we get home and see what he says."

"That's not necessary," Travis says. "If you guys hadn't helped Mikal find them at Kings Dominion, you'd have already won, fair and square."

"Let him tell us no," I say. "I'm willing to bet he won't."

"Me, too," says Seamus.

"Then it's settled." Ernie wipes his hands on the tops of his shorts. "And I'll mention something to him about coughing up two more vouchers." He glances at a roach crawling across the floor. "After dealing with the subpar lodging, it's the least he can do."

Everyone says goodbye to Travis, and after cleaning up the cake, Ernie and Mikal head out. I brush my teeth beside Seamus for a second time, and after he changes into his pajama pants, he slips under the covers beside me.

His warmth spreads slowly across the cool sheets, an invitation.

But something stops me. "You know, you could sleep in the other bed now. You don't need to cram beside me on this tiny double," I say.

"You don't want me here?" he asks.

My eyes haven't adjusted to the dark, concealing his expression, but his voice sounds wounded.

"No. It's not that. I don't want you to leave. It's just—you seem squished."

He settles against the pillow. "I'm fine."

"You are?"

"Yeah. If it was a problem, I could've been sleeping in the other bed all this time. You know that, right?"

I consider his revelation for the first time.

Wylla was never sleeping in the other bed. It was always empty.

He *chose* to sleep beside me.

On a tiny bed.

Not because he had to.

But because he wanted to.

And I was worried he might like Wylla more than me.

Oh Lord.

I slip a little closer, laying my head against his chest. His heartbeat is steady and strong, quickening ever so slightly when I weave my fingers between his. I've misinterpreted everything, and it's become pretty obvious I should get back to therapy and start taking my Zoloft again. I make a mental note to confide in Mom about not taking them when we get home. Maybe she'll have a suggestion for staving off the stomach aches.

Seamus shifts beneath me, and I close my eyes, soaking him in. Considering everything that transpired today, I honestly can't believe he didn't bolt. If Nia had confessed to secretly seeing a dead person for the better part of three months, I probably would've needed a bit more time to process. But Seamus seems to be taking it all in stride.

"I'm glad you're still here," I say.

"Why wouldn't I be?"

"I don't know." I squeeze his palm against mine. "I'm still freaking out about everything and figured you would be, too. But you're not."

He chuckles. "I sort of am. But honestly, what you've been experiencing makes some sense."

I don't know how that's possible. "It does?"

"I mean, yeah." He hesitates, running a finger across the scar on my shoulder before going on. "Remember when I told you about my mom and her bipolar disorder?"

I don't know where he's going with this, but I'm curious. "Yeah."

"Well, right after her diagnosis, she got really forgetful. Not like 'where are my keys' forgetful, but more like 'what do you mean I have a mental health issue' forgetful. I started reading about what might be going on with her. News articles, medical journals, pretty much anything I could get my hands on." He sighs, like remembering that time in his life is a struggle even now. "Anyway, it turns out some people's brains are wired to block out stuff that's too hard to process so they only see what they want. Like a defense mechanism or something. It's actually pretty common."

I bite at my lower lip and blink back tears. "You think I blocked out the accident and imagined Wylla was still around because I couldn't process losing her?"

"Maybe. I don't know. But you'll talk about it with your therapist and figure it out. Or you won't. Either way, none of it changes how I feel about you."

Silence hangs between us. While I'm relieved he doesn't think I'm a psycho, I'm still not certain where our relationship stands.

"About that," I say, clearing my throat. "I've been sort of confused about us the past few days. I mean, you came on pretty strong at first, but then, I dunno, it was almost like you stopped being into me or something. I guess that's why I thought you might like Wylla instead."

His breath is warm against the top of my head. "I couldn't see Wylla. We've established that."

"Yeah. I know now. But I didn't know then." I pause. I might've been imagining my sister, but I wasn't imagining his actions. "Admit it. You were sending me mixed signals there for a while."

He doesn't respond immediately, running a finger along my collarbone while he gathers his thoughts. "If I confused you, I'm sorry. I never meant to make things hard. But after the whole mess with Mikal, it seemed almost as if you weren't sure how you felt about me, so I wanted to give you the time and space to figure it out, you know? No pressure, or whatever."

The truth about his feelings for me comes crashing down, and I don't know how to reply in a way that doesn't make me sound like an idiot, especially since everything I made up in my head about him was wrong. He wasn't crushing on Wylla when he asked me to ride with Mikal, he simply didn't want Mikal to ride by himself all the time.

And he didn't want me to be the one riding alone.

I've never felt so stupid in my life.

I need to change the subject. "You gave up the possibility of winning the vouchers pretty easily tonight, though," I say.

He lets out a deep sigh. "Winning doesn't seem as important as it did at the start."

"Really? You were really gung-ho about it at first."

"Yeah." There's something nostalgic about the tone of his voice.

"But now you don't care if you win them or not?"

He shrugs. "I don't need them anymore."

I shift onto my elbow to see his face properly. "You gonna buy them on your own or something?"

"That's not why I don't need them." He hesitates. "I mean, sure, it'd be nice to not wait in line for the rest of the season, but impatience was never my motivation."

I reach out to trace the curve of his jawline, freckle to freckle to freckle. "Then what was your motivation?"

He chuckles softly. "You, duh."

"Me?"

"Yeah. Of course. How else was I gonna get you to hang out with me once we got back home? If we both won the vouchers, at least I'd be able to make a case for us going to Drury together a couple times."

"I'll go with you, even without the vouchers."

"I know that now. But I didn't know it then."

A beat of silence stretches out between us. And for the first time this entire trip, my sister's not sleeping in the bed beside us.

"I'd like to kiss you now, if that's okay," I say.

He brushes my cheek with his thumb, like a feather against my skin. "It's more than okay."

My lips touch his, soft and tentative. He tastes like spearmint toothpaste, and as I roll on top of him, his hand moves to the small of my back, pressing our bodies together. Time stops like it does on a coaster, teetering at the top of a hill in the last second, poised to drop. Once I crest, there'll be no turning back. We won't be just friends anymore. We'll be something more.

"Elise," he whispers against my lips, part question, part invitation.

The still of his hand tells me whatever's about to happen is my call, but I already know my decision.

It's time to take the plunge.

Like a runaway coaster, we move quickly, picking up speed. Lips pressing. Skin touching. My shirt is off, and so is his, but my stomach doesn't drop. I have no idea what comes next or where this ride will eventually take me, but this is nothing like careening into the first unknown loop of a coaster ride.

Because with Seamus there's nothing to be afraid of.

I'm safe here in his arms.

EPILOGUE

Seamus's hand is warm and familiar in mine. Sweaty, too, but it's not like either of us care. I toss him my car keys to put in his pocket for safekeeping. Since I started taking my Zoloft at night, my stomach pains have all but disappeared, and I'm back behind the wheel without incident.

I'm still unpacking all the emotional baggage surrounding the accident, but my therapist confirmed Seamus's suspicions that my brain was using Wylla as a shield against my trauma. I don't know if I'll ever get all my feelings sorted out, but I'm finally dealing with her death on my own terms.

Nia races ahead toward Mikal, his boyfriend Kevin, and Travis waiting by the park entrance. "Who's ready to ride the Blaster?" she calls with a laugh, knowing the rest of us would be satisfied to never ride the stupid coaster from the contest ever again.

"Hard pass for me." Mikal flips his towel over his shoulder and throws a coy look at Kevin. "I'm way more about hitting the waterpark with this fine thing."

Travis's nose is slathered in zinc oxide like some sort of '80s lifeguard. Between the sunscreen and his skull and cross bone board shorts, it's hard keeping a straight face. "It's hotter than Satan's sauna out here," he says. "All the Fast Lane vouchers in the world couldn't get me on the rides in this heat today."

"Not to mention we've ridden everything about a million times at this point," I add. "The wave pool never disappoints, though."

"Neither does the lazy river." Travis scans his season pass at the kiosk and passes through the turnstile. "Seamus, lead the way to the inner-tubes."

Our small but mighty coalition sidesteps the newcomers who stop to take pictures at the entrance, waving off the park photographers looking to capture our attendance for posterity as we have on every other occasion this season.

"Hey, wait," Mikal says, stopping dead in the middle of the walkway. "Maybe we should get one of these things. We've avoided these guys all summer, and I feel kinda bad."

"It's definitely been the year of the coaster," Seamus says. "I'm in if you guys are."

Kevin throws an arm around Mikal. "You know I'm always ready to mug for the camera."

"Me, too," says Nia slipping under Kevin's other arm.

Travis waves over one of the park photographers, a bored looking junior from last year's English class. "Hey, Elise," he says.

I give him my cheesiest grin, hoping for a favor. "Hey, Gavin. So, listen, we'd like to get our picture taken, and I know it's probably against the rules, but could we do it over by the Blaster. For posterity. You get it." He looks incredulous. "Come on. Not even for four of the Blaster Seven? Mr. Blankenship won't mind. And who's gonna tell?"

"Not me," Nia says.

"Me neither," Mikal agrees.

"Fine." Gavin turns toward the Blaster. "Let's go if we're going."

Once we arrive, there's a bit of discussion about poses and placement. Travis wants to make sure the first drop is in the background, and Mikal and Kevin take ten minutes to figure out the best way to center the train in their heart hands as it goes by.

Gavin is not happy. "Are we ready?"

"Ready." Seamus kisses my nose.

"Be sure to wait for the train, though," Mikal cries.

It takes six tries to get the photo the way everyone wants it, and by the time we're finished, everyone's more than ready to spend the rest of the day in the water.

We take on the slides, the wave pool, and of course, the lazy river, before stopping by the photo kiosk on the way out of the park.

"We'll take six copies," Travis tells the cashier, handing her his credit card. "On me."

Everyone protests in unison.

"No, now stop. This here's my little gift to all of you for including me this summer. You didn't need to let the old guy tag along, but you did, and it means a lot."

Mikal wraps his arms around him. "Like we'd ever leave you behind."

The cashier rings up Travis and slides photos into separate bags for each of us.

I take mine out as soon as he hands it to me.

Five of the most important people in my life grin up at me. My best friend, Nia. Mikal and Kevin—their hands creating a perfect heart to frame the Blaster as it speeds down the first hill. Travis, the stand-in father I never knew I needed. And Seamus, the guy who's stolen my heart.

To keep from damaging it, I slip the photo back into the bag, but before it's all the way inside, I notice a strange glimmery spot beside my left shoulder. I pull the picture back out for a closer inspection. The image is faint—more shadow than figure—but at just the right angle I can almost make out Wylla's beautiful smile.

Still beside me.

Still my sister.

acknowledgements

When I began writing this novel, I wanted to give a voice to one of the strongest—and arguably one of the most difficult—of the familial relationships.

Sisters.

My own sister, Laura, and I have a complicated, messy past. One where we didn't often see eye to eye and where I spent the better part of my childhood propping myself up by putting her down. Regret haunts me and probably always will, but thankfully, Laura has a forgiving and understanding soul, and today we are the best of friends.

She's the one person I can trust with my deepest, darkest secrets because at the end of it all she already knows the worst of me and still chooses love.

So, of course, *A Walk Between Raindrops* wouldn't be possible without her exceptional presence in my life. Thank you for being my partner in crime 'til the end of time.

Thank you, as well, to the best agent in the world, Ann Rose, and everyone at Tobias Literary Agency. Thank you for allowing me the space to write my truth despite the tides of the fickle publishing industry. Thanks for being an absolute champion for my work, and for caring about my stories as much as I do. Ride or die, forever and ever.

To the Rosebuds, for always having my back. For making me laugh when I want to cry. For being the best distraction and the greatest motivation. And for being the most amazing group of agency siblings a girl could ever want.

And finally, thank you to my family. After ten years of writing and dreaming and sacrificing, I'm so grateful for your gifts of patience and support. Love you all more than you will ever know.